Conquests

Vikings. Fierce warriors who terrified all in their path as they raided and marauded, enslaved and murdered during Europe's Dark Ages.

But these rough men from a rugged land were also sailors, explorers, craftsmen, and highly sought after mercenaries.

Conquests: An Anthology of Smoldering Viking Romance will transport you to the realm of fantasy where such fearsome and loyal men are relentless potent lovers. Whether the lady of the keep demands a few stolen hours of pleasure with a captured Viking warrior or the handsome Northman is the one seducing his captive, you will find plenty of lusty adventures in settings as far-flung as Ireland, Iceland, Norway, Byzantium, Moorish Spain and the New World.

Let your fantasies run wild to a time when men wearing bearskin shirts and shining iron helms could capture a fierce maiden's heart!

CONQUESTS:

An Anthology of Smoldering Viking Romance

Edited by Delilah Devlin

CONTENTS

FOREWORD

Few alpha heroes have fueled our imaginations like the seafaring Viking. The term *Viking* is thought to have come from the Scandinavian term *Vikingr*, which literally means, *pirate*. Those fearless explorers, who conquered and plundered the British Isles, northern France and parts of Russia, spent most of the year tending their farms when they weren't pillaging monasteries or burning villages. After looting riches, and sometimes stealing brides for their farms in Norway, Denmark, and Sweden, Vikings earned their reputation for cleanliness and masculine beauty by soaking in hot springs and taking baths. What's not to love about the powerful image of a handsome, blue-eyed, blond haired Norsemen rising naked from the water?

The Vikings were far ahead of other Europeans of their time with regard to grooming, and used tools like tweezers, combs, and razors to tend to their good looks. Brunet males relied on strong lye soap to bleach their hair and beards to maintain their cultural ideal of attractiveness. One can only assume they groomed for their ladies, who were also more independent than other women of their time. A natural born Norsewoman could inherit property, petition for divorce, and regain her dowry in the instance of an unfortunate marriage. A strong and handsome Viking who could support his wife and family through plunder and farming, however, was a man worth keeping.

The fierce and enigmatic Vikings have been the subject of legends, folklore, and myths since their first foreign raids in the eighth century, and remain popular figures in history and fiction. My standalone novella *Her Immortal Viking* is based on Norse mythology and Viking culture, the roots of which are still taught in Scandinavian schools to honor their heritage.

The talented authors of the anthology *Conquests: Viking Romance for Women* will ignite your senses with their virile, handsome Viking warriors and the strong women they love. You'll want to read these sizzling stories again and again.

Enjoy! Or as the Vikings would say in Old Norse, "*Njóta!*"

Adele Downs
Best-Selling Author of *Her Immortal Viking*

"Downs' clever mash-up of Viking elements and contemporary romance (and oh, the hot, hot Viking!) make this novella an absolute winner."

5 Stars! ~Words, Words, Words

INTRODUCTION

My step-grandfather's name was Olaf. Now, before you start picturing a cuddly snowman with a carrot nose, picture instead a man of medium height, light brown hair, and pale eyes—pale *blind* eyes. Grandpa began going blind in his early twenties. By the time I came along, he lived completely in the dark.

Not that blindness ever stopped him. He rarely walked with a cane. He climbed tall ladders to re-shingle the roof, clean the gutters, or prune trees. But the thing I remember most about him was his keen mind and wicked-sharp sense of humor. His parents migrated from Norway, and he spoke the language and visited cousins back home. He built a workshop in the garage and set up a micro-brewery where he and his friends would gather, and laughter was everywhere.

When I was a child, I attributed my blonde hair and blue eyes to him, but sadly realized very early on that was impossible. Because of him, I never accepted the stereotypical view of Vikings as base, marauding warriors. They were artists, poets, farmers, traders, adventurers, and yes, fearsome warriors.

In this volume, I've collected stories written by some amazing writers who've captured the breadth of the Viking experience—settlers in a brave new world, raiders and traders who travelled from northern Europe to Africa and Byzantium in wooden boats, soldiers whose superior might made them feared and sought after. More, they gave me stories about the men who remained in their cold, rugged land and the strong women who matched their courage and will.

And I can well imagine my grandfather aboard one of those Viking ships, his face turned to the wind as it caught the sail and carried him to the edge of the known world. Despite the racy content, I think he'd be tickled about this book. So Grandpa, this one's for you.

Delilah Devlin
Editor

THE CAPTIVE

Lizzie Ashworth

Near Lichfield, England, 880 AD

"Dane, do you know why you were brought here?"

Elspeth, Lady of Hystead, gathered her thick red skirts and sat on the curved stool at the side of the room, opposite the spot where the broad-shouldered man stood. Her hungry gaze drank in the powerful strength of his legs, the ripple of muscle in his chest and arms, the iron line of his jaw. Even wounded, even smeared with the grit and gore of battle, his body glistened with male vigor.

Candlelight reflected off the lime-washed walls and framed the warrior's furious stare. He strained against the bonds holding his wrists behind him and stretched the short length of rope between his ankles. Animal skins covered the stone-paved floor under his feet, one of few luxuries in the humble room with its bed, bucket of hot coals, and side table.

She turned to the two armed men who'd brought him. "Go now and bar the door until I call."

An angry string of words followed the men as they departed. Elspeth heard the bar fall into place with a heavy thump.

Pale blue eyes flashed toward her, defiant.

"What of our language do you know, Dane? Can you speak?"

"I know enough," he snarled, his words heavily accented. "What is your intent, woman?"

"My name is Elspeth, and it pleases me to see you." His anger excited her, although she tried not to reveal any hint of her swelling desire. She sipped from her cup of ale. "Will you drink?"

His tongue slid over the crease of his narrow lips, but he gave no answer.

"You must be thirsty." She poured another cup from the ewer and carried it to his mouth, tilting it forward.

He drank deeply. The line of his jaw slackened slightly, and she remained beside him, more intrigued than ever by his bristling strangeness. The grime of battle still coated his face and arms, but elsewhere, his body had been covered with clothing and armor, now mostly removed, so that he stood in rough pants that hung from his hips. Blood smeared from cuts on his arms and hands did not disguise the inked design scrolling over his tanned arms. A section of his yellow-white hair clumped against his scalp in a dried, darkened mass while the rest fell in tangles around his shoulders.

"Are all your kind so beautiful?" she asked quietly, trailing her fingertip across his chest. His nipples lay flat on the domed pectoral muscles and more ink patterned a fantastical beast between them. Hardly a hair curled there, although lower on his abdomen a faint line of darker hair collected downward to disappear at the waist of his pants. Her gaze lingered there briefly as her pulse quickened.

He made no answer, but inhaled as her finger stroked over one of the nipples. His posture shifted slightly.

"Is this beast meant to say something about you?" she asked, fingering the tattoo.

"It honors the gods," he grumbled.

"Have your gods served you well today?"

He did not answer.

She brought a basin and set it beside him before pouring water warmed near the hot coals. With a linen cloth, she bathed him, wiping the sweat-stained whisker stubble on his face to remove blood and dirt. A strong straight nose traveled from his smooth brow and centered between prominent cheekbones. His firm jaw cut sharply to a bold chin, oddly contrasting the cruelly sensual curve of his narrow lips.

Her breath stuttered as she worked, each freshened part of his body even more stunning than she had first considered. His skin, marred by various scars from previous battles, stretched like warm silk over bronzed muscle. She sponged carefully around a gash on his cheek and another shorter mark on his forehead. Bruising on his jaw had turned purplish-blue, and more bruising colored parts of his chest and back. Nicks and scrapes laced his forearms, and a crusted gash on his bicep caused him to jump when she pushed the wet cloth against it. The scalp wound proved more trouble-some. His height forced her to stand on tiptoe to reach it.

"Bend over," she demanded, pressing his head forward so that the water could soak the matted hair. He made no sound as she cleaned his injuries. At length, she set aside the basin.

"Will you take food?" She cut a piece of the cheese and broke a part of the loaf of wheaten bread.

His gaze had become speculative, watching with an almost bemused expression that softened the strained lines of his face. "Why do you trouble over me, when I am to be killed?"

"Perhaps that isn't your fate, Dane."

"Do you have the power to determine my fate?"

"It seems I do, does it not?"

"Things are not always as they seem," he replied.

But he accepted the stool she pushed behind him and sat to eat the food she fed him, and after a time, with the loaf, cheese, an apple, and considerably more ale consumed, she noted a certain relaxation in his frame.

"You mean to have me," he observed and raised one eyebrow in question.

"Yes." She noted the hint of a smile, which pleased her.

"My hands…" He shifted his shoulders to struggle with the bonds holding his wrists.

She laughed lightly, swallowing past the growing ten-sion in her neck. How she would love to release him, let him tear at her, throw her down, and take her to the ends of her reckoning. "Dane, surely you don't think me foolish enough to release you?"

He smirked. "My name is Magnus, and I don't think of you at all," he replied. "I was not aware the Saxons gave over the task of torture to their women."

Anger swept up her cheeks, and she held her skirts to kick out the stool from under him.

Unsteady, he gained his feet as the stool flew back.

"Torture?" Her face burned. "You see pleasuring me as torture?"

She thought them of equal age. But she was no maid, rather the wife of a doddering old man who couldn't keep from dribbling on himself when he pissed. On her, alone, lay the full array of tasks necessary to run such a large estate. Even the thanes sworn to her husband's service knew she ruled Hystead. Many had made suit to her, surreptitiously, for standards required decorum in such matters. In these uncertain times, she could not risk loss of respect for herself or her husband.

Torture. Her nostrils flared as she met his insolent gaze. Her copper-red hair and green eyes received regular comment from the flatterers, and she knew her form remained comely. This man meant to provoke her.

"To what end do you taunt me, Magnus?" she challenged, standing next to him so the swell of her bosom grazed his chest. "Shall I slap you, cause you pain? Would that please you more?"

He laughed, revealing white teeth and creases in his cheeks. "Battle pleases me."

She ran her hand over his chest, stroking the smooth skin and lingering over the nipples to toy until the flesh thickened. Her own nipples hardened against her bodice as she noted a hitch in his breathing. He may have seemed carved as the finest work of metal, but he *was* made of mortal flesh. Her hand slid down to the bulge pressing the front of his pants, and a sly smile grew on her mouth.

"Torture becomes you, Magnus," she said quietly.

She stroked his organ through the heavy cloth until he made a noise, until the thick swell rose tightly outward. Then she unlaced the front and pushed the garment to his ankles. Her hands traveled back up the length of his legs, over calves furred with pale hair, over straining thighs nearly as big as her waist. She walked around him, teasing the rigid curve of his buttocks with light strokes of her fingers until his skin shuddered.

At his front, his rock-hard prick angled toward her, its length corded with veins, and the head of it swollen and dark. Briefly, she grasped it with both hands and pulled, marveling silently at its fearsome size. Moisture wet the thatch of hair between her thighs, her body greedy for this stiff wood to plow her open.

With a sideways glance at his sullen glare, she refilled the basin with fresh water and scented it with lavender oil then bathed his groin, tending softly to the knotted bag of stones clustered in its dense thicket of hair. The cooling effect of the water softened him slightly, amusing her when she noticed the pulse in his jaw.

"Down," she ordered, pushing his shoulders forward. He complied, jumping tensely as she spread his taut buttocks and scrubbed down his thighs where an injury had left bloody residue.

Then seated at his front with him still standing, she began her play. Her tongue licked at the cockhead, teasing it around the rim and along the front of the shaft. He instantly regained his hardness, blood throbbing through his length until it again darkened. Her lips teased his sac, the line of his leg, around the lower reaches of his abdomen, and then returned to his prick to suck it into her mouth. Savoring his musk, she inhaled and sucked harder, drawing him to her throat, coursing over him with her tongue until she felt his issue begin to gather and burn.

She thought he trembled when she stood back, leaving him at the brink. Veins rose on his neck and temples, and his lucent gaze glittered.

"Battle it is, then," she said then laughed quietly.

She released the fastening ties of her woolen dress and let it fall, and then pulled her linen shift over her head so she stood before him in only her long stockings. Her breasts rose and fell as his glance seared over her body. She touched herself, rimming her puckered nipples and briefly caressing her mound.

With the clothing gathered in her arms, she formed a bundle and placed it in front of him.

"Kneel," she demanded, pointing downward.

"*Hunhund,*" he muttered, dropping to his knees on the bundle.

Whatever his word meant, she caught his intent. A humiliated flush spread over his cheekbones as she positioned herself in front of him, a foot propped on his stool. He did not move at first, nor did he meet her gaze. She gripped his hair, tugging him forward.

His nose pressed her thigh and rubbed sideways, sending strings of fire up her belly. Breath froze in her chest as his tongue slipped to the moist fur, parting it, stroking between her folds. A quiet moan formed in her throat, escaping in tiny broken sounds as he buried his face more deeply between her legs.

He used his chin, nose, and mouth, spreading and penetrating until her hips jumped with each hard thrust of his tongue. She gasped, struggling to stand. There had been men, of course, besides her husband, but never a man to do this so well. Her fluids oozed in heated pulses.

He nestled deep to snare the tender pearl of her sex. The contact pinioned her, bathing her instantly in a film of sweat. With the knot of nerves caught between his teeth, he tormented it with his tongue and mouth until she groaned and shuddered. Unbearable pressure throbbed to the tips of her fingers and toes, driving her mad with need.

He dried his face on her thighs before grinning upward. "Battle drawn."

She gasped, shaking with the urgency screaming through her. She clasped her hand over the coal between her legs, stroking where he had left her wanting.

Abruptly, he turned and bit her inner thigh, sending shocks through her belly.

"Ahh!" Her body reacted to the bite as if his cock penetrated her. Abandoned to her release, she shuddered against her hand as her bud pulsed. Her eyes closed briefly, her head thrown back.

"You'll want more," he observed drily.

Struggling to gather her wits, she stepped back and glanced to his groin where his cock strained erect.

"As will you," she snapped back.

He grinned more broadly.

Her options were limited. She could not release his bonds. He could easily hurt her, even with bare hands, and then perhaps make some threat at the door which could force his release. And though her private activities were known to a handpicked few, any wider knowledge would compromise everything in her careful world.

"Come to the bed."

"The women fall as easily as the men," he laughed, sneering between the loose, damp strands of his hair as he struggled to stand.

"Yet, it is you in bonds," she retorted, shoving him as he shuffled forward. "Sit."

With his back to the bed's corner post, she brought a leather tie around one wrist and fastened it to the post, then untied the rope so that one arm came free. She accepted the risk. He could still do much harm, even with only one arm loose, and if left alone, he would instantly release the rest of his bonds and try to fight his way out.

He flexed his shoulders, massaging himself with his freed hand.

She thought of how it must be for him, one moment a warrior and the next enslaved and facing certain death.

This captivity surely tore at him, and he would pursue any option for escape as keenly as he fought on the field.

The thought stilled her momentarily, as she accepted that nothing of what he did with her would carry any meaning or caring. She hadn't realized until that moment how much she wished to be cared for in that way, to have a connection between sex and her heart. All these years, since the age of fifteen when her father gave her to her husband, she had cared for these lands, holdings, and even the old man himself. But in his eyes, she was another possession. And even in the early days, when he could still more or less function as a man, his pleasuring concerned only himself and ended quickly.

She had loved no man.

It shamed her to be in this position, to feel no allegiance in her heart, to have no man who loved her, wanted her, made her tremble at his touch. She tossed her head and bit down the swell in her throat. "Lay back," she said hoarsely.

With an even greater smirk, this Dane with his splendid body spread himself upon the bed, his pants still captured around his ankles. He raked her naked form with his leer before bringing his challenging stare to meet her gaze. His heavy cock jerked slightly, teasing her with what he had to offer, what she had to have.

She straddled him, lowering herself over his chest, and slid her wet folds along his rigid length. Her breasts draped his chest, her hair fell over his shoulders, and her hands explored his powerful arms, the wide spread of his shoulders, the tangled blond hair gleaming in the candlelight. His scent filled her nose with musk and the smell of leather. She nibbled along his neck, savoring his salty taste.

War treasure in its richest form, he was hers to enjoy. For long delirious moments, she teased his throbbing manhood between her legs, reveling in the sensation.

Finally unable to wait another instant, she shifted her hips and caught his swollen tip at her eager entry. Bit by bit, she lowered herself until she bottomed at his root. His thickness spread her open. Moving at first in short desperate strokes, she soon succumbed as her hunger seized her, and she had no choice but to ply more boldly.

His hand came to her thigh, then captured her breast and firmly pinched her nipple, but she barely recognized his act so caught she had become in her frenzy. Wildly, moaning, she rode him.

Deep she drove, to the mouth of her empty womb, to the pit of her stomach where parts of herself opened for the first time and unleashed a ravening storm. Her body vibrated with longing, from the soles of her feet to the roots of her hair. She burned, crying out in each lunge as his cockhead surged in her belly.

His big hand spread over her thigh so that his thumb pressed the same coal he had tormented with his mouth. He circled it, pressing and pushing until flames ignited over her skin and erupted from the point of his massive prick. Her body convulsed around him, milking and writhing.

His groans came no less urgently than her own, his hips shuddering upward in his release. Long slow thrusts shoved up from his loins, prolonging the molten collapse of her body around their joined flesh. His hand captured her hair and brought her down to his mouth, his lips caressing hers, and his tongue searching her own.

They lay silent, her head on his shoulder, their bodies still mixed. Tears burned from her eyes, and she couldn't stop the sobs that rolled in her chest: sadness for what her life could have been if she had been free to marry a man more suited, grief for the loss she would know when this man was gone. He cared nothing for her, yet had been caring in their joining, more than she expected or deserved.

"*Valkyrie,*" he muttered. "Perhaps I have died and only now know it."

She moved to lie beside him, consoling herself within the sweep of his arm even if he meant no embrace. "I have used you in real life, I assure you," she whispered.

They rested together. Yes, she agreed with her silent argument, she should tie him. She should make this the end of it, pull on her clothing, and leave him to his fate.

But she did not. Instead, she listened to his breathing settle into sleep and let herself imagine life with him, a dream of happiness that could never be hers. And she herself slept, finally, against his chest.

A soft rapping at the door and Magnus's jerk awake startled her, until she was reminded of her circumstance. All candles but one had guttered.

"My lady," a familiar voice urged.

Aether. She threw on her dress and went to the door. As she had arranged, a meal, a bucket of fresh coals, another ewer of ale and one of water were brought into the room. Fresh candles were lit.

The Dane sat in the bed watching as Aether, his gaze carefully lowered, departed.

The tray held roast fowl, smoked fish, slices of ham, and more bread in addition to cabbage, carrots, and turnips stewed with onions and herbs. She carried the tray to the bed and set it beside his free hand, and then sat across from him. They drank ale, feasted, and conversed on issues of no consequence: whether the food pleased him and how it compared with his native fare, the nature of Valkyries, the time of day, whether the winter would again be fierce. He smiled often, each time dazzling her—a gleam of fat on his lips, creases that dented his cheeks, the sparkle of pleasure in his eyes.

"How can you smile when you are captured?" she inquired, carrying the near-empty tray from the bed. She returned with a fresh cloth moistened for their hands and faces.

"The Fates decide my future," he said, shrugging. "I am not dead yet, so they still favor me."

Her troubled glance saw that his words did not fully describe what he thought or felt, but she left him the dignity of his private fears.

"And you, free and of high rank—are you not also captured? Why are you hidden with me here?" He studied her with a half-smile.

His words caught her, forcing the truth of her situation to the front of her mind. "I don't wish to think of my life, Magnus. It tears at me. I have risked much to have you, to take some few hours of pleasure."

"Yet, you are the lady of this estate, are you not?"

"I am."

"No husband?"

"I have one, but he is old and infirm."

"And local men pose much risk." He nodded to himself. "Captured, surely. But not about to die."

"Don't say that. I wish you not to die."

He threw back his head, laughing. "So you would keep me here to service you? For how long would you carry in food, wash me, keep me from sunlight and fresh air?"

His words cut at her like daggers. "I think of only this moment," she protested.

"Can you even see me as a man, with my pants captured at my ankles? I can't mount you as you deserve."

His certain anguish speared her heart. No matter how brave a front he put up, he only marked time to the end of his days. Never to see his homeland, his brothers in arms. What if he had a woman? This wasn't what she wanted, this despair growing in her after only a few hours.

"Do you have…a woman you love?"

"No."

"If you were free to go, where would you go? What would be your future?"

"I fight. It's what I know how to do. I am a sword warrior. I stand in the shield wall and glory in spilling blood."

"Can you not go home?"

He shrugged. "Home is wherever I sleep. But for our native country, little is there. The place is overrun with too many of our kind, and the land is rocky, nothing like the green meadows here where sheep grow fat."

"Do you fight here to gain our land?"

"Your land, yes, your treasure, your food. All we need to live, we must take." His voice softened. "It is our way."

"What is the way of your women?"

"Do you wish to be my woman?"

Elspeth turned away, caught on the point of his words. "Yes, for now," she managed in a weak voice. "But I have duties here. Many depend on me for their livelihood, not the least being my husband. The entire village, the household, the thanes—all of them center around Hystead as if we were the sun. And I am the force that makes it shine."

His hand brushed her hair. "Take off your dress, force of sun. Valkyrie."

Her heart leapt at his touch. Did he treat her tenderly out of some plan to gain freedom? She couldn't think of that but simply did as he asked. When he turned to her, his mouth fastened on her mouth with what seemed to be passion, and she wanted only to feel his skin under her palms.

His mouth grazed her shoulders, and his heated breath swept over her breasts. His kiss left her weakened.

"Unbind me, so that I may fully take you," he rasped.

"You could harm me."

"What would I gain? Your goodwill is all that stands

between me and the torture of inglorious death."

"You could use me to force your way out."

"And then? Ride off with you and be hunted like an animal by an army of your men?" He snorted his disgust. "I have no escape. Like you," he added quietly.

Her choice seemed unthinkable, but as she tugged at the ropes around his ankles and pulled free his other wrist, it seemed to Elspeth the only thing she could do. He spoke truth.

And in that moment, her life shifted. So little of what she did each day mattered. A sudden vision of her future formed in her mind, herself in old age, unable to bear children and beyond any bloom of youthful beauty. She would be alone, even more alone than now, when at least the pleasure of flesh still swept her breath away.

With a growl, he pulled her to him, crushing her in his arms. His mouth slanted over hers in a fearsome kiss, ravishing with his tongue and nipping with his teeth until her lips felt stung. His hands surrounded her, firm on her breasts and coaxing her nipples to points, lifting her hips and positioning her on the bed so that he loomed over her, his golden hair hanging toward her as his hard cock nudged between her legs.

Her mind ceased, her body softened, and she gave herself fully to his taking. He ravaged over her like a wild animal. Feral noises issued from their throats as he pounded and seethed, as she rose to meet him.

"Look at me, woman."

Her gaze flew upward, and she encountered his icy blue stare. His face creased with the intensity of his effort, beaded in sweat, shadowed in his veil of yellow-white hair.

"This is to remember," he said gruffly.

He brought his knees under her thighs and lifted her hips to shove his prick to a spot she had not known. Her body curled around him, contracting, arching, cut to the core with a torch of fire that spread from her belly and blazed over her in long fiery bursts. His eyes command-ed her to watch him, see him remove her last defense, fulfill her secret wish, make her his own. His eyes spoke of his own need, his wish for life even if only in the future of the seed he planted.

He took her again and again in the hours of that long night, waking from fitful sleep to turn again in each other's arms until she was swollen and sore, and he shook with exhaustion. Everything he had, he gave. She wept off and on, delirious, consumed. The room and Magnus in it were all that mattered.

And yet, some part of her remained separate to question, worry, wonder. Grieve.

She could see faint daylight in the crack around the door when the next knock came. She drew on the dress and brought Aether inside.

He set the tray on the table. "The lord has asked, my lady," he muttered in a low voice. "What shall I say?"

"That I am indisposed and wish to see no one."

"Very well."

"Who is about?"

"No one yet, at least not on these grounds."

"Excellent." She motioned, and he followed her outside the door. "I have much to ask and little time, so listen carefully."

When she had finished her instructions, she returned to the room and shed the dress. She and Magnus ate with languor, amused at small things that passed between them in word play and gestures. Hours passed again in the bed, hours when he brought her to unknown heights of pleasure, and she wept in its joy. How unjust, that this was the man who fit her so perfectly, this man of another country, the enemy at the gate. How absurd, that she wanted him more than she wanted any of her wealth or comfort, that she cared more for him after only one night than she cared for her duties or even the dearest of her companions. They slept in fits, wrapped in each other's arms, until the door's rim had darkened with night and again, the knock came at the door.

"Aether, what is your word?" she asked anxiously through the open door.

"It is prepared, lady, as you asked. They are feasting in the great hall."

"Take care, dear friend." She clasped his hand and pulled him close for a quick embrace. "Remember, no word until you must."

She turned. "Magnus, draw on your pants. We go out."

He stood, his face suddenly pale. "You tire of me so soon? I thought I would have at least another day to live."

"You will have another day," she said with a sudden wide smile, "but not here."

Night sounds swelled as she threw the door wide. Her nerves strung tight as harp strings, Elspeth lifted her hot face to the cool fall air and breathed deeply. She had made her decision, and she wouldn't turn away from it. Tall dark horses, two of their best, stood fully packed with provisions, weapons, and all else they needed for the journey.

"We ride to the east, to Dane-held lands," she said quietly. "If you will take me."

His expression formed sharp angles in the moonlight, incredulous and wary at the same time, as he assessed the situation and adjusted to this new turn of Fate. His pale gaze shifted around them then riveted on her face with a quizzical look.

Her pulse hammered in her throat. Did he not want her?

"I will." He laughed, a gentle rolling sound that caused her heart to clench. "No longer captured, Valkyrie of the sun?"

She hadn't realized she'd been holding her breath. It released in a rush. "Only by you, warrior Dane."

He stepped close and touched her face. "What is your name, Valkyrie?"

"Elspeth."

He helped her mount, and then threw himself onto the restless stallion.

"Lead the way, Elspeth, woman of Magnus," he said, bowing his head slightly as he swept his hand toward the rutted lane.

Thrilling, she kicked the mare forward.

Ásgeirr and the Tree of Life

Mina Murray

The southwest coast of Ireland, 821 AD

IT HAPPENS SO fast…the turning of his fortunes, the treachery of his Viking brothers. Ásgeirr cannot say for certain what wakes him—whether it is the urgent whispers, or the creak of the boards—but what does it matter? The result is the same. The fumbling for his weapon in the gray half-light before dawn, hands clumsy with cold. Torvík, standing over him with a spear, about to strike. The thrust to the heart Ásgeirr manages to deflect. The thrust to his side that he doesn't. The fight that follows, with Ásgeirr outnumbered.

"You'll be dead as soon as you hit the water," Torvík sneers, before pushing him from the longboat.

And Ásgeirr believes it, in those moments of freefall, which seem an eternity but are no more than the blink of an eye.

This is no way for a Viking to die.

His woolen cloak, his tunic, his boots, weigh him

down. His sword, too, though he would rather drown than part with it. He takes off his belt, uses it to lash the sword to his wrist. He clings to his shield as the *langskip* pulls away.

The current eddies around him, and Ásgeirr stops resisting it, allows it to carry him out to the wide open sea. Now that the fight is over, the battle-rush gone, the pain of his injuries hits him. His body goes limp. The sting of the salt water penetrates his torn flesh. *It would not hurt so much if I were dead*, he reasons. *So, it seems I am alive, after all.*

FROM HER VANTAGE point atop the cliff, on the peak of Éire's southernmost inhabited island, Ashling can see for miles. To her right, the Atlantic Ocean shimmers. To her left gleams the Celtic Sea. And behind her, some way down the path to the harbor, stands the small stone cottage where she lives, alone.

Ashling knows each inch of the coastline, each rugged cliff-face, each inlet. Which is why she notices—sooner than others might—the body bobbing in the waves below, clinging to some debris. She may be blessed with a falcon's sharp eyesight, but even Ashling cannot make out whether the figure being swept into the harbor is male or female, alive or dead.

It is low tide. The harbor will be deserted. There will be no one to see this lost soul; no one to render aid.

Ashling scrambles down the path, crushing wildflowers in her wake. By the time she reaches the bottom, the man has washed up on the pebbled shore. When she sees the markings on the shield he clings to, the weapon tied to him, she is suddenly very glad no others are around.

The Vikings have not yet come this far south, but in the winter just past, they had set up camps as close as Cork. Summer is coming—raiding season—and the island folk are fearful. They would kill this man on sight. Ashling is a healer, though, and will turn away none in need. "Good day," she calls out.

The man stirs but does not rise.

"Oh gods," she gasps, seeing his condition. "I must get him home."

But as strong as she is, she cannot carry him up the hill. And she cannot call on anyone to assist them. Not now she knows what he is. There is nothing else for it. She must wake him.

She ventures closer, eyeing his sword. What if he startles when she rouses him, and he swings? Perhaps she should stand on the blade. That might slow him long enough to realize she is no threat.

She is about to tap him on the shoulder when the sun emerges from behind the clouds.

The stranger's eyes snap open, and he pulls the sword from beneath her boots with no effort at all.

Ashling stumbles backwards, stifling a scream.

But he stills his hand. A beat later, he lowers his sword.

He means her no violence. In fact, he seems to be…he *is*…kneeling before her, head bowed. As if she were a great lady. As if she were a goddess.

"Freyja," he says with more fervor than he should possess having been wounded.

She shakes her head, points at herself, and says, "Ashling."

"*Nei*," he corrects, insistent. "Freyja!" With great ceremony, he offers her his shield.

Ashling has the good sense to play along. She accepts his offering and nods in thanks. Then, regally, she extends her hand and beckons, slender fingers curling inward toward her palm.

The Northman lifts his head to look upon her.

Her breath catches in her throat. He is young. Likely the same age as she. And his countenance is striking: the sharp planes of his cheekbones, the proudly aquiline nose, those *eyes*. Slate-gray and flecked with blue, glassy-calm on the surface, but turbulent beneath, as if they held the very sea itself. His wet clothing clings to his muscled form. A silver ring pierces his left nostril. It glints in the sun.

So beautiful, Ashling thinks, *so savage*.

To her great relief, he accompanies her without question. She chooses one of the lesser-known paths. A slightly longer route, but it is hidden from view, and just as well. Their progress is slow. They stop frequently so she can press her flask on him. The water is the only aid the Viking accepts. He refuses to lean on her for support, even though he stumbles often and is ashen with pain. Finally, just before twilight, they reach Ashling's cottage.

The Northman seems struck by the great tree flanking the entrance.

"Yggdrasil," he says and pushes up his sleeve. On his

right wrist is a tattoo of a giant green ash. It is the world tree, the tree of life at the center of the universe.

Ashling recognizes it from her mother's stories. She would like to touch the tattoo, but she knows it would not be wise. She has taken enough of a risk already. All have heard about the fury of the Northmen. She ushers the stranger in ahead of her. The dagger she carries hidden on her person is still there, a reassuring presence against her thigh. Ashling will use it if she has to, as she has in the past.

When she turns to shut the door, there is a muffled thump. She pivots to defend herself, but the Northman poses no danger. At least, not at present, for he is passed out on her bed, resting uneasily on his side, long legs dangling awkwardly over the pallet. The small room fills with the sound of his labored breathing. Ashling collects the shield and the sword, hides them in a safe place, and then lights a fire and gets to work.

IT IS A blessing, the dark stranger's lapse into unconsciousness. It makes her task so much easier. That, and the opiate she trickles down his throat. To get to his wounds, she has to cut him out of his tunic and cloak. It is a shame to mar such good garments, but Ashling is as handy with a sewing needle as she is with a doctoring needle. She will mend them both. For now, she hangs the fragments of his clothing over the chair near the fire.

Ashling has heard that the *víkingr* decorate their bodies. Here before her is living proof. The stranger bears tattoos not only on his wrists, but all over. She recognizes some of the images. She will ask him about the others when he wakes.

In the meantime, she places pillows on either side of him, to support him while she extracts the arrows. Only one has gone through to the other side. It will be the least painful to remove. She selects a pair of cutters, shears off the protruding arrowhead then tugs on the fletched shaft. It comes out as easily as she'd hoped. The other two are tricky, lodged in bone. Those she has to remove with the aid of a special instrument that can grasp the metal barb.

The stranger's wounds were clean—all that seawater—but Ashling cleans them again. First with vinegar then with whiskey. She stitches up the hole in his side, quickly cauterizes those on his back and chest, and applies a healing salve.

Only now, after her delicate task is done, do her hands begin to shake. She considers the bottle of whiskey. Finds herself a glass and pours one dram, then a second, but not a third. There is more to be done. She must finish undressing him.

Ashling has seen naked men before. But when she tugs the Northman's breeches from him, and then his underclothes, an unfamiliar fire blazes through her veins.

'Tis wrong to stare at him lustfully, she tells herself, *when he may be dying.*

But when will she again have the chance?

The island folk think all Northmen are fair-haired, but this one's hair is dark. Closely cropped at the sides and back, longer on top and at the front, it falls at a rakish angle over his forehead. His dark beard, the hair curling over his chest and his forearms, all emphasize the natural paleness of his skin. Ashling cocks her head to the side, taking in the long lines of his back then letting her gaze travel lower. Over the dip at the base of his spine. Over the mounds of his arse. Over his powerful thighs, the back of his legs, his ankles, his long feet.

Ashling's heart thuds as she circles to view him from the front, scandalized at the brazenness, the *thoroughness*, with which she examines him.

A line of hair bisects the sharply-defined muscles of his abdomen. The fine trail starts just above his umbilicus and leads all the way down to his member, which lies like a sleeping dragon along his thigh.

No, thinks Ashling. *Not a dragon.*

For etched into the sensitive skin just below his navel is another tattoo. A serpent, biting its tail. She drops to her knees beside the bed to get a better look and a shock pulses sharply, sensually, through her. Down, down, down the serpent writhes. Its scaled body coils intimately around its master's cock, and then rears up again, tapering gradually to the fine point of a tail held between two sharp fangs.

Nothing can prevent Ashling from touching the Northman now, from tracing with her fingertips the tattoo's serpentine progress. She undresses quickly, casting off her overdress and her *léine,* and lies down beside him.

His skin burns against hers. The fever that threatened earlier has taken hold. For a moment, she feels a pang of guilt. But then the voice of temptation speaks. *He will not remember*, it says. *Or he will think it only a dream.*

She reaches for the stranger's prick, touches it tentatively at first, watching with fascination as she gently works back the foreskin and the plum-like head emerges, a clear fluid leaking from the tip. With the pad of her thumb, she smears it around the crown. Even through the drugged fog, the Northman's body responds, his hips canting forward. He grows harder as she uses his foreskin to pleasure him, sliding it up and down over his shaft.

Ashling whimpers and thrusts her other hand between her legs. She is wet already, so wet there is barely any friction at all. Her fingers slide clumsily over her little jewel, and she knows she will not find the tension she needs to climax. So she crosses her legs tight, and pushes her hips back and forth, increasing the pressure against her bead. The rocking motion presses her closer to the Northman, so close that the head of his cock butts insistently against her.

She kisses him then. Kisses his hard mouth and his broad chest, tugs at his nipples with her teeth, sucks the corded muscles in his neck. Her breasts rub against his battle-hardened body, and she gasps as sensation builds inside, builds like a storm does, far out at sea. Ashling holds it back, anxious to prolong this stolen intimacy as long as possible.

She crawls down the stranger's body until her mouth is level with his cock. Ashling has never done this before.

The very newness of the act is intoxicating. She drags her tongue around and across the smooth-polished head, occasionally flicking her tongue into the narrow slit on top, the eye that wept when she first touched him.

He tastes like the ocean, Ashling thinks. *Like tears and the ocean.*

Then she notices the indentation on the underside of the crown. Its very shape seems to beg for a kiss. So she presses her mouth to it and obliges, pausing every so often to dart her tongue out and lick his shaft, or to rub her face against its fleshy smoothness. She moves further down the bed to play with his heavy ballocks, to draw them deep into her mouth.

From this angle, she can see clearly that what she thought was one spiral of the serpent's tail is in fact three, each inked on top of the other.

He must *have stretched his skin taut while they did this*, she thinks. *Or else his prick was stiff.*

The very thought of such a scene—the Northman's body on display for others—makes Ashling hot with desire. She takes his root into her mouth again, all the way into her mouth, moaning around his shaft, laving the tattooed serpent's rings with the tip of her fluttering tongue.

I could taste him for hours, Ashling thinks.

But she can no longer delay her release. Her fingers move frantically between her thighs, flicking at her pearl, slipping between her slick folds. She can barely breathe with the stranger's prick so deep in her throat and is beginning to feel light-headed. But the sensation adds an edge to her bliss, and she wails like a banshee when she comes, crying out around the Northman's cock. The vibrations provoke a violent response in him and his whole body begins to tremble.

Ashling wants to watch what happens as he goes over, so she lets him slip from her mouth and takes him in her hand. His prick is still wet from her tongue. The moisture eases the way, allows her to swivel her palm over the head, as well as glide it up and down the thick shaft. He feels hot, so hot, and Ashling knows it is not the fever. She looks on, enthralled, as the Northman's cock—now an angry red—seems to grow even longer and begins to pulse.

For one heart-stopping instant, just before his seed spurts all over her hand, she is certain the Northman is watching her from beneath half-closed eyes.

Just a trick of the light, Ashling convinces herself. And to be sure, the moon *is* high now, its silver beams stealing through the windows, battling with the firelight to illuminate one minute, to obscure the next.

As the after-shocks of orgasm flicker through her like retreating lightning, Ashling raises her hand to her mouth and licks the Northman's seed from her fingers. She falls back on the bed, sated, but tired. Bone-tired. She pulls the bed-clothes over herself and her dark stranger, and, just for a minute, rests her eyes.

ÁSGEIRR DREAMS OF fire and blood. Of drifting delirious on the open sea, surrounded by the slap of the waves, no land in sight and no ship to bear him home. Sometimes, he dreams of home. Or at least, what *feels* like home. A small cottage with fresh rushes on the floor. Clean air. A fire that warms him without filling the house with smoke. A soft bed and softer furs. And a woman, slender and beautiful, with honey-brown hair and eyes the color of amber. Her gentle touch, cool against his brow. The pleasure she brings him with her hands—oh gods, with her *mouth*. The comfort of her body pressed against his.

But such golden visions are all too brief, and soon he is back on the longboat. Only this time, Ásgeirr is ready. He senses Torvík nearby and grabs the bastard by the neck, rising to his full height, lifting his enemy off the boards. The traitor kicks his feet uselessly, scrabbles to loosen the choke-hold. Ásgeirr just squeezes harder. His fingers completely enclose his enemy's neck.

But something is wrong.

I should not be able to do this, he realizes. *Torvík's neck is much too thick. And I could never have lifted him with one hand.*

Ásgeirr's grip slackens. The scrabbling stops, replaced by a percussive beating against his chest. And then by the point of a dagger, just below his sternum.

At the cold touch of steel, the fog in his head retreats.

The cottage from my dreams, he thinks, as his vision clears. *And the woman, too.* "You saved me," he says, wonderingly.

But wonder turns to horror when he realizes how he has repaid her kindness. "*Helvíti*," he curses, then releases her immediately.

The woman collapses in a naked heap, sucking in long shuddering lungfuls of air. She still clutches her dagger.

Ásgeirr does not blame her.

"Touch me again, Northman, and die," she says, when she is able to speak.

"My name is Ásgeirr," he says. He takes a moment to register her strange accent. "Where am I?"

"Éire. On an island south-west of Cork."

"Who are you?"

"I found you, cast up on the shore, stuck with arrows."

Her voice is husky, either naturally so, or from the injury he has done her.

"I brought you to my home to heal you." She rolls to her side, and then into a crouch. "But if I'd known you were going to strangle me during a nightmare, I'd have left you for dead."

He tries not to stare at her body, tries to ignore the rise and fall of her large breasts, the golden glint of hair between her thighs.

Too late, he thinks, with a groan. His cock rises, no matter that he wills it down.

When she sees his erection, her eyes widen, and in a second, she is on her feet, wielding her knife in front of her as if it was a sword.

"I'll not hurt you," Ásgeirr says, stepping back. "Here." He tosses her a fur with which to cover herself. Then he steps into his breeches, waiting for him on the bed. They do nothing to conceal his excitement. His cockstand tents the fabric in front of him.

Suddenly, his belly growls. A rumbling sound that seems to go on forever, echoing off the walls. All the hungers of his body have come to life at once. A lesser warrior might be embarrassed.

But the sound breaks the tension at least. The woman laughs, and the tightness in his chest eases. Having been speared once in the past week, Ásgeirr is not keen to repeat the experience.

"Come," his rescuer says, "if you are done trying to kill me, we will eat."

IT IS A simple repast—bread and cheese, stew and some berries—but to Ásgeirr, the food is ambrosia. He has not eaten in days.

"Slowly," the woman cautions.

Ashling. He remembers her name now. She told him at the shore, when she found him.

They eat in silence. He spends most of the meal observing her. She will not meet his gaze. Once or twice he catches her looking at him, and she blushes.

She has changed into a woolen shift and overdress. *I liked the fur better*, Ásgeirr thinks.

"*Takk*," he says, when they are finished and are seated in front of the fire. "I thank you. For the meal. And for healing me. For giving me back the chance to die a warrior's death."

"Better I had given you the chance to live," she replies softly, staring into the flames.

They are waiting for water to heat so he can bathe.

He looks longingly at the large tub, positioned close by the hearth. His skin is tight from three days in the salt sea, and his wounds are itching.

When Ashling rises to put on gloves, to lift one of the heavy cauldrons, Ásgeirr grabs her hand and says, "No, let me."

He rubs his thumb back and forth in the centre of her palm. "Such soft hands," he says. "I would feel them on me."

Ashling clears her throat, but her voice comes out in a whisper. "The water."

Her hair is tousled, her cheeks flushed, her lips parted.

She looks ready to be fucked, Ásgeirr thinks. *Ready to be fucked, and I've barely even touched her.*

But she also looks nervous, and Ásgeirr likes his women willing. So he lets her go, and says "Yes, the water," and picks up the cauldrons, one in each hand, and empties them into the bathtub. He is about to undress when Ashling hurries over with a long sheet of linen.

Next to the bath, hanging low from the ceiling, are two hooks used for drying herbs. Ashling winds the linen around the hooks, and then steps back.

The sheet falls to the ground between them.

"For modesty," she explains.

"Mine? Or yours?"

"Both."

"But you have already seen me unclothed."

"That was different." She pauses. "You were ill. You

were asleep."

"But then I woke. You saw me then, too."

"Yes," she concedes, with a blush. "I did."

Ásgeirr strips off his clothing, exaggerating his movements, knowing that the barrier between them is no real obstruction. He can see Ashling's silhouette through the fabric and knows she can see his, if she is looking. He hopes she is. He hopes he is not the only one goaded by desire.

When he eases into the bath, Ashling passes a bar of soap and some scented oil around the makeshift screen. A moment later, she hands him a square cloth, too. Ásgeirr rubs it against his face. Soft. It has been a long time since he has had such luxuries. "Will you stay and talk with me?"

There is a scraping sound as she moves her chair nearer.

"How is it that you know my language?" Ásgeirr asks.

"My father was a Gael, but my mother was from the North," she says. "She taught me her language before she died, told me tales of the old gods."

"Where is your father now?"

"Dead."

"Husband?"

"I have none."

"You should not be here by yourself, alone."

"I am not unprotected."

"Should I expect a band of angry Gaels, then, lining up to kill me at my bath?" Ásgeirr is only half-jesting.

"No." Ashling snorts. "They would not come even if I begged them. Not for a halfling like me. I protect myself."

"With what?"

"With weapons," Ashling says, and then pauses, as if she is not sure whether to continue. "With the old magics."

The curtain shifts as she leans forward, close enough that he can see the curve of her breasts, the elegant line of her neck.

"I answered your question," she says. "Now answer mine, if you will. How did you come to be here?"

He would prefer to forget. So much blood. So much death.

"You do not have to tell me, if it is painful."

"I owe you that much for your aid," he says. "So I will tell you. But tomorrow. Or the next day." He settles back in the water with a heavy sigh. "For now, I would like to enjoy being alive."

He is about to start soaping his back, but then thinks *I would much prefer her hands on me.*

"What is wrong?" Ashling asks.

Like he hoped she would, when he splashes around and curses under his breath.

"I cannot reach my back," he complains. "Not without it hurting."

Ásgeirr knows there is a long-handled brush by her feet. He can see it, just under the screen. She could hand it to him. But she doesn't. Instead, she twitches aside the screen and holds out her hand for the cloth.

ASHLING HAD INTENDED to stay behind the barrier. To stay where it was safe. Or at least, saf*er.* But then she watched the Northman undress, watched his cock bob up and down as he stretched, and knew that she was lost. *If he had not asked me to bathe him,* she thinks, *I would have found an excuse myself.*

So now she is perched behind him, on the wide wooden rim of the tub. Dipping the cloth into the soapy water, washing his shoulders, careful of his wounds. Steam rises from the bath and swirls around her in a scented cloud. Beside her the hearth-fire crackles. As Ashling relaxes, her movements gradually slow, become more sensual; her touch is no longer that of a physician, but a lover. She sweeps the cloth over the Northman in elaborate patterns. Trails it up and down his spine. Draws rhythmic circles over his lower back.

After each pass of the cloth, Ashling rubs that same spot with her fingers, creating a wave-like rhythm that hypnotizes even her. The Viking's eyes close in pleasure. Before Ashling knows it, the cloth has slipped from her hand and she is running her palms over the Northman's broad shoulders, then lower. "What is this?" she asks, sketching the lines of a circular tattoo on his chest.

"A protection symbol. A compass to guide my way, to bring me home if I am ever lost."

He shifts in the water and the serpent between his legs stirs. Ashling inadvertently grazes his nipple with her fingernails.

The Northman groans.

"Sorry," she says, sure she has hurt him. She withdraws her hands, but he snatches them back, pulling her down until her neck rests against his.

"Don't be," he says.

The rough timbre of his voice sets her belly aflutter.

"It feels good when you do that." With his hand atop hers, he shows her what he wants. "Pinch it," he whispers, "the other one too. You'll not hurt me."

When she complies, he turns his head and nuzzles at her collarbone.

"I know your touch now, *kjære*." He follows the endearment with delicate bites along her neck. "I know it was you," he murmurs, "who brought me such pleasure while I slept."

Ashling flushes with shame, but it soon turns to shock when the Northman yanks her into the water. She lands sideways, her back pressed firmly against one side of the bath, her legs hooked over the other. He gathers her hands in his and presses them to the center of his chest.

She struggles vainly in his lap, until she realizes what she is rubbing against. Her soaked garments do nothing to protect her from that thick ridge. Fear and excitement course through her in equal measure.

The Northman tugs the pins from her hair and once it has tumbled free, twists his fingers in the silken strands, winding them around and around until his palm cups the base of her head.

They are so close now that she can count the striations of color in his eyes.

"I remember everything you did to me," he says. "I

remember you kissed me. Like this."

He tilts back her head, presses his mouth to hers, parts her lips with his tongue.

"Like this, too," he says, mouthing her neck, tonguing the pulse that hammers excitedly at the base of her throat. "And then like this."

Ashling knows what is coming next, but this does not prepare her for the reality. For how she feels when the Northman bends his head to her breasts and sucks the tight-budded tips into his mouth. Or when, a moment later, he twists both peaks between his fingers.

A charge runs through her—all the way to her sex— as if a sacred circle has been completed.

"I told you it felt good, *kjære.*"

Ashling shivers.

"But you did something else to me," Ásgeirr says. "Do you remember?"

"I made you come," Ashling says. *And I will never forget it.*

"Yes." His voice is hoarse. "All over your fingers. And then you sucked them clean."

"I like the way you taste," she says.

"Well, *min elskede,* now it is my turn."

Ásgeirr seizes her by the waist, hoists her onto the wide edge of the bath, and flips up her wet skirts.

Too late, Ashling recalls the twin daggers, strapped to her thighs.

"So this is where you hide your weapons." He stops her when she tries to unfasten them. "Leave them," he rasps and kisses the sheathed blades. "I like how fierce you look." He shoots her a smoldering glance. "My shieldmaiden."

Yes, Ashling thinks. *His.* She falls on him eagerly. This time it is she who takes the lead, who parts his lips, who sucks his tongue into her mouth. This time it is she who does the claiming. *He is mine,* she decides. She will fight anyone who tries to take him from her.

The Northman breaks away first, to crouch in the cooling water. He grips her ankles like a conqueror. Spreads her legs wide. Slides his hands over her calves. Such exquisite friction, his roughness against her softness. His palms are callused. Years of carrying a sword and shield. Years aboard a *langskip.* Such power he holds in check.

Ashling feels faint. From their kiss or from the heat or from expectation? Likely from all three. Ásgeirr's hands move higher, and soon he reaches the top of her legs, her swollen sex. With broad thumbs, he spreads her open.

"I'm going to kiss you here. To taste you, as you did me."

"No one has ever done this before."

"Then I am honored."

The Northman's dark head moves between her thighs. At the first touch of his tongue, she gasps. At the second—a long flat stroke that starts right at the bottom, then snakes up and over her pearl—Ashling forgets her manners and grinds against the Northman's face.

He pulls away, blows a stream of cool air over her heated flesh.

She twitches at the contrast.

"Greedy," he teases.

"Yes," she says and pushes him back down. "Don't stop."

Nothing Ashling has done to herself, late at night, compares to this. *This is some new kind of magic,* she thinks. *Surely it cannot be real.*

But it feels real, when Ásgeirr starts licking her in earnest, with side-to-side movements, with up-and-down flicks, with twists and circles and patterns Ashling cannot begin to name. It feels real, when he tongues her bud until it is stiff, so stiff, that he can draw it between his lips. When he pulls gently on the frilled lips of her sex. When he tells her to split her legs wider, as wide as she possibly can, and rest them over the sides of the bath. When he slides his pointed tongue inside her, just a little, and makes her scream.

"You like that," he gloats.

"I like it all. Whatever you give me, *a stór.*"

"What does that mean?"

"My treasure," she says and smiles.

Ásgeirr puts his mouth on her again, flicking at her bud with the tip of his tongue, slowly at first, then faster and faster.

"Oh," she cries out. "Oh, more, more." She clutches at his head, presses him closer, arches her back, and shudders.

Ásgeirr crushes her to his chest, then, and takes her mouth.

Ashling can taste herself on his tongue. "Please," she

begs, against his open mouth. "Please let me touch you."

"All right," he says, stripping off her wet clothes, "but not here. This water is freezing."

He carries her from the bath as if she weighs nothing.

"Your stitches!"

"You will mend me if they tear."

He drops her unceremoniously on the bed.

"I like watching you bounce," he grins and joins her. "Will you do that on my cock, too?"

"Later," Ashling says, reaching for him, eager to have him in her grasp. But before she can touch him, he drags her up to the top of the pallet.

"What are you doing?"

"Kneel over me," Ásgeirr orders, "but facing the other way. Rest your knees here, either side of my head."

When she comprehends his meaning, Ashling is aghast. "But you'll see…"

"Everything. I know."

"But—"

"*Elskling*, I've seen most of you already," he says.

Ashling shrieks as the Northman manhandles her, hauling her over his face. His fingers sink into the pillowy flesh of her buttocks. A second later, his tongue explores the furrow between them, finds the tight little hole Ashling wanted to hide. But she needn't have worried. Her Northman is not squeamish, Ashling realizes, as he pushes his face into her and plunders her arsehole enthusiastically with his tongue.

"Yes," she cries out. "Oh gods, yes."

Her legs collapse, and Ashling falls forward on top of him. His prick is right in her face. She props herself up on one elbow and swallows him down to the root.

Ashling both hears and feels his shouts, reverberating between her legs. *Tongue my bud*, she silently begs, *use your fingers in me*. And he does. Oh, he does. Ashling's whole body quivers. When he adds a second finger, stretching her deliciously, she breaks apart in bliss.

A moment later, Ásgeirr tries to roll her onto her back, and she panics.

He will split me in two without realizing it.

"No!" she cries. "I mean, not on my back."

"But *kjære*," he says and starts to sit up.

Ashling unsheaths her daggers quick as a flash and straddles his body, pinning him with her thighs.

"Only if I'm on top," she growls, rubbing her sex against his flat stomach, "only if I'm in control."

"I'll take you any way I can, *valkyrja*," says the warrior, surrendering.

She flings aside her daggers and lowers herself onto his cock, inhaling sharply as the bell-like tip breaches her. She wriggles back and forth, working it into her gradually, and the pain eases.

Beneath her, Ásgeirr hisses. "So tight," he says, and then looks at her in surprise. "Ashling, surely you are not… Are you a *virgin*?"

"Yes," she gasps and drops down onto him.

"*Min elskede*, you should have told me."

"So you could refuse me for honor's sake, because I saved you?"

"No," he says. "So I could be gentle."

Within a heartbeat, he flips her, and for a moment Ashling is frightened. But the Northman is true to his word. He moves slowly and their first joining is not a plundering, but a steady sinuous dance that is no less devastating.

Ashling soon grows accustomed to the singular pleasure of his thickness inside her. To the roll of his hips, to the unrelenting advance of him into her body, into her heart. She lifts her hips to match his thrusts, learning the way of it.

"I will take my time with you later, love," he groans. "We will do it any way you like. But for now I am done."

"Then come for me," she urges.

"Look at me, Ashling. Watch what you do to me."

His rhythm grows faster, his length burns like a brand inside her. Just when she thinks he will burst into flames, he pulls free of her tightness and spills his seed on her belly.

LATER, AFTER THEY have rested, they will talk of the future. And Ashling will ask to go with him when he leaves the island.

He will turn to her and say, first, we need a ship. And she will suggest they can build one or steal one—she is part Viking after all. When she asks which he prefers, he will laugh, and her heart will leap in her chest.

"That depends," he will say, "on whether you are as skilled with a hammer as you are with those daggers."

A Varangian Guest

Melissa Fuchs

Constantinople, 1036 AD

THE SMELL OF roasted meat, expensive spices, and rich fish sauce wafted through the house of Melite's brother, Chrysion. Slaves rushed through the dining room, carrying plates and bowls full of select delicacies. Melite stopped a young slave girl, who carried a bowl full of deeply purple and dark green olives and took one to try before she waved her off.

Her brother's wife was too sickly to care for the arrangement of the feast, and so it had been her responsibility to make sure everything was ready for Chrysion's return from his troop's campaign to Sicily. She made another round through the dining hall while the slaves scurried through the row of columns separating the room from the patio, and she put a vase that had been standing in the corner onto the small table below the large mosaic of some legendary ancestors of their family, one of which had gained sainthood. Quickly, she made the sign of the cross, once again thanking the Lord for her brother's safe return, and again turned to the sumptuously set table.

First, cheese and olives and pieces of baked octopus, grey mullet roe, clams stewed with garlic, onions and olive oil, and wheat bread baked with anise and fennel then sprinkled with sesame and poppy seeds—those dishes were laid out on the table, accompanied by jugs containing three sorts of spiced wine. Then, the *monokythron* – their mother's recipe, cabbage and slices of cold fish, eggs and rocket, a little celery, more olives and cheese—in a bowl and drenched in sweet wine. The meat would come after that. Then the saffron dishes and the spoon sweets. No grilled fish—after so many months of hunting down pirates, her brother would likely be sick to death of grilled fish.

When she looked up from the table again, her brother's wife entered the room. Callinice was pale and gaunt as always, but the dark blue gown she wore—the color of the Virgin, the divine patroness of Constantinople— endowed her with saint-like beauty. Once she had been an incredibly pretty girl, but since her sickness started after her third pregnancy, she faded like an eremite of legend.

Melite didn't like to admit it, but the bad health of her brother's wife had been a blessing. Her own husband had died five years ago before, leaving her in the house of his mother, a woman painfully pious. Melite had outright kissed the icon of the Virgin in her brother's antechamber when his wife's illness gave her a reason to return, if only to lead the household she had grown up in and to care for her niece and nephews.

Callinice's pale grey eyes flitted over the laid table. "Do you think we will have enough?" she asked anxiously.

Melite smiled and walked towards her. "It will be just Chrysion and a handful of his comrades. We have enough to feed half a *theme*. Don't you worry, Callinice."

Her own four pregnancies hadn't emaciated her like her brother's wife. The Lord had already blessed her with wide hips and an overall elegantly curved body when she had bloomed into a young woman nearly fifteen years ago. Her hips had become more ample with her two boys and her little baby girls, but the looks other women habitually cast her in the bath house told her she still had an enviable figure. For tonight, she had chosen a ruby red gown, the neck and hem embroidered with pearls, a gift from her late husband.

Suddenly, they heard a commotion from the antechamber.

"Well, that will be them," Melite said with a smile and motioned her brother's wife to follow her through the patio and along a short colonnade.

She could hear her little brother's laughter before they rounded the corner and her niece's squeaks, as well. As she saw just seconds later, Chrysion had hauled his daughter over his head and was now spinning her around like a spear in battle, which sent the four-year-old screaming and squealing with joy.

"You might want to put down your daughter or you will shake out her brains," Melite teased as she came to greet her brother with open arms.

He laughed and put the girl onto his shoulders to properly hug his sister. "Ah, Melite, what a comforting sight you are. And where is—" He let go of her and looked around searchingly before he spotted Callinice standing next to a pillar. While he went to greet his wife with a kiss (far too ardently for Callinice's weak body), Melite was able to look at the men her brother brought home. Two were known, and she greeted them with a wide smile, which they returned with words of reverence.

"The domes of Constantinople might be the first thing for a returning soldier's weary eyes to see, but the beauty of the Roman women is what makes a man truly feel at home, *Kyria*," Philonas, one of her brother's oldest friends, told her with a grin.

Melite smiled politely. "Just wait until you see the feast I have had prepared for you. There are plenty of other things that will make you feel at home, my friend."

She turned toward her brother, waiting for him to introduce her to the other three men, when she caught the gaze of one of those strangers. He was young, maybe four or five years younger than her own twenty seven, but tall and broadly built, light-eyed and golden haired. A foreigner.

Chrysion beamed as he approached them with fast steps. "Sister, let me introduce Arestes, my friend from the far-off Northlands. He serves in the Varangian force. The men under his command have taken out more pirates than any other squadron."

The foreigner bowed. "It's an honor, *Kyria*." His Greek was heavily accented—this was not a descendent of the Norsemen who came to Constantinople a hundred years before like the Varangians that made up such a large part of the palace guard. This was a man who had traveled far and fought many battles in his young life, judging by the scar rising above his collar.

She wondered how far down that scar reached… "Welcome to our home, Arestes," she said with a smile. "I noticed your accent. Are you from Varangia?"

A grin appeared on his face. "I am, *Kyria*. From a country by name of *Norvegr*." The country's name sounded like a growl coming from his lips.

"Arestes is a nobleman's son, and he served the king of Kiev before he came into the service of our empire," Philonas explained.

A nobleman? She hardly heard the names of the other two men Chrysion introduced, though she still greeted them politely while she did her best not to stare too openly at the young Norseman. Just looking at him—his broad jaw, his blue eyes and light hair—made strange feelings rise inside of her.

Struggling to recall her duty, she led their guests and newly returned master of the house into the dining room, where they attacked the first course as if it was a pirate-infested Mediterranean island.

Melite, who was familiar with the behavior of sailors newly home, had already served clams, cheese, and bread onto her and Callinice's plates, just to be on the safe side, and did her best to chat with her brother about their campaign while Chrysion ate heartily of octopus. While she picked the flesh out of her own clams with a little skewer, she let her gaze wander over the rest of her dinner guests. Before she even knew it, she was looking at the Varangian again.

He definitely had the table manners of a barbarian. He broke his clams with his fingers, licked the juice from his hands instead of swiping it up with bread, ate whole handfuls of cheese, olives, and mullet roe, and washed everything down with wine before he had even swallowed. When the *monokythron* arrived, he didn't even look at the fork next to his plate but kept using his fingers. Melite had heard the barbarians of the North thought forks were the work of the devil, but she really couldn't say whether this man didn't want to use one, or if he just didn't know how.

He did use his knife for the meat, and he complimented the fish sauce in which the kid and antelope had been cooked.

"The Slavs of Kiev sadly don't fancy fermented fish, *Kyria*," he told her with a wide, wickedly handsome grin, wiping sauce from his stubbly chin. "In my homelands, we ferment the fish whole or eat them dried, and their taste is quite similar to this sauce. But I would never have thought of using this sauce with meat."

Melite smiled—his grin was contagious; it crept into her flesh and sent tingles down her spine. He might have been a barbarian, but who cared about table manners when a man's smile made the sun rise in her dining room?

"We might have more in common than is obvious on first glance, then," she answered, and when he next licked the juice off his fingers, keeping his gaze on her, she couldn't stop the blush that spread from her cheeks to her chest at the sight of his tongue caressing his wet fingers.

For the rest of the dinner, she scarcely looked away from their Varangian guest. And he, in turn, kept casting her glances while eating and laughing with his brothers in arms.

They ate and drank until late into the night. When their friend, Philonas, left to seek his bed, only Chrysion, Melite, and the Varangian remained. Callinice had gone hours before. Outside the open windows, the moon stood high above the domes and towers of the city.

"You don't have a place of your own, Arestes, do you?" Chrysion asked the young Norseman who had caught Melite's eye so many times during this evening.

"I have been assigned to the barracks of the garrison for my stay in the city," he replied. He had emptied a good two jars of wine on his own, and still, there was no sign of drunkenness neither in his posture nor in his voice.

That was more than could be said for her brother. He was leaning heavily against a pillar while his face distorted into a comical frown. "That's far too far away to w-walk at this hour. Stay here. We have guest rooms."

Melite wasn't sure if she imagined Arestes cast her another glance before he nodded at Chrysion. "You are too kind, my friend."

A little smirk snuck onto Melite's face at that answer. "We will see how kind you will find it once you wake up tomorrow to the racket of five small children."

"Five? Are two of them your own, then?" Arestes asked while Melite motioned one of their slaves closer.

"I have four children," she said, smiling. "But only my two daughters live with me. My sons stay with my late husband's brother, a veteran who can give them a proper military education." Melite paused to instruct a slave to take Chrysion to his rooms.

"You must miss them," Arestes said in his rasping accent.

Melite's smile turned slightly rueful. "A Roman mother's sons belong to the Empire, my friend."

An earnestness she had not yet seen appeared on Arestes' face. "I am sure they will make you proud one day, *Kyria*."

Another slave arrived to lead Arestes to his rooms, and the Varangian bowed one last time to Melite before he walked away.

Exhausted and confused by the warm feeling in her chest, Melite trailed slowly to her bed.

SHE AWOKE A few hours later and then was unable to fall asleep again. With a sigh, she got out of her bed and threw a *palla* over her shoulders to cover the tunic she wore to bed. Then she left her bedroom, barefoot, and walked toward the patio.

Melite couldn't see the moon from the lushly planted inner yard, but knew the sun would come up in a few short hours. She sighed as she drew the cool night air into her lungs. The days were getting hotter and hotter, and soon even the last lingering coolness of the early morning hours would disappear. With her eyes closed, she leaned against one of the columns and listened to the noises of the night: the call of the night birds, the chirruping of a cicada, the low hum of a male voice…

That last noise made her open her eyes, and she frowned as she tried to catch the sound again. It came from close by. Now curious, she followed the humming to the other end of the patio and through a short hall into the humid warmth of the bathroom.

She didn't know which poor soul he had woken up to have the water heated, but Arestes was sitting in the sunken pool, faced away from the entrance. One of his naked, muscular arms laid languidly on the edge. His head was tilted backwards. And while she couldn't see what his other hand was doing, she could very much see the muscles in his shoulders moving. The noises she heard hadn't been humming, but low, rough moaning.

Heat rose in Melite's face. She wasn't sure if it was because she had intruded on a very private scene, or because those rasping moans sent sparks through her body and between her legs.

The prudent thing would be to leave him, and she slowly began to retreat. But just when she had set one foot over the threshold, her *palla* slipped from her head, and the soft noise of silk sliding over wool was enough to alert Arestes to her presence.

With the reflexes of a soldier, he jumped up and turned.

She managed to duck into the hallway before he could see her, but now that he was standing, his body was on full display. Bared of clothes, his shoulders looked even wider, his arms more powerful. Curls of golden hair covered a broad chest dripping with water. The scar she had noticed earlier ran from his neck down his chest, white and slightly luminescent in the dim light of the tallow lamps. It continued over taut muscles down to his navel, where another thin line of hair led to a bed of more curls between his legs where his sex jutted, long, thick and glistening, and still hard despite the sudden disruption.

Melite's mouth watered and her fingers started to itch. Never had she seen such a large, beautiful cock before.

"Who is there?" he called, not loud enough to alert the slaves, but loud enough for anybody in the hallway to hear. The thick muscles of his thighs tightened as he made a move to leave the pool.

In this moment, Melite decided that five years of celibacy had been enough. Prudence, propriety be damned. She was a widow—even if he did tell anybody, who would believe the words of a barbarian over those of a noble Roman lady?

All those thoughts rushed through Melite's head in a split second. She stepped into the bathroom again.

Arestes' eyes widened. "*Kyria*, I…"

She cut him off with a motion of her hand, and while fixing his gaze with her own, she slowly let her silken *palla* slide to the floor. His eyebrows shot upwards, but when she started to walk towards him, the light blue of his eyes vanished as his pupils widened. Staring from black eyes, he swallowed.

Melite smiled as she neared to the edge of the pool, though her mind was overflowing with doubts that came too late. Would he reject her? What if he laughed at her? After taking a deep breath to calm herself, she opened the lacings that held her tunic at her shoulders, allowing the soft wool to pool around her feet and revealing her voluptuous body.

A low growl came from his throat. Rough hands reached to grasp her hips and pull her toward him, leaving her no room for doubt concerning his attraction.

He pulled her in for a hungry kiss, and Melite couldn't hold back a needy moan when his hard, thick sex pushed against her belly. His tongue thrust into her mouth so fiercely she smiled against his lips and chastised him with a tiny nip at his tongue.

He growled into her mouth again, but pulled away obediently when she gently put her hand on his chest.

Her lips felt wonderfully swollen, and she could feel her own sex pulsing with need, but she wanted to draw this out as long as possible. "You seem to have a bit of a head start, my friend…" she said, her voice deepening to a sultry whisper.

A sound he must have liked because he drove his loins against her hips again.

She licked her lips and ran her fingers over the scar covering his chest. "I know that those from the icy north have lava in their veins," she whispered, "but try to bridle your youthful energy just for a few moments, and you will experience the bliss of a Roman bosom in its entirety…" She could feel him hesitate, but then he pulled back a little more, though his hands stayed at her hips, their grip even tightening a little, as though to keep her from running.

As if she could now that her body was awakened and needful of Arestes' beautiful length.

"Sit down," she whispered.

With a slight narrowing of his eyes, he let go and did as he was told.

A true soldier, after all, she thought with a smile, before she stepped downward, joining him in the pool.

She straddled Arestes' thighs and kissed him again, while her fingers ran down over his chest once more. His strong hands in turn found the mounds of her breasts, soft and large from feeding four hungry little babies in their time, and began to knead them so thoroughly that she had to stop the kiss just so she wouldn't choke on her moan.

His eyes were keenly trained on the flesh between his fingers, but after a few moments, he looked up into her eyes.

"I have been thinking about this all night," he confessed, and then he leaned forward to kiss her neck, to bite her tender skin.

She gasped, but put her hand onto the back of his head when he tried to pull away. His tongue swiped over the abused spot, then one of his hands left her chest and started to trail over her soft belly.

"Your image has followed me into my dreams, *Kyria*..." His warm tongue licked down over her chest, to the breast his hand abandoned. "The swing of your hips... The curve of your breasts underneath that red gown..." He growled again as he nipped the side of her chest, and Melite inadvertently thrust her hips forward, where they were met by his hand which now reached the black curls between her legs.

"I have been dreaming of sucking your teat just like this..." His lips closed around the tip of her breast, and delicious suction followed, paired with just a hint of teeth. He stirred in the water, and she could feel the little waves dancing around her hidden folds, adding to the pulsation between her legs. Her fingers raked through his golden hair, and her moaning turned into whimpers as he teased her by letting his fingers dip just half an inch beneath her curls, and then pull back again.

Only when he let go of her breast did he finally shoved his thick, calloused finger between her legs, where he unerringly found her nubbin and began to torment her with slow, circular movements.

"I have dreamed of pushing up your gown, *Kyria*... Of making you quake and shiver under my touch..."

His other hand left her chest, too, and grabbed her jaw, holding her in place as he kissed her roughly, possessively, in the same second as one of his thick fingers thrust into her slick, open entrance.

"If you had not been the sister of a comrade I respect as much as Chrysion," he growled against her lips, "I would have thrown you over that table right then and there," his thumb brushed over her nubbin again, making her hips buck," ripped that dress from your body," he pushed his first finger into her, up to the second joint, and swallowed her shaky moan in a rough, but short, kiss, "and fucked you between the clams and olives until your cries of ecstasy became so loud that they'd even make the whores at the waterfront blush." A second thick finger pushed into her, and she cried out with need and fell forward against his chest.

The heat of the water, the crudeness of his words, the touch of his fingers between her folds made Melite's head swim. Lord, he was good for somebody so young. But with a body and a face like that, he had surely never experienced any lack of willing bedmates.

But even though the feeling of two of his fingers inside her seemed like heaven on earth, she straightened again. Now was her turn.

Gently, she pushed away his hand from her lap. When he looked at with slight confusion in his eyes, she pulled his hand out of the water and lifted it to her lips, so she could slowly, deliberately, start to lick the traces of her own sex that had survived the warm water off his skin. Keenly aware of his gaze on her, she cast hers down to look at his sex, her thick lashes deliberately casting shadows over her eyes.

A groan escaped his throat when she let one of his fingers slip between her lips, and she couldn't help a grin as her other hand ran over the side of his body, down into the water, over the muscles of his thigh, and right between his legs to cradle his sack between her fingers.

She sucked his finger deeper into her mouth, let her tongue swirl around it as her thumb gently explored the skin over his heavy globes, until one of her fingers dipped behind them to rub over his taint. He cursed in a foreign language, and Melite pulled away from his now spit-slicked fingers and gave his balls a little tug, just enough to make him wince ever so slightly.

She made a low tutting noise, and then she kissed his lips again with a smile. She could feel his grin form against her lips, and his hands started to run over her back, up and down and into the dips of her shoulder blades. The gentle caresses made her shiver, made her shoulders twitch—her back had always been one of the most sensitive parts of her body—but she still pushed backward into those strong, rough hands, whose callouses caught on the sensitive skin over her spine.

When she pulled back, there was pure animalistic lust in his eyes. She'd not be able to keep up her little games for very much longer, she knew that; but she had always liked to test her limits, and those of other people.

With a motion as dexterous as those of a lyrist, she wrapped her fingers around his thick, pulsating cock. Then she leaned towards him, pushed her breasts against his chest, and pressed her loins so close to his that he could feel her curls against the tip of his sex.

She leaned in to his ear, licked her lips, and whispered, "You have travelled over such long distances, my young friend, but has this mighty sword ever been sheathed in a noble daughter of Rome? Have you ever felt the heat of flesh born and raised in a house descended from Augustus himself?"

She squeezed the hot flesh of his cock between her fingers, then she started to slowly stroke up and down. "Since I set eyes on you, I have been wondering how your cock would feel like… How heavy it would be in my hand…" She squeezed again, and a broken moan came from Arestes' lips. "How hot it would be, pushing against my skin…" She lowered herself slightly and let the tip of his cock run through her folds. "How hard it would be, plowing into my body…"

She closed the last distance between their loins and then pushed down. His sex slipped into her, spreading her open, filling her more and more and more…

He groaned against her ear, and then his strong arms were around her, his grip holding her in place as he pushed her whole body down onto his thick cock. Only when he couldn't push farther did he stop, but he still kept her in place.

Melite was breathing heavily, her face nuzzling his neck – it had looked big before, but inside of her, it felt huge, filling every inch. Her heart was beating so loud that Arestes could likely hear it, but she didn't care – she just tried to get her breath back under control. Then, when they both had calmed a little, she leaned up to his ear once again, her voice hoarse and hot against his skin. "Fuck me."

That seemed to be all the encouragement he needed.

With a feral snarl, he lifted her out of the water as if she was no heavier than a rag doll and turned both of them around. Then he pushed her onto the marble tiles next to the pool. She gasped when he spread her legs and lifted them onto his shoulders, and her moan echoed from the bathroom walls when he thrust back into her with one swift motion.

And then he stopped holding back. The slapping of wet skin against wet skin reverberated through the bathroom, intermingling with her breathless moans and his growling and grunting as he drove his hard cock into her wet heat again and again and again, making her body explode with wave after wave of raw, pure lust.

Trapped between the hard muscle of his body and the cold marble of the floor, Melite could do nothing but to give her body, all of herself to the large, calloused hands of the barbarian who pounded into her with voracious hunger, who made her loins sing and her heart stutter. His hands let go of her legs and grabbed her breasts again, squeezing them with feral strength as his thrusts got even faster, even harder, but more erratic.

She came when he slammed his body into hers with one last, brutal thrust, and the wave of her climax nearly pushed her over the threshold of consciousness. For a second, her vision went black, but she could still feel Arestes spill deep inside, before his body collapsed on top of her.

She needed half an eternity to regain enough control over her breath to gasp out, "I have never been taken so thoroughly in all my life, Arestes…" She opened her eyes to see his face above her own, a little grin playing in his exhausted features.

"Haraldr," he said, cradling her head and kissing her

forehead.

Melite frowned. "What?"

"That is my name. They call me 'Arestes' because they can pronounce it easier, but my name is Haraldr Sigurðarson."

She felt a smile spread on her face. "It's not so hard to say, though, is it? Haraldr."

His grin grew wider, and he gently kissed her lips again. "My name sounds beautiful from your mouth."

"Haraldr," she repeated, answering his kiss with one of her own. "Haraldr…"

She could feel his sex, which he had not pulled out after his climax, stir inside again. Oh, the blessings of youth…

"Say it again," he whispered as he slowly rocked against her body.

She grinned and started to stroke his golden hair, which had dried and framed his face in angelic waves now.

"Haraldr," she whispered against his lips, and his rocking turned into thrusts again. "Haraldr… Haraldr…"

They still had hours left before the sun would rise.

How to Train Your Skjaldmaer

Delilah Devlin

Norway, 924 AD

"THAT CREATURE IS a Jarl's daughter?" Left unsaid in Lothar's wide gaze was the fact she would also be Torvald's wife.

Given the sight that beheld their eyes, Torvald might have felt it unfair to chastise his companion, but he couldn't overlook the disrespect. So he jerked his elbow backward and up, neatly breaking Lothar's nose. While the man groaned and bent at the waist to keep the blood streaming toward the rushes covering the rough dirt floor, Torvald stepped deeper into the taproom.

The brawl was well underway. His bride seemed to have things well in hand. Something that might have amused him in his younger days, but he had a position to uphold and ambitions beyond his own jarldom. Bringing back such a wife to his holdings could prove a hindrance to his plans.

Not that she wasn't a handsome woman. Beneath the

dirt on her cheeks and the blood smeared on her chin, her face was nicely formed and her eyes a direct and chilling blue. Her hair was such a pale shade as to be nearly white, and so thick it escaped her braids to fly about her back and buttocks like a wild mare's mane. And she had surprising strength and stamina in her tall robust frame, which admittedly intrigued him.

As he watched, she turned sideways, gripped the edge of a table, and flipped over it, planting her feet in the center of a large, brutish man's belly to topple him. The man went down with a roar then kicked out his feet, pulling himself to stand in a single, astonishingly graceful motion.

His bride glanced up the big man's frame then planted both fists on her hips in a fearless stance. "I tipped a bull once. He thrashed a bit, but didn't get back to his feet nearly as quickly as you."

Her words were brusque but admiring, and her expression gave away her cheeky lack of contrition.

The red-headed brute glanced down at her, nostrils flaring, his cheeks so flushed Torvald feared he'd pop a vein—and then suddenly, he tossed back his head and laughed.

The sound was large and loud inside the small, ale-saturated room. He clamped his arm around the woman's shoulders and turned her toward the bar. "Mead for the lady," he roared.

The brawl ended in an instant. Laughter and loud claps to shoulders filled the room.

Lothar sidled up beside Torvald, a cloth pressed to

his nose as he stared through bruised and swelling eyes. "Will you break something else if I say she's not exactly the woman Hagar promised?"

Torvald blew out a breath and nodded. "It can't be the same woman. A sister, perhaps."

Hagar, the chieftain of the neighboring jarldom, had promised a girl so fair roses blushed in dismay. A woman as slender as a reed, as graceful as a soaring falcon, with hair as dark as midnight, skin as pale as snow.

This harridan's tall angular frame and blonde hair were the exact opposite of what he'd been promised, and her ruddy complexion was berry brown from exposure to the sun and weather.

"Is it a trick to save his treasure for a higher bidder for the beauty's hand? This one's more *skjaldmær*—shieldmaiden—than bride."

"I don't know, but this…" Torvald said, pointing toward the sturdy figure dressed in a man's breeches and *kyrtill* wasn't an acceptable trade. "This will never do." No matter that she appeared strong and would likely birth warriors full-grown. She'd never stand up to the scrutiny a future queen would face.

Taking a deep breath, he indicated to Lothar to watch the door and strode toward the woman who'd raised a full horn of mead and drank it like water. He tapped her shoulder.

Her gaze swung toward him, a scowl digging a crease between her cold blue eyes.

"Are you Solveig, Hagar's daughter?"

She set down her empty horn with a thump. "And

who is asking?"

"Torvald Haroldson. I have come for you."

SOLVI FELT AN unwanted prickle of attraction as she eyed the big man's stony face. She'd noticed him the moment he'd entered the taproom. Who wouldn't? Standing as tall as her opponent, he was leagues more handsome. With the sides of his head shaved, and brown hair worn in braids down his back, tattoos ringing his wrists, he was an imposing sight. "I don't know you."

"Your father sent me."

"Again, we've never met, and I know all my father's underlings."

His green gaze narrowed. "I am not his man. Do you not know my name?"

She squinted up at him, noting the irritation clear in his expression. "Torvald, huh? Wasn't that the name of the poor sod my father sought to give my sister to?"

"Poor sod…?" A frown dug a line between his dark brows.

A crooked smirk stretched her mouth. "I take it you haven't met Runa."

His mouth twisted into to a frown. "I was sent to re-trieve *you*."

Strangely, she liked annoying him, liked the way his body stiffened the longer she argued. She guessed there were few who would risk his anger. "Father knows I'm sailing with Halvar. He doesn't expect me to attend the wedding. In fact, he told me he'd prefer I didn't." She leaned close. "He thinks my behavior and appearance will reflect poorly on his house and name."

His mouth straightened into a firm line. "'Tis two days' travel. Best gather your things. We'll leave at dawn."

She grinned. "I sail at dawn."

"You would refuse your father's command?"

"I have doubts he issued the order. He was quite adamant I make myself scarce."

"Well, he's changed his mind."

The red-headed brute drinking beside her gave a growl. "Solvi, do you want me to toss them out the door?"

The way her friend's body tensed, he was likely to start another fight. And already, she ached from the pounding she'd given him. "No need, Halvar," she said, patting his arm. "I'll see them away. I'll meet you on the docks in the morning."

Halvar snorted and gave the interloper a deadly glare before his gaze fell on Solvi.

Solvi grimaced because she noted a hint of lust in her friend's hot stare. She'd started the brawl to convince him she was as strong as any man and to make sure his interest would be dampened. What man wanted someone built as sturdily and manly as she was? Now the thought of months spent escaping his attentions in the cramped confines of a long boat didn't seem the fine adventure she'd imagined. But one problem at a time…

She led Torvald from the taproom and into the chill air outside. "Give my regards to my father and my sister when you see them," she said, glancing backward. But he'd moved beside her, snaked an arm around her, trapping her arms against her sides. "What are you——?"

A sack settled over her head and his arm slipped away, but before she could drag the burlap off her head, she was upended, her stomach hitting one of those strong shoulders she'd admired.

"This is completely unnecessary," she said, kicking her legs, her toes connecting with an iron thigh, but an arm clamped around the backs of hers. Trapped, she wriggled, knowing she was wasting breath and energy in vain, because he had her. "I'm telling you, he doesn't want me at your wedding."

"Not my wedding, Solveig," he said, his voice coming through the fabric muffled and pitched low. "*Our* wedding."

"What…?" Her mind reeled. "You're mistaken. He'd never——"

"He sent me to fetch my bride. Said you were unaware of the arrangement. I thought it odd until I realized he'd switched daughters."

"Well, see?" she said, stopping her squirming. Relief rushed through her body. "He's tricked you. You can break the arrangement. Call foul."

"Except that I need your father's backing. The arrangement stands."

"But he tricked you. He'd give you his backing just to save face."

"Maybe so, but I promised to wed his daughter. *I* don't break my word. Ever."

Footsteps hurried toward them. "I have the horses

saddled," came another gruff voice, likely his bruised and bloodied companion.

"Good. We should leave before that red-headed troll looks outside and sees we've stolen his sweetheart."

"We aren't sweethearts," Solvi grumbled. "We're just friends."

"Men don't befriend women."

She wriggled again, anger making it impossible to hold still. And she itched like crazy from the rough burlap. Never in her life had she been treated like this. Thor's balls, she'd never been bested by a man.

That thought hammered through her mind at the same time a slithering heat curled inside her belly. She'd never been bested. But here she was, slung over a man's shoulder. One who wasn't breathing hard from the effort. One who'd tossed her around like she was a waif. The thought tantalized.

Torvald slid her off his shoulder and into another man's arms. She kicked out, the toe of her boot thudding against soft tissue. From the quick exhalation and the gagging that followed, she'd hit him squarely where he deserved it—whoever *he* was.

Again, she was thrown over a hard curved surface—from the smell, a horse.

"Lothar, you're in no condition to sit a horse for hours," Torvald said, his voice harsh. "Rest. Follow us to Hahn's tomorrow."

"If you're sure..." Lothar's voice came, sounding strained.

She snickered, glad of the burlap because she knew

men were sensitive to laughter regarding their dangling parts. A slap landed against her bottom.

"Sorry, I meant to nudge the horse," Torvald murmured.

And then the horse bolted forward, jerking her against it. Without hands to reach for a mane or sturdy thigh, she flopped with each rolling gallop. Torvald turned the horse with a nudge of his thigh, heading to higher ground, away from the docks, away from the small village that hugged the edge of the waterway leading to the ocean. Up and up they went, the horse's smooth gallop becoming choppier as it strained against the incline.

"I'm going to be sick," she cried out.

It wasn't until they leveled off that he halted the horse and lifted her, dropping her to the ground where she landed on her bottom. She wrestled with the bag until she freed herself, and then glared. From the ground, peering up at him sitting atop his tall horse, he appeared almost frighteningly large. Moonlight highlighted bladelike cheeks and the bumpy ridge of his nose. In shadow, his gaze gleamed like dark hollows, seeming sinister now. Perhaps he'd taken her father's betrayal to heart and intended to retaliate with violence.

Did he know he was better off without Runa? If her sister had thought to pass off the child growing inside her belly as Torvald's, one glance at his hard, implacable features must have frightened her enough she'd confided in their father. Why else would her father have offered her to Torvald? Solvi had bolted from her father's fortress at her sister's confession, knowing she'd never keep the secret safe. Her disgust at her sister's behavior wasn't something she'd have kept hidden.

She pushed back her wild hair. "I'm not the bride you bargained for. You can tell him I sailed. That I was gone before you arrived at the dock."

"I don't break my word. Neither do I lie."

His tone was so deadly even, it made her gulp. "You won't let me go, will you?"

"You are promised—already my bride by right, to do with as I see fit. If the wedding is what you fear, we will forgo it. A ceremony is not required. What is required is that we lay together."

Solvi swallowed then coughed. Her cough wasn't convincing, but she didn't want him to know that she'd conceded she really had no choices here. She wasn't going to win an argument, but she might delay his intentions long enough to escape. "I think I may have broken a rib. In the brawl. Hanging on a horse didn't help."

"We don't have far to go. We'll stop at one of my holdings. And then I'll take a look at those ribs."

Maybe she should have opted for a fracture somewhere less embarrassing.

He held out a hand and crooked his foot. "Ride with me. Or walk. Your choice."

Since she preferred saving her energy for battle, she accepted his hand and stepped onto his foot, settling against his large frame, her legs spread over his warhorse. Something she'd not considered risky until she was there, trapped between the front of his hard saddle and the equally stiff appendage pressed against her backside.

His arms bracketed her body as he held up the reins. His right thigh tightened, pressing into the horse's side and nudging the back of her leg. As intensely intimate and awkward as the moment was, Solvi couldn't help the smile tugging at the corners of her mouth. Well, she'd wanted an adventure.

WITH THEIR BODIES pressed together by the saddle's high pommel in front and the cantle at the rear, there was no hiding his reaction even through the thick wool of his breeches and Solvi's *kyrtill*. Torvald's cock was full and hard, and after an adjustment to ease it upward for comfort, it nudged beneath the rising hem of her over-tunic to ride the soft division of her buttocks.

And she was aware, he knew, because she sat rigidly in front of him, barely breathing.

He cleared his throat. "The house we're going to isn't far."

"Then you have river access. Have you ever sailed?"

"Twice. In my youth. Before my brother's death."

"Second son?"

Second choice. And his dreams dashed, but he wasn't going to complain. "Yes."

"Where did you go?"

"Rusland. Ireland. I had plans to go farther west."

"I would like to see those places."

By the way her voice softened, he knew she spoke from her heart. "Well, you won't," he said brusquely. "We are both land bound for the foreseeable future."

Likely for the remainder of their lives, given the ambitions of his family.

They rode in silence for another hour, her sighing and shifting. His erection waned as his body relaxed. Moonlight shone from a cloudless sky, reflecting off patches of snow in rough rock outcroppings. Enough light he knew where he was, knew when they drew near Hahn's longhouse.

Shouts rang out in the still air. The doors to the lodge were flung open. "You have her?" came Hahn's voice.

With servants arriving with lit torches, Torvald handed down Solvi to Hahn, who set her on the ground, and then blinked as he eyed her up and down. "She's a beauty, Torvald. If she proves too much for you to handle…"

Torvald slid to the soft turf and delivered a fierce glower, which caused Hahn's mouth to twitch with merriment.

Hahn raised his hands. "I only meant it as a compliment to your fair bride."

"I'm not his bride. He was tricked," Solvi said, her hands fisting on her hips.

To forestall another brawl, Torvald latched his fingers around her wrist and pulled her toward the open doors. "We'll take your bedcloset, Hahn."

"The covers are already turned down," Hahn called after him, and then laughed.

Once inside, Solvi shook off his grip and stood, rubbing her wrist.

"Is it your wrist bothering you now, rather than your

ribs?"

Her glare was blistering, and Torvald realized with a start that he enjoyed teasing the woman. She was a prickly as a hedgehog. But egging her into anger wouldn't aid him in achieving his goal. "Hahn's wife, Inga, will lead you to the bedcloset," he said, giving the brunette hovering at his elbow a nod. "See that she has water to bathe and clean clothing."

Inga nodded and pasted on a smile before turning to Solvi. "If you will follow me, milady."

Solvi didn't move for a long moment, her glare locked with his steady stare, but perhaps she read his resolve. He was offering her a choice—comply or be forced. He was almost disappointed when she shrugged and followed Inga down the long central corridor to a doorway that led to another corridor and Hahn's private quarters.

The moment she was out of sight, Torvald turned to Hahn. "Set guards on the horses and the doors. She might try to slip away. The fool woman planned to sail in the morning, to go a-Viking. Don't underestimate her determination."

Hahn grinned. "What happened to the dark-haired beauty you were promised?"

Torvald snorted. "We won't ever speak of that again. I think I have the better bargain." And although he said it partly to save face over the fact he'd been gulled, Torvald was beginning to think Solvi was indeed the better prize. So she was rough around the edges. She was strong of body and of will. Qualities he hadn't considered essential before. Manners could be taught. A lady's skills in managing a household could be learned, and his mother would be there to see to her education.

The thing he wondered about most was how they'd fare in the marriage bed. Something he was eager now to test.

The pleasant smell of woodsmoke from the central hearth followed him as he strode down the high-beamed corridor to the door leading into Hahn's private quarters. Just as he pushed through it, Inga sailed out, her eyes wide with fright. "She threatened to toss me from the chamber. I left water, but she refused my help."

Torvald stood aside to let her flee then suppressed the smile threatening to widen as he stalked down the narrow hallway to Hahn's alcove. A curtain enclosed the end of the hall, providing privacy from curious gazes from sleeping berths built into the corridor walls on either side. He slipped behind the curtain and halted, his breath catching as his gaze raked his bride's long, muscled frame.

She was lean, legs like a racehorse, wide hips, lush round bottom. Turned away, she waved a hand behind her. "I told you I don't need any help. I've bathed myself since I was babe." She stood on a towel before a basin, a cloth in one hand as she bent and washed her feet, one at a time.

The view of her glorious arse stirred his arousal. "Would you so deny your husband?"

Solvi straightened and her head swung toward him.

But she showed no maidenly modesty, never attempted to shield her form from his interested gaze. Instead, she turned to face him, offering him a view of her full breasts and toned belly. His gaze snagged on her pale ruff, and his cock slowly hardened.

"I am done. Sorry you missed it." She bent sideways to retrieve a garment hanging over the back of a chair, something Inga must have provided because it was embroidered at the neck.

He waved his hand. "Don't bother to dress."

Her breasts rose on a sharp breath.

The nipples were tight, the tips beaded—but from the chill air or his perusal?

"You would take me now? Without ceremony? Don't I deserve better? Don't you?"

"What I deserve was what I bargained for—a wife."

The way she stood, still as a granite statue, bothered him. He wanted the heat he'd seen earlier, even if it was only anger, but something he could stoke into passion. He wanted no cold union. Taking a deep breath, he glanced away, staring at the log wall. "We are bound, Solvi. The deed is already done. If you resist, you will lose. Would it not be better to concede this battle graciously? We could begin as you wish to continue our alliance—the choice of whether we will war or love is yours?"

"Love?" She shook her head. "I am not what you wanted, and you would settle for less than you bargained for?"

Torvald met her gaze, locked with it, determined she would see he spoke the truth. This once, he would treat her with the respect he'd show any valiant adversary and explain himself. "I have come to realize you are a greater prize than the sister I was promised."

Her ice blue gaze narrowed. "I have no wifely skills. My mother gave up long ago teaching me to cook and sew."

"I have wealth enough to pay servants to do those things." He studied her expression, noted the way her gaze fell away, and her mouth softened. Did she fear marriage because she thought she would disappoint a husband? Knowing this was the most important negotiation he might ever enter, and sensing she was giving way, he pushed forward. "I have ambitions higher than my own jarldom. One day, I will challenge for the king's high seat. I will need a strong wife. Someone I can trust as a partner. I have heard your sister thrives on intrigue. Is that true? I would have truth spoken between us always."

Solvi's chin lifted, but she gave him a quick nod.

"She would never have suited me." He tipped his chin, indicating her body. "Your sister is slim, yes?"

Again, she nodded.

"I am a warrior, not given to gentleness," he said softly, waiting until he saw a hint of curiosity in her glinting stare. "And yet, I think you could bear my rough attentions."

Her tongue snuck out to slick her bottom lip. "Rough attentions…do you intend to beat me?"

Her voice was tight, but there was a gleam in her eyes. Was it interest? Could he hope it was lust? He raised his arms at his sides. "I am not a small man. And I am strong. I would never beat you, but my hands might leave bruises along the way if I loose my passions."

She swallowed hard and blinked before glancing away. Her breaths came faster, her nipples quivered. "I am not a waif. Not…delicate," she said, glancing up from beneath a lock of thick moonlit hair.

She was like a wild creature, poised to take flight. But he sensed she was intrigued, that she could be seduced, and the challenge she embodied set fire to his loins as no other woman had ever managed before. His doubts over her suitability as his mate were gone, perhaps from his first sight of her brawling in the taproom. She was his match in every way. 'Twas no doubt why he hadn't fled the moment he'd realized he'd been duped.

Her mouth pursed around her quickened breaths. "These rough attentions…"

He nearly smiled, but knew she might think he was only playing her for a fool. Instead, he moved closer and held out his hand.

She stared for a moment, and then slid hers atop his open palm.

"Are you a maiden?"

An instant frown drew together her light brows. "Of course, I am. I'm not yet married."

"I'm not impugning your virtue, Solvi. But a husband should know."

Her frown lessened, and she nodded. "Does that mean I will have to wait for your rough attentions?"

He closed his hand around hers and lifted it to his

mouth, pressing a kiss against her tanned skin. "It means I will be gentle taking your virtue, but there are other acts, things I can do which will bring you pleasure, if Hahn's bed is large enough and the ropes sturdy."

Her eyes widened, and her mouth snapped close. "You mean to do this tonight?"

"Yes."

Her chin nudged higher. "Then for the sake of my father's bargain, I guess I should concede."

If it helped her to think she was bending to save her father repercussions, he'd let her. And now that the negotiation was over, he let go his lust, full-fledged. Solveig was his.

SOLVI HAD WONDERED all through the long ride how she would find a way to gracefully concede the battle. The longer she'd leaned against his strong frame and let his scent surround her, the more excited she'd grown. This battle of wills they'd begun at the taproom was better than any seagoing adventure, although she wasn't giving up on that dream altogether. She'd watched how woman used their wiles to get what they wanted. She'd just figured her lack of flirting skills would make that task impossible, but she was here, wasn't she? About to bedded by this ruggedly handsome man. She'd seduced him into forgetting about her lack of wifely skills and believing he had the better bargain in her.

She'd known it was him watching her bathe. She'd bent over, even though her cheeks were flaming, just to incite his lust. He'd seen her only in mannish clothing, but she'd planned to make him see there was nothing mannish about her desires.

And although he'd kept blathering on about the concessions he'd give her, the power she'd wield, she knew he'd had to keep a tight rein on his growing lust. His cock had stirred and hardened, visible even through the layers of his leather breeches and long tunic.

How she'd managed to stand nude for so long beneath his hot gaze… Well, perhaps she had learned a thing or two from watching Runa attract lovers. Men loved breasts. And hers were generous and round.

She had thought she'd give him a glimpse of her body, and then beg for time to know him first, but the mention of rough attentions, that hint of unrestrained lust, intrigued her. She stepped closer, until her bare nipples rubbed against his woolen *kyrtill.* "I would see all of you," she whispered.

His pupils flared and he lowered his head. She rose on tiptoe. Their mouths met in a kiss. Her first. And not the least gentle—something she was fiercely glad of. Their mouths supped, teeth nipped. When his tongue thrust inside, she pressed her thighs together to stem the rush of liquid that slid from inside.

When they broke away, they both panted. He gripped her shoulders and pushed her back, then toed off boots, raked up his tunic and the linen undershirt. While she ogled his massive chest, he thrust down his breeches.

When he straightened, there was challenge in his eyes. Her gaze dropped to his cock, thick and long, and lifting from his groin. She'd seen cocks before, laughed at them when her father's men ran naked from the sauna to plunge into cold pools, but nothing was funny about Torvald's.

Reaching out, she wrapped her fingers around him, stroked him, marveling at the smooth texture of the skin that cloaked his iron rod. His hand closed around hers and forced it up and down his length, gripping harder and twisting as they approached the bulbous tip. When his hand fell away, she continued the motion he'd shown her while his breaths deepened, and his shaft lengthened.

When she glanced up, she caught his half-smile and grinned. "This pleases you, but what of my pleasure?"

His smile stretched wider. And before she could gasp, his hands closed on her waist and lifted her, turning to set her on the edge of the down-filled mattress. With a hand pressing against her chest to force her to lie sideways, he knelt between her spread thighs.

Out of reflex, Solvi covered her mound.

He shook his head, tsking, and pulled away her hand. Then he bent toward her.

Never had she imagined what he did next. His thumbs parted her folds and his tongue stroked her center, delving into her, lapping upward, touching on the hard knot at the top, and then drawing away.

She drew a deep breath, thinking he was done, but he dove again and again, licking her sex until she arched, breasts lifting. She groaned and gripped his hair, pulling hard. "Stop. Stop."

His tongue flirted again with the hard knot. "You

don't like this?" he murmured.

"I like it too much. But I can't breathe."

"You need breath?" he teased, wagging his head, his whiskered cheeks raking her open inner folds.

"Oh," she gasped. "But there's more. I want more." Oh, she wanted him. Wanted to feel his weight atop her, wanted to know the feel of his cock entering her. Innocent, but not ignorant, she knew greater pleasure was yet to come.

"I'll give you more, Solvi. Let me do this first, little shieldmaiden." His finger swept inside her and swirled around her opening, calluses catching on the membrane guarding her entrance. The pain she'd heard of was negligible, over in a moment and forgotten when he rose and pushed her fully onto the mattress. He climbed into the alcove bed, parting her legs with brusque impatience, and then settled between them, raised on his arms and knees, his cock poised at her entrance.

"Solvi, this is it," he whispered. "From this moment, you are mine."

The gruff texture of his deep voice filled the shadowed space. "Do you think I still resist? Do you want me to?"

"Yes."

She grinned, loving the hiss of his word. Reaching up, she raked her fingernails across the bristles at the sides of his shaved head and pulled on his braid. "If you want a battle, I will bring one. Every night, Viking." Then she lifted her hips and pushed against his cock, forcing it inside her.

He tensed for a moment, holding still as she shoved. And then he groaned and came down on her, his chest crushing her, his cock sinking deeper. Trapped, beneath him, she couldn't move, but resisted the only way she could, tightening her entrance around him, trying to reject his intrusion, but only in play, because the deeper he stroked, the more intense was the pleasure.

Heat from friction drew more moisture from inside. Her inner walls were stretched and raked with each deep push and pull. Her hips followed his withdrawals, trying to capture him, fighting to hold him now. Her hands roamed his back, nails digging into his skin.

When he rose again, he thrust his arms beneath her knees and lifted her bottom, and then thrust unimpeded into her, the slick glides ending in snapping motions pounded against her center.

A keening cry tore from her throat. "Torvald!"

"Yes," he hissed. "Gods, yes!"

Pleasure exploded, causing her body to arch and hold. He hammered several times more then paused. Hot liquid flooded her, and she knew he'd spent his seed. When the spasms slowed inside her, she opened her eyes to find his gaze on her, his hands cupping her bottom and gently kneading, while he rocked back and forth, their flesh still connected, the pleasure receding, more comforting now.

She couldn't believe she was there. Beneath him. His wife. It had happened so fast. But the attraction hadn't palled. Solvi had no regrets.

Slowly, he lowered her bottom, his cock sliding from

inside her. He settled beside her in the narrow bed and turned her to face him. His hand cupped her breast, a finger tracing the circumference of her nipple. "I neglected these."

"A slight I won't forgive." She slid her hand between them, blocking his touch, and then gave him a narrow-eyed glare, letting him know she was holding to her promise. Their war had just begun.

THE NEXT MORNING, Inga held up a wrapped bundle of food. "For your journey."

Torvald took the package and set it his wife's hands. "My wife thanks you."

"Yes, thank you, Inga," Solvi said, adding a dig of her elbow against his ribs.

Torvald grinned at Hahn, careful not to let Solvi see, and then pulled the reins. Lothar, whose eyes were almost swollen shut, still managed a smile as he stared at Torvald who'd refused a second horse although it forced his wife to once more share his saddle. He didn't understand that Torvald planned to enjoy her discomfort. No matter which way she leaned, she couldn't escape the ache between her legs. He'd done that. Likely every person in the longhouse had heard her keening cries each time he'd sent her flying toward Asgard.

He whistled as they headed back down the mountain they'd climbed the previous evening.

"Um, Torvald?"

His smile deepened at the husky sound of her voice

when she said his name. "Yes, wife."

"Are we not heading toward my father's lands?"

"No."

"So, we aren't returning for the celebration?"

"No."

She stayed silent for a moment, shifted again, and then let out a breath. "Are we going to your home?"

"No."

She leaned away and turned her head to give him a hot glare. "If not to my father's or to your holdings, then where are we going?"

Torvald couldn't help himself. He grinned like a boy. His pleasure in his wife had been there for everyone to see that morning. Thor's balls, he hadn't been able to keep his hands from her shapely arse throughout their morning feast. "We are taking a journey. Consider it my wedding gift."

Her frown lessened, and her gaze dipped to his smile then back to his eyes. "Where are we going?"

"Do you fancy Iceland for the summer?"

Her jaw dropped and before he knew it, she climbed awkwardly around until her legs wrapped around his hips and her arms hugged his neck in a surprisingly strong grip. Her kiss was hard and not well-placed, landing on his chin, then his nose, and cheeks, but finally, finding his mouth.

When she drew away, tears filled her eyes. "You would do this for me?"

"I would do this for us," he said softly. "Soon enough, we will have to face our responsibilities. But first, we will get to know one another doing something we will both enjoy."

Her radiant smile was beautiful, her ice blue eyes melting with tears. "Thank you."

Torvald gave her a smug smile. Training a *Skjaldmær* to be a wife was a pleasurable task indeed.

THE VIKING'S PRIZE

Emma Jay

The coast of Newfoundland, 1078 AD

CALDER GEIRSON SAT near the fire and studied the dark-skinned woman as she moved about her people with the basket of bread. Her hair fell in sleek lines around stark features, and beneath her fur shawl, her body was lean and strong. Her deep-set eyes, tilted up at the corners, remained lowered as she served. She kept her distance from his men, who gathered at the edge of her village, close to the forest that surrounded it. Their boisterous behavior was partly ale, partly thwarted aggression. They'd come to this land expecting a fight. Instead, they'd been given a peace offering—or at least, he had.

The girl before him.

He wanted to tell her his men wouldn't bother her, not after her father had made her a gift.

Her expression was stony, as if she didn't understand the treaty that bound her to him. Not in marriage. That was made clear. She was not his wife, merely his chattel.

He had never owned a woman, though he had been

once wed only to watch his wife die struggling to bring his son into the world.

This woman's copper skin fascinated him. He wanted to stroke it, but something in her closed expression stopped him. She hadn't met his gaze since her father presented her. Perhaps direct eye contact was against her people's custom.

To test his theory, he looked around the fire. Several women met and held his gaze, some with inviting smiles that transcended the language barrier.

So the avoidance was her.

He shifted his attention to her people. He understood when she was given to him that she wasn't highly valued, but he accepted the insult because her beauty and his curiosity overruled his good sense. In his years as a warrior, he had learned it best to let the enemy think they knew something he didn't. But now, as he watched her with her people, he witnessed the disdain they held and worse, saw them laughing behind their hands. She didn't acknowledge any of this, but he had had enough. Any woman associated with him would have respect.

He tried her name silently, *Odina,* then aloud, "Odina."

But she didn't respond.

He tried again, louder, his tone commanding, and several women tittered.

Reluctantly, Odina raised her gaze.

He expected to see fear, but what he saw instead was defiance. The idea that she would be defiant toward him angered him. She was his property.

He rose and reached for her. She looked at his hand for a long moment, and again, he wondered how different their customs were. Did she understand she was to take his hand? He bent to demonstrate what he wanted her to do when she placed her slim fingers in his.

She was almost as tall as he, towering over the others in her tribe. He was used to tall women—his wife had been only two fingers' width shorter. But the way Odina slouched made him wonder if her height was one of the things for which her people rebuked her.

The village chief had shown him to his lodgings on the edge of town—a pleasant little hut with a fire pit in the center and a hole in the roof to vent the smoke, a place of honor, he understood, for the leader of the warriors. If not for Odina, Calder would have slept outside with his men in the forest with a view of their ships, which bobbed in the inlet. But he had been too long without a woman, and his curiosity about this woman was overwhelming.

Odina kept her gaze on the pile of furs, wolf, and caribou, as Calder closed the flap behind them. She stiffened as he walked behind her and ran a rough hand down her glossy hair and frustration rose in his chest. He wished he knew how to communicate with her. Was she afraid of him? Angry with the chief for making a gift of her? In love with someone else?

He turned her to him and tucked his finger under her chin, forcing her to meet his gaze. This time, he didn't see defiance in her eyes. This time, he saw something he didn't recognize. Not fear, exactly, not caution. He couldn't put a name to it, adding another frustration. He hadn't expected a language barrier within himself.

"Odina," he said her name again, and then, wanting to hear her voice, pressed his hand to his own chest. "Calder."

She frowned, and he smoothed away the furrows with his thumb. The gesture caught her off guard, and her lips parted, that expression he couldn't identify disappearing.

He repeated the act. Her name then his.

"Calder," she finally echoed.

Her voice with a rough edge that sent lust, already simmering, rolling to a heat he had trouble reining in. He touched her cheek and that lovely smooth copper skin. "Beautiful."

The furrow reappeared, and again, he smoothed it. "Beautiful," he said again, tracing her face with his finger, then pointing to her heart. "Beautiful. Pleasing."

Of course, she didn't understand. He leaned forward, his hands on her shoulders, and with his lips, followed the same path. She quivered beneath his hands, but didn't move. When he reached the curve of her cheek, she gave a little gasp that might have been pleasure. He circled his thumbs on her shoulders, pushing aside the fur to find flesh, firm and smooth. He wanted his mouth on it, on her, everywhere. Never had he seen a woman so striking, so compelling. He wanted her naked, now, beneath him.

He wanted her to want him, as well. So he would take his time.

He removed the fur from her shoulders and tossed it in the direction of the bedding. Her shivering increased. He wanted to pull her closer, into the heat of his body, but she was too anxious. He angled his mouth over hers, let his breath wash over her lips, and touched his to hers, very lightly.

She snapped back her head, eyes wide, but he didn't hesitate. He slid his hand through her hair, holding her still as he repeated the caress and tasted the softness of her mouth. He touched his tongue to her lower lip, and she tried to pull away again, but he held her fast. He flicked his tongue against her upper lip, and she made a funny little strangled noise. This time, she closed her fingers around his upper arms and angled a little closer, her lips parting against his.

Her acceptance sent his blood, hot and thick, to his groin, and he stopped himself from grinding his hips into hers. No, he wanted to savor her like a fine feast, savor the differences between them. He wanted her to respond, wanted to feel her go taut beneath him, wanted to feel her body clasp his as he moved inside her.

She released his arms and softly, so softly, touched his beard. She made a humming sound in her throat that he felt against his lips as she stroked her fingers over the hair on his face.

Of course. None of the men he'd seen in her village had beards.

"Wo'gwet," she murmured.

"Beard," he said, scrubbing his own fingers through it.

She nodded. "Beard." She eased back a little, to look as she combed her fingers through it. Then she nodded again, and her mouth eased into what he might almost call a smile before she stroked her fingertips over his lips.

He captured her hand and kissed her fingers before moving aside her hand and bending to capture her mouth again. This time, she came in closer, her mouth parted, her tongue imitating his strokes. Her breathing was faster, heavier. Encouraged, he slid his hands down her back, stopping above the curve of her buttocks, and pulled her fully against him. He wanted to touch her skin, and the way she was squirming against him, trying to get closer, made him think she wanted that, too.

Her garment had lacings between her breasts, something he'd noticed during the meal. He reached between them now to untie them, to push the soft leather apart and off her shoulders. She held her breath, but didn't stop him as he trailed his fingers along the line of her shoulder. She shivered, but he wasn't sure if it was arousal or a chill, so he edged her closer to the fire as he pushed down the garment, baring firm high breasts, her nipples tight. His mouth watered, eager to take them deep, to savor the sensation of her nipple between his lips, between his teeth.

Calder was not used to denying himself, yet he found himself intrigued by his own desire to wait. His cock throbbed with need, but he took a strange delight in denying it. Instead, his fingers descended the slopes of her breasts. He captured her nipples in tandem, first dragging his callused touch across the tender flesh, which tightened further.

She gave a soft moan and her head rocked back on her neck.

He pinched her nipples lightly, and then leaned forward to kiss the curve of her shoulder, down the curve of her breast, before he bent and took her nipple into his mouth. He teased the hardened tip with his tongue, and then drew it deeper until she pressed against him, wordlessly asking for more.

He moved his mouth to her other breast, tugging harder, and she responded by threading her fingers through his hair, holding him to her.

He couldn't wait any longer. He tugged the garment down her slim hips, hearing a rend but not caring. Kneeling, he pushed away the gown and stared up at her.

She was breathtaking—all that dark skin, and curly black hair between her thighs. He could smell her arousal, and trailed his fingers up her thighs, intending to push her legs apart to get to her cunt, but she parted her legs without his urging, inviting his touch. When he stroked his fingers along her swollen lips, he found her already wet. The discovery delighted him. He slipped his fingers through the crisp hair and into her channel, one finger entering her first, then two, pumping gently.

An odd sound emerged from her throat, and then she gripped his shoulders and pushed against him, fucking his hand. Her abandon took him aback for a moment then he added his thumb, sweeping it back and forth across the bundle of nerves at the top of her cleft.

She cried out, which made him smile as her body

grew wetter around his fingers, as the scent of her arousal filled the small hut.

He could no longer wait to be inside her. He withdrew his hand to untie his breeks, freeing his erection. At the same time, she knelt before him and reached for his tunic. As his cock sprang free, she pushed the fabric of his tunic up his body and patiently waited for him to raise his arms to remove it the rest of the way. Her gaze focused on his chest, and she placed both hands there, fingers spread.

As eager as he was to be inside her body, her fascination with his body intrigued him. She slid her fingers through the curling hair and folded her fingers against his chest, as though she was savoring the sensation.

"Wo'gwet," she said again.

He frowned. He'd thought she'd meant "beard" before, but maybe her people didn't have a word for beard, since the men didn't grow them. "Hair," he said, reasoning the word addressed those same qualities.

She gave him that half-smile again, this time looking up through her lashes as she trailed her fingertips over his stomach and closed her hand around his cock. He jolted at her directness then gritted his teeth to hold onto control as she explored him with her nimble fingers. He folded his hand over hers and showed her how to stroke him, up and down, which seemed to delight her, but tortured him.

Impatient now, he pushed her onto her back on the furs, and that half-smile brightened. Needing to deny himself just a moment more, he levered himself over her and kissed her mouth then her throat, and then an up-thrust nipple before parting her legs and sliding deep.

She went stiff beneath him, her nails digging into his upper arms, but he was beyond reason. Her cunt was tight and hot around him, and it had been so long since he'd been inside a woman. He wanted nothing more than to stay inside her, to experience this pleasure forever.

But she wriggled beneath him and pushed at his chest. When he gathered enough control to focus on her, he saw real distress in her face. But by Odin, he didn't want to leave her body. Instead, he leaned down to kiss her mouth, but she turned away her head. He rubbed his beard down the line of her throat, since she had seemed to like that before, but she continued to push at his shoulders.

Gripping her hips, holding her tightly against him, he rolled onto his back so she was over him. Her mouth was stretched tight over her teeth as she rose, her hands braced on his ribs, like she would push away. He lifted his hips into her, the rhythm harder as he dug his heels into the furs for leverage. He gripped the tops of her thighs, marveling at the differences in their skin, hers so soft and smooth, that beautiful color against his paler flesh. He fucked her, guiding her to match his rhythm, but she wasn't as eager as she had been. Her cunt was no longer as slick with desire. Had he frightened her? Hurt her?

With his thumb, he parted her cleft and slid his touch over her soft petals. No, she was no longer slick for him, so he licked his thumb and returned it to the little nub, circling it as he pumped his hips. He watched her face as her lips parted and her eyelids drifted shut, and at last, she began to match her body's movements to his.

Gods, she was beautiful, her long hair falling forward over her shoulders, swinging with her movements, her breasts peeking through the black strands. Her face was awash with pure pleasure—eyes half-lidded, lips parted, chin angled down. She moved into his hand, rolling her hips more and more forcefully, seeking her climax.

He should have made her come before, so he could watch her face. But her frantic movements sparked the beginning of his own orgasm. Her erratic rhythm, her wet cunt, her clasping channel drove him into a frenzy. He dug his heels into the ground and thrust upward, his fingers between her legs stilling as his orgasm swept over him, pulling from the base of his spine and shooting through his extremities. He was aware, vaguely, of her swollen flesh rubbing against his hand as his seed pumped into her, aware that she didn't climax, that her movements had moved from frantic to frustrated.

For a moment, as the energy drained away, he couldn't be bothered to worry about it. But when he slid free of her body, he sensed the tension in hers. When he tried to turn her onto her back beside him, she shoved at him again. Gone was the expression of arousal. Instead, the furrow had returned.

He pushed her with more force this time, coming over her, parting her legs with his body. She used her strong slim thighs to try to rid herself of him, but he was determined to show her pleasure.

He captured her nipple between his lips, flicking his tongue over the tip, and felt some of the tension leave her legs. He hadn't become leader of his village by being lulled into a sense of security, however, so when she pushed again, he was ready.

And he sucked harder on her nipple. Her cunt grew slick against his bare belly, but she refused to let him closer. He released her nipple and slid down her body, dragging his beard over her skin. She gasped and arched toward his mouth. He smiled his satisfaction as he continued down the length of her body, parting her legs wider, using his thumbs to open her cunt to him. He blew a soft breath over her petals, and she cried out, letting her legs fall apart, making room.

He settled her legs over his shoulders, held her nether lips open with his fingers and teased his tongue over the tender flesh. The flavor of her filled his mouth as he lapped at her, feeling her tense, but this time in a good way. She moved against him, and he flattened his tongue against her petals, letting her rub, her moans filling the hut. Easing back, he flicked his tongue against the sensitive nub until she was absolutely still.

Then she softened against him, the pearl pulsing against his tongue, her body moving in long, undulating movements. He drew the essence of her scent into him and stretched out beside her on the furs. She turned her head and grinned. He grinned back and pulled her close against his side.

THE NEXT MORNING, Odina lay in the dying light of the fire and rubbed her hand over the soft fur on the stranger's chest. Not a stranger any longer, not the way he now knew her body, every part of it. She shivered with delight at the memory of his head between her legs, the way his light eyes, the color of the cold blue sky, glinted at her, like the wicked pleasure he'd given her was a secret they shared.

She had known a man before, had a man between her legs when she was young, and had shamed her father, which was why he now gave her to an enemy.

An enemy. That wasn't the word for him, either.

Calder. He'd said that was his name. At least, she thought that was what he meant when he repeated the word over and over. And he'd said her name in a way that made her warm throughout.

She liked the way he looked at her, liked the way he was covered with light-colored fur that didn't hide the scars marking him as a warrior. The fur was at once soft and scratchy against her, making her skin feel tight and tingly. Just thinking about it made her want to feel him against her again. She traced a puckered scar that ran from the top of his shoulder almost to his nipple, and he grunted but his eyes remained closed. Keeping her touch light, she followed another scar across his ribs. What kind of man survived wounds like these?

After he'd brought her to pleasure, he'd talked to her last night. She hadn't understood most of what he'd said, but she understood that with his ships, he'd been to many lands. She couldn't imagine the freedom, the adventures he'd had, though his scars proved how dangerous a life he led.

She shifted her weight, pressing her breasts to his chest, sliding her hand down the soft hair of his stomach to the coarser hair of his groin. She found him already hard, and the shift of his breathing told her he was awake and waiting.

She slid her leg along his, up over his hip, and rose over him, taking him into her in the same motion. He grunted, watching her through half-lidded eyes as she bent over him, sliding her body against his furred chest, rubbing her tender cleft against the heat of his body. She wished he would touch her as he had before.

Instead, he folded his arms behind his head and watched. The glint returned to his eyes as she moved over him, seeking a rhythm that would please them both.

When she struggled, he smiled the same smile he'd given her after he brought her to pleasure, and then sat up and looped his hands around her back, pushing up into her, until she found a way for them to move together. She hooked her hands around his neck and matched his rhythm, then took one of his hands and pushed it down her body.

He chuckled and acquiesced, just as the door to the hut swung open and two women stepped inside.

Before Odina could process what was happening, Calder had his sword—which she hadn't even noticed—in his hand. He relaxed a little when the women addressed Odina.

"You must come now. Make breakfast," Odina's younger sister ordered.

As the youngest, she was always ordering. She was too indulged by their father.

Odina shook her head, tightening her hold on Calder's shoulders.

Calder shouted at them, something Odina didn't understand, but combined with his sweeping hand movements, frightened away the women, but not without a hateful glance from Luntook, the second woman, with whom Odina had grown up.

Once the women left, Calder smoothed his hand down Odina's back to gain her attention. She shivered, despite the heat from the fire, and turned to meet his blue-eyed gaze. He curved his hand around her neck to kiss her again, his lips and tongue coaxing as he slid his other hand between their bodies to find her.

Only a few caresses, and she'd forgotten the interruption, was moving against his hand, kissing him back. This time, the climax was not as powerful, but her body slumped bonelessly against his as they struggled to catch their breath.

ODINA EMERGED FROM the hut a short time later, knowing that without her contribution, Calder, and possibly his men, wouldn't be fed. She belonged to them now; they were her responsibility. She joined the other women at the campfire preparing the stew that would make the last of the game stretch to feed so many. The women, including her sister, were less talkative than usual, and she caught several sidelong looks. Were they resentful of the night she'd spent in Calder's arms? Was not her position to appease him? Or worse, did they think less of her for enjoying the foreigner's embrace?

Lost in her own thoughts, she prepared Calder's meal. Suddenly, a sense of awareness washed over her. She looked around and saw no men, not her tribe, not Calder's men.

Where was everyone?

A movement at the edge of the forest caught her eye, and she caught sight of an unfamiliar young face. A moment passed before realization struck. Another tribe? Here now? But why?

Pretending not to notice anything out of the ordinary, she finished spooning Calder's meal into a wooden bowl and rose, scanning the forest. Yes, the young face was not the only stranger here. And they could have only one purpose.

Moving quickly, but not fast enough to draw attention, she returned to the hut where Calder waited, trying to reason out how to convey the information to him. They had no words except their names.

Calder stood, relieving his bladder into the provided pot. He was still gloriously naked, all muscle and strength, and for a moment, she was distracted. But then she remembered the faces in the woods, and she lunged for his sword. It was heavier than she expected and pulled her off balance, but she kept her grip firm.

Instantly, his body tensed, and his hands came up in a fighting stance. The fierceness of his furrowed brow and curled lips chilled her heart an instant before she shoved the sword at him, hilt first. Surprise relaxed his posture, and he took the sword reflexively, his gaze not leaving her face as she swept a hand behind her and raised an arm over her head and made a face, mimicking an attack.

Understanding bloomed instantly. He pushed past her and gave a bloodcurdling cry, which was echoed by his men from a distance.

She ran after him, watching his bare hindquarters flashing white in the dappled sunlight through the trees, his long silver sword raised.

The enemy warriors swarmed forward, surrounding him, blocking him from her view.

She screamed, straining to see him through the clothed bodies. She heard his shouts and the clang of his sword striking axes and spears. Bodies thudded as they hit the ground, but since her tribe was still fighting, she knew Calder was not dead. She thought of the scars she'd stroked on his body and hoped he'd walk away with nothing more. But she knew, witnessing the violence of the men before her—strangers intermingled with her own people—the hope was unlikely. They wanted him dead.

The ground thundered beneath her, and beyond the battle, where Calder was sorely outnumbered, rushed forward his pale-skinned men, weapons raised, a terrible cry rising as one.

She scrambled up the trunk of a tree, needing to see Calder, to make sure he was on his feet. Dread knotted her stomach—would she see him killed? The man who had shown her such kindness, such passion—was she going to see him die?

She couldn't find him among his own men who had surged forward to even the odds, who had pushed their way into the thick of battle to fight for their leader.

And then there he was, yellow braid swinging, flecked with blood, his naked skin coated with it. His, or someone else's? She wished she had a weapon, too, that she could join the fight at his side.

Her thoughts were disloyal, she knew. To fight against her own people was traitorous. But for them to give her to Calder as a distraction so they could call for reinforcements to battle the new arrivals? Strange men who had up to this point been peaceful? It was a trick without honor, and she was ashamed.

Calder's men were not peaceful now, however, hacking and slicing and thrusting with abandon. Men she'd known all her life dropped at their feet; strangers fell in a swirl of blood-soaked mud.

But just when she thought Calder and his men were winning, another surge of warriors emerged from the forest. They were outnumbered and certain to be defeated.

Calder staggered under a blow from behind.

Odina's heart leapt to her throat, and before she could think, she was scrambling down the tree and running toward him. She lost sight of him a moment before she saw two of his men lift him up and head toward the water's edge.

To their boats.

Retreating. Leaving. Leaving her behind.

Fear pumped her legs faster. She would not stay here, not when she'd been given to him, been given a glimpse of another life, one other than as the whipping girl to the village. She wanted to know the adventure Calder had spoken of. She wanted to be by his side.

The pebbles of the beach dug into her feet as she pounded across them toward the boat where Calder's men hoisted him aboard.

"Calder!" she cried over the sound of clashing weapons and bloodthirsty cries. "Calder!"

She didn't know if he was dead or alive, only that he was limp between his men. Were they merely retrieving his body to return to their homeland? The idea was unfathomable. She could not accept the thought that he could be dead so soon after leaving her bed.

"Calder!"

He lifted his head and turned, searching, finding, pinning her with those blue eyes. She ducked beneath a Northman swinging his ax at a man she didn't know, slipped, and scraped her knee when she swerved to avoid a warrior racing after the retreating Northmen. But her gaze never wavered from Calder.

She reached his boat and held up a hand, bracing her foot on the hull to hoist herself inside. She felt the boat drifting from shore, and her foot slipped, but then a strong hand wrapped around her wrist and hauled her upward. In less than a moment, she was in the boat, and face to face with Calder, surrounded by his men.

He looked terrible, his hair matted and bloody, a cut running the length of his face and oozing blood, more cuts on his body, disguised by more blood.

He said something to her that she didn't understand, but he was frowning. Was he asking her if she wanted to go with him? She didn't know how to make him understand, so she pressed a hand to her heart, then took the same hand and pressed it to his. She repeated the gesture in case he didn't understand, keeping her gaze on his, hoping he wanted her to come with him as much as she needed to go.

Around him, his men grumbled, and she sensed they wanted her left behind, but she looked into Calder's eyes and waited.

With one arm—she saw now that his other arm was wounded and hung loosely at his side—he pulled her against him and kissed her soundly. He drew back, pushing her hair from her face with a bloody hand and nodded.

"Mine," he said.

And that word, she understood.

THERE FOR THE TAKING

Nym Nix

The Skagerrak Coast of Norway, 842 AD

IDONEA WIPED A stray strand of red-gold hair from her face and glanced around. The man, Einar, and the woman, Sigridr, sat together on one of the platforms that served the cottage as both bench and bed, their fair heads bent close. Talking about her. She could tell, even if she couldn't understand a word of what they were saying. It was the way they looked at her.

Heat rose in Idonea's cheeks, and she turned back to stir the pot over the firepit to hide her discomfort.

She knew *he* desired her. He did nothing to disguise it. Every time she caught his clear blue gaze it made her pulse race, even while that sharp stab of fear twisted in her gut. She had been here two nights now, under his roof, and both nights he had wordlessly invited her into his bed. What puzzled her was why he had let her refuse.

Vikings took what they wanted. Didn't they? Wasn't that how she came to be here?

Idonea wrapped her filthy skirt around her hand and swung the pot away from the heat. She ladled stew into two bowls, ignoring the way her skin prickled under their twin gazes.

The woman puzzled her, too.

She'd been on the boat. At first, Idonea hadn't realized she was a woman. She'd been dressed the same as the male raiders, carried the same weapons, worn the same bloodstains. Later, Idonea had seen her in the huge hall at the centre of the Viking village where they'd divided up the spoils and the captives. But Einar alone had led Idonea away from the settlement, over steep hills to this lonely farmstead. Idonea was fairly certain no one else lived here. Yet, Sigridr had arrived with the sunset this evening, dressed now in a kirtle and with her hair let loose.

Idonea did not know what to make of the pair. Were they betrothed? It seemed unlikely Sigridr, in all her ferocity, would countenance the presence of a young, female slave in the house of her husband-to-be. Siblings? Sisters did not look at brothers the way Sigridr gazed at Einar.

Idonea offered them the bowls. She tried to keep her gaze down, but could not help darting him a nervous glance.

He smiled.

It caused an answering curling sensation in the pit of her stomach. But she was too afraid to let herself smile back.

She backed away, looking at the ground.

The woman spoke.

Einar laughed, his expression sheepish.

Idonea did not understand their words, but Sigridr seemed to have exposed some guilty secret.

He leaned forward and said something to Idonea. She stared at him helplessly. He beckoned her. Reluctantly, she edged back around the firepit. He held up a spoonful of the stew toward her lips.

Idonea took a step back, but he made gentle shushing noises, as though she were a shy animal. She bent her head and took the mouthful. It was warm and rich and made her empty belly clench. Fear had stolen her appetite of late. He made a satisfied noise and offered another spoonful. She ate that, but when Sigridr said something derisive, she backed away again, feeling her face flush.

Idonea could not understand his kindness. She was a slave—he was the master. She understood the nature of the contract that had been forced upon her. What else did he want from her? The question made her sweat with fear. And something else she did not know how to name.

Beside him, Sigridr was speaking again. Einar answered her, without taking his gaze off Idonea.

Idonea wished he would look away. Her face was burning, and her heart beat too fast.

Sigridr set aside her bowl and leaned into Einar, murmuring into his ear. Einar nodded and Sigridr began to nuzzle at his neck. One hand slid down the front of his shirt, playing across his chest in a manner unequivocally sensual. Idonea's eyes widened. Einar smiled again, his gaze never leaving hers.

Sigridr dragged off his shirt, clearly taking pleasure in the broad expanse of his chest and the slope of his bare shoulders, gleaming ruddy in the firelight.

Idonea's chest felt tight. *What are they doing?*

Sigridr ran her hands over Einar's skin, her fingers tracing the paths of old scars and dancing over the peaks of his nipples where they stood out from the sparse whorls of dark gold hair over his chest.

Idonea's breath caught in her throat.

Einar grinned at her. He rose, and Sigridr's hands plucked at the drawstring of his trews.

Utterly discomposed, Idonea turned away. It was clear they had no requirement for privacy. If she did not want to witness this, she would have to leave. They murmured to each other. There were thuds as footwear was discarded onto the floor. And there were other noises, soft, intriguing sounds that filled her with humiliating warmth.

Idonea moved to the door. As she laid her hand upon the latch, however, Einar spoke a sharp word. She needed no knowledge of his language to understand it. She halted and let her hand fall.

Reluctantly, she turned back to them. He was naked, now, standing with his arms wrapped around Sigridr, his hands full of her exposed breasts. He frowned at Idonea and shook his head. Sigridr twisted around to glance at Idonea, and then drew Einar's head back down to kiss her neck. He complied, but his gaze stayed on Idonea.

Idonea slumped against the door, her eyes filling with angry tears. She did not want to stay in here while they took their pleasure with each other. She did not want to see any more of the handsome Viking's naked body. She dashed the tears from her eyes and discovered, when her vision cleared, he was still watching her, even as he caressed Sigridr's body. She set her jaw and glared back.

Einar tugged at Sigridr's dress, baring her bottom. He slid his hand around her body and squeezed it. He might have been squeezing Idonea's throat, for the trouble it was costing her to breathe. He bent to take Sigridr's pale, pointed nipple in his mouth, and Idonea felt an answering tug in her own flesh as her nipples grew taut in response. Sigridr uttered a low, voluptuous moan that set off echoes in Idonea's belly.

Einar raised his head from Sigridr's breasts and called to her. "Idzunn!"

He had a strange, burred way of saying her name.

His arousal was clear. Idonea could feel how warm and wet her own sex was, and when he put a hand around the proud curve of his organ and gave it a teasing pull, she felt a throb of pleasure so intense it made her knees tremble. If it had not been for the door at her back, she might have sunk to the floor.

He beckoned her, and Sigridr turned to give her a pleasure-dazed smile.

He wants me to join them.

Idonea tore her gaze from his groin, her face scarlet. She shook her head, the bright little shard of fear in her heart momentarily vanquishing the building pulse between her thighs.

He shrugged, a smile dancing at the corners of his mouth. He sat on the edge of the sleeping platform and pulled Sigridr towards him. She cast an amused look over her shoulder at Idonea, and stepped out of her crumpled gown. In one smooth movement, she straddled Einar and sank down over him.

Idonea's insides clenched as they came together, each with a hard exhalation of breath. Sigridr tipped back her head and moaned. Over her shoulder, Idonea could see Einar close his eyes in ecstasy.

In the sudden freedom from his scrutiny, Idonea's fear abated. She drew in a deep shuddering breath, conscious now of her own arousal.

Sigridr began to move up and down. Idonea could see the muscles in her thighs working as she rode Einar. Einar ran his hands down over her back, past her waist, pulling her down harder, holding her down. Sigridr growled at him through her teeth and began to rock back and forth. Idonea watched Einar's strong fingers digging into Sigridr's buttocks as they moved together, and was surprised by the burst of fierce envy that suddenly filled her chest.

Einar dipped his head to take Sigridr's teat in his mouth again. She cried out, arching her back. They were both breathing hard.

Enraptured, Idonea panted as they panted, pushing herself back against the door in time with the rhythm of their urgent rocking. She was shocked to find she had shoved her hand between her thighs, pressing hard upon her sex through the layers of her clothing, feeling her own pleasure build. But she couldn't stop herself. And for once, Einar was not looking at her.

She rubbed and kneaded, watching the way his brow

furrowed with every heave of Sigridr's naked body. Just as the mountain of sensation inside her reached its peak, Einar opened his eyes.

Idonea gasped out loud, her knees giving way, and she slid to the ground. Stars crowded across her vision, and her blood pounded in her head. *He saw me!* When her vision cleared, Einar was grinning. Then he threw back his head and gave a guttural roar, bucking into the woman on his lap.

Idonea sat on the earthen floor, breathing heavily, watching the two of them as they toppled languidly into the furs, the sweat on their skin gleaming in the firelight. Einar asked Sigridr a question, and she gave a contemptuous answer in the negative, hitting him on the shoulder. Einar laughed, and said something, pointing at Idonea. Sigridr twisted to stare at her, hard, and Idonea almost stopped breathing.

Sigridr pulled herself free from Einar and got up from the bed, stalking towards Idonea. Afraid again, Idonea tried to scramble out of the way, but there was nowhere to go. Sigridr seized her arm and dragged her to her feet. She pulled Idonea over to the bed where Einar was still sprawled, looking bemused.

To Idonea's consternation, Sigridr began to tug at the ties at the front of her dress. Idonea protested, but Sigridr slapped aside her hands and yanked open her dress. She pulled on the cord at the neck of Idonea's shift.

Idonea fought her, and tried to cover herself, but Sigridr hit her squarely across the face. Hot tears sprang to Idonea's eyes again, and her cheek stung. She stood, shaking and helpless, as Sigridr held her dress and shift open to give Einar a clear view of her naked breasts.

The pleasant sensations of a few moments before had vanished. All she was conscious of now was the cutting fear twisting in her belly.

She felt, rather than saw, Einar get up from the bed. He stood so close she could smell his warm musk and feel his breath soft on her face. Tears burned their way down her cheeks as she waited for what must surely come next.

Instead, she felt his fingers tugging up the front of her shift, pulling her dress closed. She looked up. Through tears, she saw the rough gold of his beard, and then his blue eyes. The hunger was still there, lurking in the depths; she could sense it. But mostly, she saw the crease of concern between his brows. She searched his face, hardly daring to believe her reprieve. He hadn't even so much as brushed her breast with the back of a finger.

He looked down at her a moment longer, his face serious, and then gently touched her cheek, where her skin still hummed from Sigridr's blow. Then he took hold of her shoulders, turned her around, and pushed her towards the sleeping platform on the other side of the firepit, where she had spent the last two nights huddled alone.

Idonea took a stumbling step towards her bed. Behind her, Sigridr said something angry. Idonea looked over her shoulder to see Einar pick Sigridr up bodily and toss her roughly onto the bed. When Sigridr tried to rise, he pushed her down and knelt over her, speaking low and sharp. As Idonea crawled onto her bed, Einar took hold of Sigridr's legs and forced her knees apart. She cried out angrily, and Idonea turned away, dragging her fur across her body. But the next moment, the other woman gave a cry of a very different nature, and despite herself, Idonea looked.

Einar was lying on his belly, holding her knees wide apart, his face between her thighs. Sigridr was arching her back against the furs, groaning in pleasure. Idonea went hot and cold in shock, watching as Einar's head dipped and Sigridr cried out, her arms outflung, her hands clawing at the furs. Whatever he was doing to her, she liked it. Safe under her own fur and with Einar completely occupied, Idonea felt her own arousal building again.

Sigridr panted and twisted, spreading her knees wide, crying out Einar's name as he tongued her cleft hungrily. Idonea could hardly bear it. The sounds seemed to go on forever. When Einar began to thrust one of his hands into Sigridr's sex, Idonea could no longer resist. Under the privacy of her own fur, she dragged up her skirt and worked her hand beneath it, suppressing a gasp as she found her own point of pleasure in the moist, heated folds of her sex. As Sigridr cried out across the room, calling Einar's name over and over, Idonea closed her eyes and succumbed to another melting crisis that consumed her right to the very ends of her fingers and toes.

Afterwards, she didn't open her eyes. She could feel

Einar's gaze upon her again. She couldn't bear to return it. She dragged the fur up over her head and sank away into a dream-fevered sleep, even as the noises from the other bed began all over again.

IDONEA WOKE IN the grey light of morning to find Sigridr standing over her. She recoiled, breathing in sharply, but the woman did nothing more than crouch down until their faces were level. She was dressed, a cloak wrapped around her shoulders.

What does she want? Livid images from the last night sprang into Idonea's mind's eye, and her breath began to flutter in her chest.

Sigridr reached out and brushed Idonea's bruised cheek. Idonea flinched as her touch woke a faint ache under her skin. Sigridr's mouth twisted and her brow puckered. She spoke a handful of incomprehensible syllables Idonea understood instinctively.

I'm sorry.

Idonea stared back stonily, not in a mood to forgive.

The woman retracted her hand and stood. She looked resigned.

Idonea watched her leave, and then glanced back to where Einar lay under his own furs. With a jolt in her belly, she saw he was awake. He was leaning on his elbow, the bright blue of his eyes burning through the haze of heat over the slumbering firepit. He grinned. Idonea was filled with inescapable certainty. He knew what she had done to herself last night, whilst she watched him service Sigridr with his tongue.

Unable to bear the suspense of Einar's gaze, Idonea rose and went outside. Here, in the early morning sun, there were a dozen tasks with which she could easily busy herself. None of them were any different from her chores at home. She gave a bitter laugh. After all those days and nights, huddled in the bottom of the raiders' boat, cramped and freezing, sick with fear and the movement of the heaving sea—she'd found things were no different on the other side of the world.

At least, she mused, watching the pig snuffling in its pen, *it is not Wybert waiting for me inside.* She felt a sudden fierce burst of satisfaction at her last memory of him, lying on the floor of the burning wreck of their home, Einar's axe in his neck and Idonea's dagger in his belly.

As if in response to her thought, the door clattered open and Einar appeared. He had put on his trews and cast his shirt carelessly over one shoulder. After all she had witnessed last night, the sight of his bare chest made Idonea feel warm. He gave her a crooked smile and strode over to a trough of water, standing against the south wall of the house.

Idonea stayed where she was by the pigpen. He was not watching her now, apparently satisfied in the knowledge that, this time, she was watching him. He scooped up handfuls of water from the trough and rubbed them over his face, and then did the same for the back of his neck and his armpits. Idonea watched breathlessly as the fine, gold hair on his chest turned darker and clung to his skin. A familiar ache was building between her thighs. She wanted to touch the wet tendrils of hair on his chest, to brush the drops of water from his skin and—

She looked away abruptly. Her gaze fell upon her own hands. They were so filthy. She rubbed at a smudge of soot on the back of one hand. It did no good. Grime lurked under her nails and in the creases of her skin. The sleeves of her dress were filthy and ragged. She looked back at where he stood, clean and damp, leaning against the wall. Watching her again.

"Idzunn!" he summoned her, beckoning. Reluctantly, she went. He took a cup hanging from a peg on the wall above the trough and gestured for her to put out her hands. Hesitantly, she held them up. He poured cold water over them, and she rubbed them together, watching the dirt drip away.

He gestured for her to stay where she was, and disappeared back inside the house. A minute later he returned, carrying a short stack of folded garments. He set them on a bench beside the trough and motioned for her to undress.

Idonea went red.

He folded his arms and gave her a meaningful stare.

He cannot mean…

She glanced around uncomfortably, as though she did not understand what he wanted her to do. But he made impatient motions with his hand, and she had to relent. Slowly, she dragged her ruined dress over her head and threw it aside. She stood in her shift, shivering in the cool air, waiting for him to show her what next.

But he wasn't satisfied. His next gesture made it clear she should remove her shift, as well.

Yesterday, she would have been terrified. She *was* still frightened. But last night something had changed. Half in terror and half in trembling excitement, she pulled off her shift and sent it after her dress.

Einar smiled.

Then he dipped the scoop into the trough and poured a torrent of icy water over her head.

Idonea shrieked.

Behind the curtain of sodden red hair plastered over her face, Idonea heard him start to laugh. Furious, she shoved aside her hair and glared, wrapping her arms around herself as her skin turned to gooseflesh. Still laughing, he made a helpless gesture. Half-apology, half-plea for her to see the humor. Shaking his head, and making those soothing-shushing noises, he scooped up more water, this time pouring it more thoughtfully over her right shoulder.

The slow trickle was still so cold it made her bones ache, but it was bearable. She rubbed at her skin briskly, then bent her head and pointed at her scalp, gasping as he drenched her there. After that first piece of mischief, he was most considerate. He poured where she pointed, and made no move to do anything else. Still, she couldn't help noticing, as he scooped and poured, and she scrubbed and clenched her teeth against the cold, the growing bulge at his crotch.

When she was done, he handed her his shirt and indicated she should dry herself.

"Are you sure?" she asked, even though he could not understand her. He gestured for her to go ahead. When she was dry, he gave her the clothes he'd brought out. They were much like the clothing Sigridr had worn, although made for someone shorter and stouter than Idonea.

When she was dressed, Einar stood looking at her for some moments, a different smile on his face. He crossed his arms over his still-bare chest and nodded.

Idonea ducked her head, partly out of a sudden fit of shyness, and partly because she couldn't look at him anymore. He was unbearably attractive, with his damp, tousled hair and powerful shoulders. She didn't know what to want.

SIGRIDR DID NOT come again that night. Einar made her sit and eat with him, but when he turned towards his bed, Idonea could not bring herself to join him, even though the thought made her pulse race. She turned away to her own bed. She didn't want to see the disappointment on his face. She didn't look his way as she rolled herself in her own fur. So when she peeked from under her lids to see what he was doing, she was surprised. He'd piled up his furs so he could lean back on them and watch her across the firepit. He was also stark naked with the most enormous erection. Idonea's eyes grew wide. Her whole body flushed with heat.

As she watched him, he reached down and took himself in his fist, jerking himself slowly at first, then faster and harder. Excitement boiled in Idonea's belly, making her bold.

She sat up. Her heart drumming, she pushed off her fur and shrugged her way out of her dress. Einar slowed again. Hardly daring to believe herself, she sat on the edge of her bed and lifted her shift high, clutching it to her chest so he could see her body, naked from her breasts down.

His fist began to move faster.

Idonea eased apart her knees, and then reached down with her free hand between her legs. She was already wet, her thighs slick, her sex swollen. As she slid her fingers between her ready folds, she could hear Einar's breath coming in gruff pants.

She began to rub.

She was almost too aroused. Her fingers kept sliding aside in the hot, wet mess of her sex, and she had to pinch at her nubbin to get any traction. The sensation made her gasp. Einar groaned. He was using his other hand to knead his balls. Idonea imagined him using his mouth on her, the way he had on Sigridr, and a yearning rose up that made her whimper out loud. She *wanted* him...

Einar came first. He closed his eyes and tipped back his head, drawing up his knees and digging his feet into the furs, his legs tense. Idonea watched as he thrust up into his hand, creamy spurts of his seed splattering across his belly. The sight of his legs, spread apart, exposing him completely to her gaze, pushed her over her own edge. She cried out, grinding down on the hand thrust between her legs. The fingers of her other hand found one of her nipples and she pinched hard and shattered. Warmth flooded between her legs and sensation rippled through her body.

As it ebbed away, she opened her eyes. She looked at Einar lying there, his chest heaving. The smile on his face showed his satisfaction. Not wanting to take her gaze off him, Idonea let her shift fall and lay down, tucking her feet beneath the thick fur beside her. She stared across the fire to where he smiled back at her, feeling quite satisfied herself.

THE NEXT DAY was different. As usual, Idonea felt him watching her from the moment she awoke. But today, she did not feel preyed upon. She also found herself doing plenty of watching of her own. The sight of Einar bare-chested, chopping wood, for example, was enough to make her stop and lean against the sun-warmed side of the house until he split the last log, kicked it aside, and put the axe over his shoulder. He grinned, shifted the axe horizontal, and hooked his hands over both ends, then walked off whistling, leaving her to admire the view of the muscles playing across his back.

Later, Einar showed her a small stream flowing down the hill behind the farmhouse, sheltered by wind-twisted trees. Idonea found a stand of hazel trees and began to gather nuts into her skirt. Einar hunkered down by the buckets of fresh water they'd collected and waited for her, watching. As she picked, she summoned the courage to ask the question plaguing her since *that* night.

She turned back to him, nervously clutching the hoard of nuts in her skirt.

"Sigridr…?" she asked eventually.

He raised his eyebrows and appeared to be considering what her question might relate to.

"Sigridr?" she asked again, feeling helpless without the right words.

Understanding dawned on his face. He picked up a twig and drew a simple outline of a house in the sparse dirt. He pointed to himself, and then the farmhouse. Then he drew an arc beside the house, and on the other side of it, another house. He pointed to the arc, then up the hill, then the second house, and said "Sigridr."

He drew a stick figure beside the house and tapped it. "Sigridr," he said, looking up at her to make sure she understood. Idonea nodded. He drew another figure beside Sigridr. Then three smaller figures. Idonea frowned. *A husband? And children?*

She looked at Einar, trying to understand why, in this fierce world, a woman with a husband and children would risk spending a night with the neighbor, handsome though he surely was. Her confusion must have shown on her face, because he tapped the second adult figure then, with a finger, obliterated its legs. He paused, then, almost as an afterthought, erased half of one of its arms. Then he looked up at her again, hooking his fingers into claws and drawing his lips back in a snarl. He growled.

Idonea's eyes widened. Einar nodded, his face serious. Then suddenly, he grinned, his eyes alight with mischief. He drew the figure's legs on again.

"Danr!" Then he wiped them away again. "Halfdan!"

"Half… dan," said Idonea slowly. The meaning dawned on her and a laugh escaped her lips. Einar shot her a pleased look and glanced down at the tableau he'd drawn in the dirt. His face grew rueful again. He muttered something and scratched at his beard.

She followed Einar as he carried the water back down to the farmhouse, thinking about Sigridr, with her three children and a husband mauled by… some animal.

There was no doubt. Sigridr was a woman in her prime. She was beautiful and—the image of Sigridr on the boat rose in Idonea's memory—as strong and fierce as any of the men in her village. *Why should she not spend a night with a handsome man when she's of a mind?*

Idonea gazed critically at Einar, walking ahead of her on the narrow path. *Vikings take what they want.*

Idonea went inside the farmhouse to find something to put the hazelnuts in. She took a basket down from a peg above her bed then halted in surprise.

There, lying in the centre of her bed, was her dagger. Beside it lay a new leather sheath attached to a braided belt.

Quickly, she dumped the nuts into the basket. Hardly daring to believe it, she picked up the dagger, feeling its familiar weight in her hand. She let out a breath she hadn't known she'd been holding.

Last time she'd held this, she had buried it deep in Wybert's belly. *After Einar nearly hacked off his head.*

But the axe-blow hadn't been enough. He'd still been alive.

In all her fear, in the chaos of the raid, with the huge, blood-spattered Viking standing over her, knowing she was about to die, one last, sharp desire had risen in Idonea's breast.

She had plunged the dagger home and had the satisfaction of seeing the light die in her cursed husband's eyes.

Now, here it was.

Einar must have retrieved it. Cleaned it. Left it here…for her.

Why?

Einar spoke from the doorway. She turned. He was leaning there, one hand scratching at the back of his head. His eyes told her he wanted her to be pleased.

"Thank you," she said.

He came inside. Idonea's heart began to beat faster as he came close. He gave her a crooked smile and picked up the belt. Idonea stood still as he wound the belt around her waist and tied it in place. He grinned down at her. Then his face grew serious. He reached out a hand and tapped her chest.

He uttered a string of words Idonea had no hope of being able to comprehend. But his blue eyes spoke volumes, and somehow, Idonea understood him.

You have a Viking's heart. You killed that man, even though you were about to die, not because it might have saved you, but because you wanted to take his life.

He gestured to himself, still speaking. Then he

reached out and took her hand and pressed it against his chest. His heart was beating almost as fast as hers.

Another Viking heart, she realized. *There for the taking.*

Suddenly, a gleam of humor appeared in his eyes. He covered his belly with his free hand and assumed an expression of mock fear. Idonea had to smile.

With her own free hand, she reached up and tangled her fingers in the hair at the nape of his neck. She pulled his face down to hers and kissed his mouth. He kissed her back, hungrily.

She would join him in his bed tonight.

Vikings take what they want.

SWEET SILK

Megan Mitcham

The Persian Empire, the North African coast, 820 AD

KROAN LEAPT FROM the *knörr*'s sturdy wooden deck, over the rail, and onto the bustling dock.

Forget the walls of black water that had attacked his ship in rolling waves. Forget the fury of the sky with its suffocating rain and blinding bolts of lightning. Forget the sea creatures with their blade-sharp teeth that had stalked them in the calm of day. This act, tying to port under a clear blue sky on the serene jade gulf, rankled his peace the most.

He'd traded his warship for a merchant one long ago. Yet, the need to anchor off shore in a defensive position weighted his shoulders far more than the battle axe he still carried. His fingers caressed the thick leather strap across his chest, securing the weapon. The move steadied his misgivings—at least, the ones about docking. He turned to his crew. The men stood straight as the mast, their gazes intent, and jaws waggling for the spoils of land.

"One day men. Two bands. The first of you, go—

have your fun, but do not stir trouble. I don't particularly feel like having to tell your families your peckers got the best of you. Buy your supplies, and then swap. Same goes for the rest of you. Is that clear?"

A chorus of baritone aye's carried above the commotion caused by the loading and unloading of all manner of cargo from the ships near them.

"Good," Kroan said. "I have business to attend to. Be ready to sail in two days' time at sunset. And, men, if I do not return by midnight, shove off without me."

They grumbled and sneered at his words.

The largest of the crew, save for himself, stepped forward. His arms, as big around as the gut of a spit-roasted hog, folded over his chest. "The ship will await its captain," Broden said.

"As first mate, you become the Swaran's captain. And you will follow my orders. Understood?"

"Aye, sir," his friend growled.

"On we go," Kroan barked.

With begrudging nods, half his motley crew followed. Their sturdy frames *thunked* onto the mooring. The others stayed behind to guard the vessel, while he and the first group headed to market.

Though the crew wasn't looking for trouble, harbor workers scurried from their path, making way for the band of behemoths. When they hit solid ground, Kroan stepped to the side, ordering his men to precede him with a jerk of his head.

He eased from the stone path to the brilliant sand. It sucked his feet to the ankles and warmed them through the tanned leather. The last time he'd set foot on the parched Persian earth, he'd saved an old man from certain death and gotten settled with a child bride as his prize.

Of all the tainted luck.

She'd been a virgin to life, much less lust. But her eyes had shaken his stalwart morals to rubble. Dark as pitch in the midst of the sea. Vibrant as a million stars glinting in the eve. Everywhere he'd ventured in her father's silk hut, her knowing gaze had followed. Those attentive orbs fanned with lashes long enough to tickle his skin and were framed with a jeweled headdress and thin veil that had shown only a glimpse of her smooth walnut skin.

Anticipation wrestled every nerve in Kroan's body, threatening to topple him onto the blistering ground. Steeling his spine, he strode onto the path an older, and hopefully, more worthy husband than he'd been at twenty-one. The city itself had matured in the time he'd been away. Its streets filled to bursting with patrons. But he wondered about the girl.

At twenty-three, she'd likely be ripe enough to bring him to his knees, assuming he could find her after all these years. He weaved through the sea of people to the main fair of vendors in search of his wife.

"PARDON, MY LADY. I am in need of silk, and I'm told you have the finest in all the world," a booming voice spoke gently in her native tongue.

Shîrîn's heart shuddered. What pleasure and pain that voice—or, more accurately, the memory of that voice—brought her over most of a decade. When a shadow large enough to accompany the man cast her in darkness, her hands faltered. The point of the needle missed the fabric altogether, stabbing into her finger.

"*Angra Mainyu*," she cursed the devil and his destructive forces.

The piercing sting was restitution for turning her back on the hut's entrance, beginning yet another bolt of silk in the obsessive pattern sure to put her family out of business. None of her countrymen wanted silk with a Viking astride a dark horse, his chest wide and bare with one sinewy arm brandishing an axe above his long blond locks.

"Are you hurt?" The voice and shadow grew bigger until both leaned over her shoulder. "Please, let me help."

A hand, large enough to completely encompass her throat, gathered her smaller one and lifted it high. Though strong enough to inflict damage, his hand cradled. Heat radiated from roughened fingers.

Her breath lodged in her windpipe. Desire ran amuck in her mind, creating a desire for things she wanted more than all the silk in the land. She clamped her eyes shut. With a fast back and forth, she tried to shake away the absurdity of her thoughts.

An acute burn snapped her lids wide. Shîrîn rocketed from the woven rug, dumping the roll of expensive fabric and spools of vibrant threads to the ground. She turned, anger perched on the tip of her tongue.

"Have mercy on…"

A mountain of a man stood over her. It seemed his shoulders spread almost as wide as her arms could. She tilted her head and found her hand nestled inside his much-larger one, and snugged against the cleft of two bulging pectorals.

Shîrîn's gaze locked there for far too long, mapping the thatch of light hair and tautness of the sun-kissed skin. In his other hand, the needle stood pinched between his thumb and forefinger. Crimson tarnished its point. Her cheeks suddenly grew hot, no doubt matching the vibrant red of the feather-light veil threatening to suffocate her.

She struggled to swallow, to speak, but her mouth grew as dry as the dunes. She should feel ashamed, ogling this man who conjured every fractured memory of her long-lost husband, as well as every carnal fantasy she'd entertained over the years. But she didn't turn away, only continued the tour. This man's jaw was wider than the man in her dreams. The scowl deeper. His nose sat proudly, if not a little crooked, between sky blue eyes flecked with cloud white fissures. Her palms slicked with sweat and her pulse stuttered.

She knew those eyes, would know them anywhere in the cosmos. "Kroan," she gasped.

"You're bleeding, Shîrîn."

"I don't care." Her words were thin as Mand river reeds.

His grimace deepened still, but faltered with the rise

of one brow. A smile played at the edge of his lips. He inclined his head and opened his mouth. Firm lips engulfed her fingertip in silk rivaling any she'd had the pleasure of experiencing. Chinese, Byzantine, Indian—none came close to the soft heat of the Scandinavian silk bathing the smallest bit of her skin. The rough give of his tongue caressed her pad, and then all too soon his lips dragged off her finger.

"I care," Kroan said.

The spell broke as surprise morphed into outrage. "You care?" She yanked her hand from his grip and surged into his space with a brashness she'd never dared to display. Since he hunched forward her covered face crowded his own.

"A husband shows concern for his wife by sharing the responsibilities of life. By speaking with her every day and holding her close every night. By loving her mind and worshiping her body with his own. But not you, my husband. You leave me alone, without the favor of your smile or the heat of your body."

Heat indeed. It radiated from his exposed chest and arms. His hands balled into tight fists. The muscles in his jaw danced.

But she couldn't stop. Words held captive for too many years tumbled out between them. "Was our courtship not pleasing? Did you find me boorish, stupid? Fear me ugly? Kroan, I am not any of those things."

She ripped the covering from her face in what would have been plain view of the passing throng of market goers were it not for her husband's Herculean frame.

Her gaze dared him to call her unsightly, begged him to enfold her in his arms and kiss her as boldly as he had in her imaginings.

Instead, his grip encircled high on her right arm. He drove her back from the storefront, his hold careful and strong. With his other hand, he pulled down swaths of silk, which hung from the ceiling. The fabric barricaded the light of day and hid them from the sight of the street goers. It plunged them into a dim cave of luxurious textiles.

Kroan scrubbed a hand over his face. His muttering came hoarse and in a language she didn't recognize. The lilt of the words caressed her in a velvety wave, priming her as if his hand had done the work. Her nipples beaded, and she flushed lower still, in the place she'd only toyed with in the dead of night when her imagination forced her to the brink of sanity.

"I don't understand. Kroan, please." Shîrîn didn't know for what she begged, but she did, and would at his feet, if necessary. She clutched her loose dress to keep from throwing herself at him, to keep from exploring the feel of his pale locks. Everything about them was so different. Size, coloring, beliefs. But she prayed their desires were the same. Like her, he held himself in invisible restraints.

"You are more provoking than a harem of willing women at my feet, wife, more fascinating than any scholar. Our courtship dared to please me too much."

"Then why leave?" she shouted.

He placed his fingers over her lips. His gaze tightened, but he whispered, "Are you set on getting us in trouble? Do you not realize that married or not, the guards will arrest us for being together? You're a Persian beauty meant for a pretty Persian man, not a brute like me."

She pressed her mouth more firmly to his fingers. Her soft lips molded around them. After placing a chaste kiss, she eased back. "This body is meant only for you, ruffian. So why did you leave?" she breathed.

"You were barely fourteen," he answered.

"I was the proper marrying age. The laws of church and man deemed it so."

"But not the proper bedding age."

She huffed a breath. All she heard was a thin excuse. "Are you really so savage?"

"Don't mock me." His hand cupped the side of her face and then tangled amongst the hair at her nape. He crushed the small space between them with one step. That mesmerizing blue gaze slid to her mouth. "You weren't bedding age, but you are now."

SHÎRÎN LIFTED HER chin and parted her lips. For him? Her delicate bone structure, perfect skin, and rosy lips were refined enough for royalty. His peasant blood and warrior's face couldn't begin to compare, but with her this close, this willing, he couldn't deny the need.

"Your father promised you long ago. But, wife, do you wish to be mine?" Kroan's breath seized as he studied her features and awaited her reply.

Her lips trembled and moisture welled in her dark

eyes. "All those years ago, I set out for the harbor with a package a customer had left behind. When I reached the city gate, I saw you, bare-chested and dripping sweat, working on the deck of your ship. I watched you heave sacks of spices over your head, and before I realized the day turned to dusk. You dried off and headed into town, not even sparing me a glance." Her small pink tongue wet her lips, while her rapid breaths did their best to dry them.

It had been his first voyage on a merchant ship and he'd been greener than his homeland in spring, learning everything the hard way and loving every backbreaking minute. She'd been young and covered head to toe. He wasn't surprised he hadn't noticed her, but the fact she'd noticed him had him swollen with more than pride.

"I thank Ahura Mazda every day that you spared my father a glance for it was my fault the men wanted him dead. I had forgotten about the package clutched to my chest for those short hours, but the customer had not."

Her petite hands released the dress and settled over his heart. "Don't you see, Kroan? I was yours before I became your wife."

He lost himself in her words and hungry gaze. With a dip of his head, he sealed his mouth over her lips. Saffron and sex mingled on his tongue. To his surprise, her tongue artfully delved inside his mouth, fumbling and exploring. Shîrîn's hands spread on his chest. Her back bowed, pressing her soft body against his.

Kroan groaned his agonized pleasure as she cuddled his erection with her belly. Knowing he shouldn't, here in the center of market, he skated his left hand over her shoulder to the small of her back and pulled her closer. He longed to pump his hips into the pressure, but didn't dare move, fearing he'd forget himself entirely and take her on the floor of the hut.

Shîrîn's hips rolled in a tiny circle, spurring his lust higher until it filled him to bursting. He stabbed the needle into the hut's wall and barred her hips with his hands, but knew his mistake the moment his fingers sank into her soft bottom. He molded the supple flesh through the aggravating layers of clothing.

She moaned into his mouth, and her fingers roamed his shoulders. His back. His neck. She wound her fingers through his long hair.

A whimper gargled at the back of his throat, threatening to mark him as the enthralled sapling he was. Shîrîn broke the kiss before he could embarrass himself. She held firm to the hanks of his hair, so they didn't stray far. Her breaths cooled his cheek.

"Kroan, I am yours, but I want to make you mine. Please, let me."

Unshed tears glistened in her eyes, and he couldn't have denied her, if he'd wanted to. He nodded his approval.

The grip on his nape loosened. He in turn loosened his grip and allowed her to step back. Her hands went to the top of her wispy orange gown. With two easy sweeps, the fabric fell from her shoulders to her hips.

"Praise be your gods and mine," he rasped.

Dusky brown circles crowned two luscious breasts,

not large, but enough to overflow his hands. The tips of each stood for him, begging his attention. He couldn't yet give them their due. Her hands smoothed over her flat abdomen and his gaze followed, starving for the next morsel of her skin. With deliberate movements, she pushed the dress over her hips and let it fall to the floor. Enraptured by the curve of her hips and the patch of midnight hair covering her mound, he froze.

She stepped out of the heaped fabric, her feet as bare as her beautiful body. Only the gold jeweled hairdressing draped across her forehead, which kept her long hair from her face, hid any part of her from his gaze.

She turned and stepped deeper into the tent, tormenting him with the full globes of her bottom. Loose tendrils of her hair brushed against the small of her back, and he wished they were his fingers. He stepped forward to do just that, but she turned and stayed him with an arch of her brow.

"I'm pleased you are impatient. I have the mind to make you wait as long as you have made me. But I haven't the will." She yanked on the pile of silk she'd been threading. The fabric billowed wildly, and then landed in wavy pools across the carpeted floor. Her body arched and bent as she layered four more hills of textile in the same artful way.

"I've waited as long as I can, Shîrîn."

She stepped boldly forward. "Wait no more." Her hands reached for the leather straps crossing his body and holding his weapon in place. He moved to secure it, but she waved away his hands. "Let me take care of you, husband. I'm not worldly practiced, but I have pleasured you enough in my dreams that my skills rival the prince's harem."

Why in hell had he stayed away so long? Her touch was swift and sure. Kroan's blood rushed in his ears as it did when he headed into battle. His wife wasn't armed, and still he knew this was one battle he'd lost long ago. She'd owned his heart as assuredly as she owned his body now.

The weight of the axe left him. She weaved with the thing, but set it to the ground without incident. Next the leathers covering his skin fell away. His erection stood heavy, bobbing between them. Her sweet hand fisted his length, and though he fought the sensation, his head lolled. His body took over, hips pumping into her hand.

A prick of pain skimmed a nipple as his pure, but not so demure, wife, nipped and then sucked the sensitive area. He'd always been a quiet lover, but his lips tingled with the need to praise and love her with his words. Of all the weak-natured gestures.

He clamped his mouth closed, focusing on the steady strokes of her fingers and tongue.

Her mouth left his chest. One of her hands kept a steady rhythm, while the other slipped between his spread legs. A groan bled through his lips as she cupped his sack and tugged. "Yes, wife, just like that. Oh, the gods, you're too good."

Each brush of her hand ratcheted his hunger, tightened his muscles until they threatened to bust through his restraint. Then her cool lips encircled his head. "I'm yours, Shîrîn, and have been for these nine long years."

Slurps and moans whirled about the tent. Hers. His. Kroan was too far gone to worry about the other merchants overhearing, patrons entering without warning, or city guards checking the disturbance.

When he could no longer temper the violent thrusts of his hips, he pulled from her mouth, plucked her off the bed of silks where she knelt, and pulled her to his chest. "Put your legs around me."

Kroan kissed her slicked red lips and sank into the kiss as he knelt and laid her onto the makeshift bed. Her ruthless heels dug into his back. With the finesse of a rutting oxen, he positioned at her wet opening and rammed home. Sweet silk overwhelmed his senses. Her cry, though muffled by his hand, cut him deeper than any blade. He kissed her cheek and buried his face in her hair, holding her as close as they could ever be, as close as he planned to be for the rest of his days.

"I'll not move until you're ready." Perfect rows of teeth clamped down on his pinky. He ground his own to keep from hollering. As soon as the vise of her jaw loosened, he yanked back his hand.

"Had I known this awaited me, I may have altered my daily prayers," she muttered.

"Don't curse me," he ground out. "I swear the hurt will ease. Just relax and feel."

"Feel?" she said, her voice rising. "Oh, I feel—"

Kroan bravely placed his hand over her mouth again, leaned back, and tweaked her raised nipples in turn. Her lips parted, and he braced for her bite. Hot breath dampened his hand on a soft moan.

"That's it," he coaxed, relieved pleasure now edged the pain.

He molded the supple flesh, jostled it this way and that. The wet of her tongue skated over his pads as he moved his hand to her other breast. He gathered them together for a feast, the generous curves stacked against one another. With a dip of his head, he suckled them one, and then the other, laving and lashing with care.

Shîrîn's fingers tangled in his hair. She pulled and bucked beneath him, setting a frantic pace he could never maintain—not for the first time with her, and probably not ever. She pushed him past reason, past humanity, to the base of animal instinct. He shifted to his elbows and met her thrust for thrust.

The fine silk scuffed his knees, but his pain did not exist in her pleasure. Leaning to one side, Kroan mapped her contours with his hands. The hollow of her neck. The peak of her breasts. The dip of her hips. The folds of her pussy. He forked his fingers over his hot penis and pressed his knuckles against her receptive nub. A hint of blood sheathed him, and a Viking's yell rumbled deep inside his chest at the proof of his claim.

Sensations multiplied like the waves on the sea. They rolled together in the tumult of their coupling. Her breaths came shallow and quick. The dusk of her cheeks reddened.

"*No. No,*" she said, her head thrashing side to side. "Oh. Yes. Oh. It feels—"

Kroan clamped his mouth over her incoherent, and

far too boisterous, ramblings.

A fresh wave of moisture bathed his cock. Her muffled keen filled his ears and pulled him into the undertow. He suffocated in ecstasy, in Shîrîn, spilling his seed into her womb. The possibility of making a baby with his wife revived and renewed him.

"Darling, Shîrîn, you are more exquisite than I imagined," he said, brushing damp strands of hair from the side her of face.

"You thought of me while away?"

"You were with me always."

"And I will be from now until the end of our days," she said softly.

As his lust retreated, he met her dreamy gaze. "I dread taking you from your home. From this life you've made for yourself. I have only a boat and what wealth I've earned to share with you."

Her soft hands bracketed his cheeks. "You are my home, Kroan. We will find our way together." She glanced around her tent. "If I can bring silk and thread…"

He smiled. "Bring it all. We'll sell what you do not use."

A dark brow winged upward. "I am quite good at haggling. I will be useful."

"You continue to bargain?"

"I will be your shadow until we sail. I won't allow you to leave without me."

"You do know I am twice your size."

"And you know I am quite relentless," she said, her

small hand encircling his cock.

With a laugh, he kissed her, filled to the brim with joy at his good fortune.

LITTLE WARRIOR

Evey Brett

The coast of Dorsetshire, 981 AD

I WAS UP on the cliffs with my sister when the North-men came.

From our vantage point, we could see the single-sailed boat with the prow carved into the head of a fantastic beast. Oars were on either side and shields lined the rails. At the head of the craft stood a man who had to be Sweyn, their leader. The sun glinted on the sword hung at his hip and the two golden braids on either side of his face. My heart pounded with excitement at the sight. He was the most fantastic creature I'd seen.

Beside me, my sister shuddered. "I can't believe my father promised me to him."

I couldn't either. Ethelfleda was a timid creature, more content to stay in her rooms sewing or singing. Much to my father's dismay, I loved the outdoors and the wildness and would have accompanied him hunting if he'd allowed it. I longed to travel, not stay home and be a good wife to whatever noble he decided was my mate. "I want to talk to them."

"Come away, Ailith." Ethelfleda tugged on my sleeve. "You know what Father said. We're not to have anything to do with them until the feast."

Father had arranged to meet with these visitors to open trade negotiations, but I knew Ethelfleda was thinking of the terrible stories about what they did to women and anyone who opposed them. Our tutor, a man who'd escaped slavery from the Northmen, had been hired to teach their language to Ethelfleda and I. During our lessons, he'd shown us the scars from his beatings and told us tales of what had happened to disobedient slaves. And yet, I was more afraid of being trapped in my father's keep the rest of my life than of these wandering brutes.

I followed my sister for a short way then, when she wasn't looking, doubled back, heading for the thin trail leading down the cliff to the beach. My skirt whipped around my legs as I strode toward my sister's intended husband. Up close, he was huge, tall, broad-shouldered, and more daunting than any of my kinsmen. The entire party, no more than eight, paused at the sight of me. I bowed then said clearly, "I, Ailith, daughter of King Aelfraed, greet you in his name. Please be welcome in our land."

"The king sends a mere girl to greet us?" one of the lesser men said, elbowing one of his friends. "She's not even pretty."

"Do you deny a woman's right to welcome a man into her home?" This, to my surprise, came from a woman. Now that I looked, I saw two of them among the company, both armed like their male companions and as equally fierce. I'd heard tales of shieldmaidens but had never expected to meet any.

"Enough," Sweyn said. He waved a hand and his jostling warriors fell silent. "Where is your father, child? It's he we've come to speak with."

I bristled. I was well into womanhood and did not like being belittled, even by a man so handsome as this. No doubt I would have answered sharply were it not for the hoofbeats sounding behind me as my father and his guards rode up. One glare was all it took for him to convey his fury that I, not he, had been the first to greet the visitors. At his gesture, one of the guards swept me up and carried me on horseback all the way back to the keep. I didn't protest. I'd gotten Sweyn's attention.

THE FEAST WAS interminable. Sweyn and Ethelfleda sat next to each other, but no matter how the warrior tried to be kind to her, she shuddered and drew away, refusing to even look at him. I was seated on my father's other side, too far away to speak to any of our guests. I'm sure he planned it that way. I'd embarrassed him, and he was doing everything short of punishing me to let me know it.

Except for Ethelfleda's reticence, Sweyn and his people seemed to be enjoying themselves. The wine flowed, and a boar had been slaughtered and roasted. His men jostled each other and partook of the meal using their knives and intricately carved spoons made from horn.

The two women appeared more feminine now, dressed in linen blouses and flowing blue skirts. Silver and amber jewelry draped their necks and wrists. They were beautiful but likely no less deadly in this incarnation. I wished I had such presence as they.

Just as the entertainment started, Ethelfleda made some excuse and left the table. Everyone's gaze followed her.

"Worry not. She'll come around," my father said, although I didn't think either he or Sweyn looked convinced.

The two shieldmaidens bent their heads together, whispering.

I leaned over. "Father, I would be happy to—"

"Not now. Sweyn and I have a great deal to discuss. See to your sister. Talk some sense into her. I can't have these negotiations fail."

Angrily, I stalked up the stairs to Ethelfleda's room. Her maid was already tending to her, brushing her long hair until it shone. When I entered, the maid bowed and left, handing me the brush.

Ethelfleda didn't bother to hide her tears as I took the maid's place. "I can't marry him. I can't. I'll throw myself from the tower first."

I found it hard to sympathize. We'd both grown up knowing we wouldn't be able to choose our husbands, and I failed to see what was so terrible about a man so handsome, rich, and kind. Sweyn was also near our age, unlike some of the suitors Father had considered before who'd been old enough to be our grandsires.

Ethelfleda twisted around to face me. She gripped my hand with fingers like iron. "Please. Intervene for me. Speak with father. You have the adventurous soul."

I'd already tried and failed on that account, but I didn't say so. "I'll do what I can," I promised.

Much as I wanted to, I didn't go back to the feast. Let Father think I kept Ethelfleda company. I had plans for later that night.

GYRID, ONE OF the shieldmaidens guarded Sweyn's room. The torch left her face shadowed, but I admired her sharp, chiseled features and the ropy muscles in her arms. Her eyes narrowed at my approach. "What do you want?"

"I've come to speak with Sweyn on Ethelfleda's behalf."

"Does your father know?" She crossed her arms and stared.

I met her gaze and kept it. "No. I came of my own accord."

She laughed. The sound drew Gunhilda out of the next room. "Ah. It's the plucky sister."

I clenched my fists. I had enough teasing from my sister and didn't need it from two women I admired. "Will you let me see him or not?"

"And you're sure it's only speech you're seeking?" Gyrid's pointed gaze raked me up and down. "A young, unmarried woman sneaking around at night only has one thing on her mind. Go back to your room, child. You don't have the stamina for a man such as my brother."

Heat flared in my face, and I was grateful for the lack of light to hide my embarrassment. I turned to go when Gunhilda caught my arm and asked, "What's this?"

I couldn't see the mark she was pointing to on my shoulder, but I knew what she meant. "I've had it since birth."

"It looks like a tree. Don't you think so, Gyrid?"

She went behind me to look and traced the mark with her finger. "Definitely." Coming in front of me again, she asked, "Do you have any sacred trees near here?"

I shrugged. "Not sacred, but a single ash tree grows upon a tor near here." I wondered why they were so interested.

The two women exchanged a glance I could not decipher. "Come," Gyrid said. "Gunhilda will join us shortly."

Inside, the room had been made comfortable. The women had a fine collection of swords, knives, and shields, all displayed prominently and within easy reach. There were other niceties—braziers full of incense, combs and bottles of scent. They might be warriors, but they had not forsaken femininity.

I was nervous at being alone with her. "Are you sisters?" I asked, as much to hide my nervousness as because I was curious.

She laughed. "Sisters in battle but not by blood." She cupped my cheek in her palm. "You are not as pretty as your sister, but no matter. We will make do."

The words stung, but they were no more than the truth. Ethelfleda had inherited Mother's softness and delicate features. I'd taken after my father, tall and rugged.

"Have you ever known a man?"

My father had kept me so pent up I wasn't allowed to be alone with a man, whether servant, tutor, or guard. My maid had lain with men and told me things, so I wasn't entirely naïve, but I didn't dare to lie. "No."

"Thought so. How did you think you'd be able to pleasure Sweyn if you don't even know what pleasure *is*?"

I gazed downward, unable to answer. All thought of tempting Sweyn into ruining me, and therefore forcing a marriage, fell to pieces.

Tilting her head, Gyrid touched her lips to mine. The touch sent a tingle through me. This was no sisterly kiss, but something hinting at more. I didn't draw away. I took in the scent of her skin, warm and fresh from bathing, and was overcome by a sudden, indescribable need.

I didn't notice Gunhilda slip in until she wrapped her arms around my waist and tucked her firm body behind mine. Without speaking, the two women worked as one, untying the laces on my dress then pulling it over my head. I stood there in my shift, trembling despite my determination not to be afraid.

"What's wrong, little warrior?" Gyrid kissed my cheek, my neck, and down the slope of my shoulder.

"We won't hurt you. Quite the opposite."

"Indeed." Gunhilda drew off my shift.

I shivered in the sudden chill, but her body warmed me as she embraced me from behind. She cradled my breasts in her hands and I froze, shocked by the presumption.

"These people are such prudes. So afraid to feel something good," she said.

"Mmm," was Gyrid's only reply. Her fingers found that private place between my legs. I flinched, but Gunhilda held me too tightly for escape. Gyrid's gentle fingers probed me, rubbing at tender parts I'd never dared to touch, until I squirmed from the tingling discomfort.

Gunhilda drew me backwards until she sat on a stool and I on her lap. She continued to massage my breasts while Gyrid forced my legs on either side of Gunhilda's and knelt. The kiss she placed upon my nether regions sent a shudder through my entire body. Wetness coated me, only to be lapped up by Gyrid's eager tongue. I wriggled, unsure how do deal with the building pressure in my lower body, but Gunhilda held me fast and made my head swim with kisses on my cheek and neck. She pinched my nipples until they were tender and sore, adding another layer of sensation.

I whimpered and dug my nails into Gunhilda's arm. Gyrid didn't stop; she kept licking a particularly sensitive spot until I could hold back no longer. My body clenched and burst forth in a series of spasms so sharp and delightful they left me breathless.

For several breaths, I lolled against Gunhilda, dazed by the aftermath. "Sweyn can do that?"

"All that and more," Gunhilda said with such satisfaction that I knew she'd lain with him and enjoyed it.

Gyrid guided me over to the bed then pushed me down. "A man will do something else. You know that."

I nodded, although I didn't know the details.

Drawing my legs apart once more, she fingered me there. I trembled, but Gunhilda sat beside me and stroked my cheek. "Breathe. There's nothing to fear and everything to savor." She whispered to me, telling me things of such a coarse and intimate nature I couldn't help but blush.

And all the while, Gyrid stroked me until I'd lost all shame at being exposed and gave myself over to the pleasure. When she slipped one finger inside me, I hardly noticed. At the addition of another, I murmured in appreciation. Three, and I'd grown tense again, but Gunhilda smothered me with kisses to allay the discomfort below.

Gyrid thrust her fingers in and out, slowly at first then with increasing speed, mimicking what Sweyn was apt to do. Pressure built inside my belly as it had before, but deeper. Climax erupted in steady, aching waves. Any cry I tried to make was swallowed when Gunhilda covered my lips with hers.

So spent was I that they both had to help me dress. I felt entirely different. New. Shorn of all I'd once been and ready for the next step.

"In the morning," Gyrid said, "we will ride out with

Sweyn. Take my brother to see the ash tree you spoke of. You will have your chance to impress him then.”

I nodded, both exhausted and perplexed by the request. “I’ll do my best.”

The kiss she laid upon my forehead was filled with love and tenderness. “I’m sure you will, little warrior.”

“WELL?” ETHELFLEDA ASKED when I returned to her room.

I took her hand, marveling at how soft and fragile it seemed after being with the shieldmaidens. I wondered how it was possible she did not notice the difference in me. “Don’t worry. I have it all in hand.”

She let out a sigh of relief. “Thank you, Ailith. Thank you.”

The kiss on my cheek was wet and cold, but I did not tell her so. I was too eager to reach my bed and recount every touch laid upon me by the shieldmaidens in preparation for meeting Sweyn.

MY FATHER WASN’T keen to let me ride out with Sweyn and show him our lands, but neither did he want to deny his honored guest’s request. When he tried to include my sister in the party, Ethelfleda pleaded illness and asked not to be disturbed. Gyrid and Gunhilda assured him they would be along to keep an eye on me and wouldn’t let anything untoward happen. I kept my gaze on the ground, unable to meet my father's look of concern. He had no idea of the true reason behind this journey, and I wasn't going to enlighten him.

It was a fine spring morning when we rode out, cool and misty. The horses snorted and pranced in the dew-laden grass. We passed through the village which nestled in the keep's shadow. I was used to the deference paid me, due to my father's rank, but when I rode by with the northerners, the people gaped and stared. A few children ran up to openly gawk at my companions, and Sweyn patiently allowed them to touch his fine leather boots and fur cloak. My father usually had no time for such niceties, and it warmed my heart to see Sweyn being kind in a village he so easily could have burned to the ground.

For a while, I did as my father had expected, showing them my favorite places, including the pond where I'd caught frogs and salamanders and the woods where my father hunted deer and boar.

A hawk flew overhead, and Sweyn watched it with interest.

We came at last to Roald's Tor, a hill of rock bare save for a few large boulders and an ash tree jutting from the center. I was both surprised to find that no one had accompanied us to the summit. The shieldmaidens waited nearby within easy reach, but they made no move to join us.

A pair of ravens croaked from the branches. Sweyn looked up and grinned. "Odin blesses this meeting."

Some of my anxiety lessened. "I'm glad, my lord."

He caught me around the waist and pulled me to

him, back to his chest. His hands were large enough that if he put both around my waist, he could enclose it. "My sister tells me you're quite the little warrior."

"I've little training as such, but my heart longs for the sea and distant lands." I tried not to sound pleading, but I probably did. "I am no tame woman to be kept inside for the rest of my life."

"No, I don't think you are." One of his hands roved to my belly. That queer tingling began between my legs, and I wished he were brazen enough to touch me there. "I need a wife to bear me strong sons and daughters. Do you think Ethelfleda is up to the task?"

I didn't like to demean my sister. I loved her, but I daren't speak anything but the truth. "No, my lord. She belongs to this land. Any attempt to take her from it would end her life." I wriggled a little, pleased to feel the growing bulge within his breeches. "I would be pleased to provide you with sons."

He drew down the shoulder of my dress and traced the birthmark. "Your father could slay me for dishonoring his daughter. I would do the same to anyone who dared lay a hand on mine."

I twisted around to face him and fingered his rough blond beard. "He won't. He's afraid to risk war with your people. There is too much for us to lose. Besides, it's I who am asking you."

He had not worn armor today, which allowed me to place my palms against his chest and breathe in the scent of salt and sweat. I felt the heat and firmness through the woolen tunic and was suddenly desperate to touch his bare skin. Impishly, I reached beneath the hem and he rewarded me by undoing his leather belt so I could reach all the way up to his belly and savor the warmth. I had not realized how cold my hands were until he shivered and covered them with his own.

He stripped off his tunic, and I discovered why the shieldmaidens had been so interested in my birthmark. Tattoos covered his skin, the most elaborate and detailed being that of a tree on his torso. In the branches, an eagle sat at the top while a dragon nestled at the bottom. A squirrel climbed in the middle. The trunk ran down the center while the branches spread across his chest. I couldn't help but touch it.

"*Yggdrasil.* The tree of life," I said, and was rewarded with a smile of approval. I don't think he'd expected a Christian like me to know. But I'd pounced eagerly on all the tales my tutor could relate, especially those of Ygg-drasil.

He stood quietly while I drew my finger down his chest, stunned by the knowledge that I had brought him here to my favorite place, and that we shared matching marks upon our bodies. In my childish fancies, I'd dreamed the tree atop the tor was Yggdrasil, and if I looked hard enough I would find a way to reach from my world to the next. I'd managed no such magic on my own, but with Sweyn, I might be able to accomplish something at last.

I wrapped my arms around his neck, grateful beyond words. His answering embrace nearly crushed the wind from my lungs.

He released me and pulled off his breeches. Yggdrasil's three roots spread downward, the first to Asgard, the home of the gods, which flowed around his right leg. The dragon curled by the third root, guarding the way to Niflheim and the well Hvergelmir.

I couldn't stop the giggle at the second root, Jotunheim, home of the giants, which pointed to the man's sizeable prick, already thick and erect.

"You think me amusing?" he asked with a smile.

I thought him more than that. I clasped his manhood, surprised by the softness of its skin while the rest of him was so rough and hard. He made a sound of approval then slowly began to rake up my skirts. I aided him by undoing the laces so he could draw the garment over my head.

I stood before him, naked and unafraid. With huge hands, he grasped my arms and turned me around, pausing just long enough to kiss the mark on my shoulder.

Then he spun me, pushing me up against the tree. The bark scraped my back in long, burning streaks, but I didn't care. He nipped at my neck and shoulder, and I bucked against him, but he held me fast. I loved his wildness, the absolute domination while he somehow remained aware of just how to please me. Each nip sent bolts of sensation all through my body, and when he kissed me, his tongue invaded my mouth, exploring and seeking and tasting of the wine we'd brought in our flasks.

He let go and swiftly grabbed his fur cloak, draping it

over one of the boulders with a fairly flat surface. Returning, he lifted me beneath the buttocks and carried me over, laying me down none too gently. As Gyrid had predicted, he spread my thighs and set to work with his tongue. He was more forceful but provided no less enjoyment as he dipped into tender, secret places.

He glanced up just long enough for me to see his barely concealed restraint. He was a scant distance away from the brutality the Northmen were known for. I could sense it within him, a caged beast seeking to act as the wild thing it was.

I sat up and clasped his weathered face, lightheaded with nerves and excitement. His masculine scent hit my nostrils and filled me with a feverish hunger of my own. "Do what you will." Wrapping my legs around his waist, I drew him in until I felt the rounded hardness of his sex seeking entry. Roaring, he speared me in one swift stroke. Pain flared then died away as he filled me. I arched backward, panting and moaning, as he drew out and then pushed back in, deeper, harder, thrusting fiercely while I clung to him.

Maybe it was the sheer freedom of offering myself or the magic of the place we'd chosen, but I couldn't get enough. I raked his shoulders, his back in an attempt to bring him nearer. Yggdrasil's roots dug deep, reaching within me to call me home. I clawed at him, desperate to hold on, as if I might climb his tattooed tree and find my way home.

How long this continued, I couldn't say. I was so lost in the frenzy of our coupling that I didn't know where his body ended and mine began, whether it was he or I who'd first reached the pinnacle and fell beyond it. My body spasmed around his. Moments later, his member throbbed as he released his seed. I prayed it would take hold and grant him the wished-for son.

He had the good sense to roll to the side once he'd expended himself to prevent crushing me beneath his weight. As it was, he pulled me to him, and I lay there for some time, curled within the warmth of his arms and utterly content.

WE SHARED A horse as we rode back to the keep. The villagers spoke in hushed whispers. No doubt they could tell by my tousled hair and rumpled dress just what had occurred between Sweyn and me. But I didn't care. For the first time in my life, I had made my own decision, and I would live with the consequences.

A messenger must have ridden ahead, because my father met us at the gates. "Take her to her room," he told one of the guards. "See that she does not leave."

Sweyn's grip tightened around me, but I patted his hand. "Don't fight. I'll be fine."

Seeing how badly he was outnumbered, he let go. I allowed myself to be unceremoniously escorted upstairs and heard the door bolted from the outside. There would be no leaving unless my father allowed it. The window, even if it hadn't looked down upon sheer cliffs, was too small for me to squeeze through.

Angry as I was, I hung on to the memories of

Sweyn's body against mine, the way his cock had moved so securely within me. I'd known bliss, and I wasn't going to let it slip away.

Just past dusk, my father entered, his face purpled with rage. "He was your sister's betrothed. Now…" he shook his head. "You are a wicked, ungrateful girl and have ruined everything I sought in these negotiations. Sweyn refuses to wed Ethelfleda. He claims she is too weak and finds you more to his liking. I would have killed him for touching you, but I know your sinful heart that lies within."

Usually, I would have cowered a little at his raging, but now I stood steadfast, pleased rather than dismayed by his consternation. "Ethelfleda is afraid of him. I'm not."

The backhanded slap stung my face. I staggered, caught off-guard. It was my father's stubborn pride that kept him from seeing the truth. He didn't like being shown his mistakes. But his expression when he met my gaze was filled with anguish.

"Don't you see, Ailith? I *can't* let you marry him, not even after you've become his whore."

The word stung, although I deserved it. But there was something more than just a father's anger over a child's disobedience. His agitation seemed tinged with grief. "No. I don't see. Perhaps you'd better tell me, Father."

He sank limply into a chair, skin ashen, and for a moment, I worried that he'd been stricken ill. "You're not my daughter."

I stared, uncomprehending as the world seemed to crumple away beneath me. "What?"

"Your mother went to visit her sister. While there, the keep was raided, and she was misused. She tried to pass you off as mine, but I knew. I *knew*, and I kept you anyway."

I'd never before suspected such a thing, despite all the whispers and constant comparisons to my sister. Painful as the news was, it gave me hope. "Then I am no kin of yours."

"No, but I have treated you as if you were. Haven't I?" he asked, sounding tired.

"I am grateful, my lord," I said, and meant it. He had treated me well and given me opportunities few maidens had. He'd loved me, in his own way. "Do you know my true father?"

He flinched at the word. "One of these Northmen. She did not know his name."

And there, I had the answer as to why I'd always had a wandering soul and a need to be outdoors. It also gave reason as to why he was so adamant about peaceful negotiations; he wanted to prevent any further raiding on his people. How painful it must be, to sacrifice his only true offspring to those who'd cost his wife her life when she'd birthed me. I was no longer angry with him for keeping me sheltered and protected or for denying me congress with Sweyn. I understood him, but I no longer had to obey him.

"Let me out, my lord. I'm no longer under your command."

He rose unsteadily and came over to me. Brushing back my hair, he placed a kiss on my forehead as he had so often when I was a little girl. "I will miss you, my child."

I would miss him, too, as well as Ethelfleda.

He stumbled out and did not close the door behind him.

When I told Gyrid and Gunhilda of my father's confession, they smiled.

"I knew," Gyrid said. "I could see it in you, little warrior."

Gunhilda hugged me. Gyrid kissed me, a promise of more to come.

Our wedding was held with all the proper pomp and circumstance. Sweyn finalized trading agreements, insisting he'd received a glorious gift in me and couldn't have asked for a better wife, even if she was a bastard.

When the boat prepared to leave, it was filled with crates full of treasures. Sweyn carried me aboard as carefully as if I was one of his new trinkets while his crew laughed and made crude jokes about privacy on the way home. As the ship turned and headed away from shore, my warrior husband stood at the prow, more magnificent than any man I'd seen. I curled my arms around his waist, already home.

Protecting Her

Regina Kammer

Constantinople, 860 AD

AELFRUN STARED UP at the shadowed stone ceiling and tugged back the linen tunica bunched around her hips. The blackness just before the rite of First Hour was the best time for self-pleasuring. In lonely cells all around her, the monks of St. John Stoudios slept heavily. They wouldn't hear her panting breaths or muffled moans as she frigged herself to fantasies of nude novices in the bathhouse.

She slid her anxious finger through her slick sex, recalling that afternoon's sensual inspiration—brothers preening and joking as they disrobed in the changing room, others unabashedly parading their sleek oil-sheened athleticism, all unaware the attendant folding towels was a woman hiding in their midst.

She vigorously stroked her awakening pearl of pleasure. Surely, the more lustful acolytes also lay awake, gripping their cocks, sliding palms over rampant shafts, seeking erotic release in frenzied masturbation—

A crash shattered the night. A scream. Aelfrun froze

under the thick woolen blanket, her hand stilled between her legs.

Beyond the wooden door of her cell, the clap of leather soles hurrying down the stone hall accompanied the worried whispers of monks unused to clamor. Whispers intensified becoming shouts of fear and warning.

Invasion! The monastery was under attack. Tall men. Blond men. The army of Satan. The End of Days had come.

Aelfrun jumped from her bed, threw on her robe, not bothering to bind her breasts, one thought impelling her. She had to save Father Damianos. He would be in the sacristy performing Matins.

She peeped out the window of her door. To the right, tall men wielded double-bladed axes, their blond braids flying as they slaughtered all in their way.

The path to the left was clear.

Her heart pounding, Aelfrun tore down the hall. Behind her, cries of terror were silenced in mid-scream. She stumbled down the narrow staircase to the sacristy. Her hands trembled on the latch as she cracked open the door.

The room was empty. On the other side of the antechamber, the door to the chapel stood ajar, the grunts of men and the clank of metal striking stone filtering in from beyond.

Aelfrun quietly padded to the open chapel door and peered around the corner.

She was too late.

In the pale glow of oil lamps, Father Damianos knelt

before the altar, his ancient lips murmuring his last prayer, his wrinkled hands clutching a jewel-encrusted cross while a blond giant clad in a thick leather cuirass and fur-fringed garb raised an ax above his head.

Aelfrun tried to scream but terror held her mute. A shout from behind halted the ax-wielding giant. He let loose a string of guttural noises as an even larger warrior strode forward brandishing a sword. The warrior punched the giant in the jaw, knocking him to the ground. The giant flailed limply then lay in a lifeless heap.

Father Damianos' aged body crumpled to the stone floor.

Shock. It had to be shock. *Please, God.* Father had to be alive.

Aelfrun screamed.

A large hand clamped over her mouth. She clawed futilely at the insistent restraint. A beefy arm wrapped around her chest, thick fingers inelegantly crushing her breast.

Her captor chuckled. "Hush, little one. I am your protector now." His heavy accent was one she had never heard.

She struggled. He muttered in his foreign speech as he clasped her firmly, then moved forward and grabbed Father's arm, yanking him off the floor. Her captor dragged them to the sacristy, shoved them in a wooden cupboard, and then slammed shut the door to the chapel.

Aelfrun held her breath, exhaling only when silence

descended. As Father Damianos murmured orisons, she cried herself to exhausted sleep.

Hours later, she woke alone, the heat of the day penetrating the close space, mingling with her fear, dizzying her. She tore off her woolen robe and tried to pray. An hour passed before Father returned to retrieve her. He held her steady as she staggered into the courtyard.

Aelfrun shielded her eyes against the noon-day sun beating down blindingly on the travertine and marble, finding relief from the glare only where the white stones had been darkened by blood.

All around the courtyard, monks moved the bodies of their dead brethren, meekly sniffling their terror and anguish, their wails and screams quieted from nine hours before.

Aelfrun stared blankly at the pile of corpses.

They shall hunger no more, thirst no more; neither shall the sun light on them…

"Brother?"

The vaguely familiar voice of a man, his accent foreign, came from above.

"I do not wish to give insult to your grief, but I am covered in blood."

They have come out of great tribulation, have washed their robes, made them white in the blood of the Lamb…

Dazed, Aelfrun looked up at the man who had spoken, meeting the sky-blue eyes of the barbarian who had saved her and Father Damianos from certain death. Blond braids sprouted serpent-like from under his scuffed and dented helmet. Above his close-cropped beard, a streak of red crusted on his cheekbone.

"Show our guest to the bathhouse, Brother Albinus."

Aelfrun livened at the soft voice of Father Damianos. *Brother Albinus.* That was her.

The barbarian's gaze swept over her. A twinkle sparked the cerulean irises as a smile played on his lips.

Aelfrun flushed and glanced down. The sight of her white hem stained with mud and gore gave her cause to glimpse up at her savior once more. His knowing glint had vanished, replaced by an imploring crinkle to his brow.

"Follow me, please." She led the way across the bloodied courtyard to the bathhouse, heavy steps thumping one pace behind and reverberating up her spine. Once inside the small structure, the air changed, humid, fragrant, a respite from the horror.

Behind her, the barbarian gasped. "I have only heard tales of your pictures in stone," he said.

She turned to see him gawking at the mosaic floor, his gaze tracing the pattern of vines as they looped around medallions of sea creatures, and then following the border of cresting waves and twining guilloche.

This barbarian from a murderous race was in awe of simple beauty.

He looked at her, his blue eyes gentle. "I am Rakki." His gaze flicked to her hair, shorn like that of a novitiate.

She found courage. "Why are you here? Why did you kill my brothers?"

"'Twas not I," he said gently. "Those men, I sent away."

While she and Father Damianos were locked up.

"Who are you?" she asked.

He tilted his head with a slight smirk. "I am Rakki. From the north. Some call us Rus. We have taken your city."

"Constantinople?"

"Yes. It has a good port. We need access to the sea."

Her heart sunk. If these men had reached St. John's, they must have obliterated Constantinople in their path. Once again, she faced an uncertain future.

Or, perhaps…freedom?

Rakki scratched his beard. "I do not believe in killing your Christian monks. They do not take up arms and have offered respite to our broken warriors." He took off his helmet and tucked it under an arm. "I tried to stop my men from slaughtering your brothers." He speared his fingers through his roots. "But was too late. I regret some were killed. It was not meant to be."

He looked at her. His smirk softened to supplication, his face was suddenly…handsome. Too handsome.

Aelfrun flushed and glanced away.

"I am left alone to hold this place until my chieftain arrives." He offered a smile. "Am I to bathe in my clothes? Perhaps that is how they can be cleaned."

"No. We bathe without clothes." *Naked.* She flushed again.

"And after?"

She swallowed. "I can provide such a garment as what I am wearing."

His gaze raked down her body as he licked his lips

and lifted a brow. Her nipples puckered under his stare, tenting the fine fabric.

She crossed her arms over her chest. "You may place your soiled clothes over there." With a nod of her head, she indicated the stone bench along the wall.

He chuckled and strode to the bench, removing his sword belt on the way. With his back to her, he undressed. His boots were first, and he made a display of unwinding the straps from muscled calves as if purposely trying to draw her attention. He unfastened and pulled off his cuirass, revealing delicate patterns on his knee-length blue tunic. He stripped off his stained leggings, carefully laying them on the bench.

He turned to face her, stretching his arms overhead then bending at the waist to the right, to the left, exaggerating the exercises, the tunic sliding provocatively along massive thighs. He grabbed the garment at his shoulders and in one swift movement stripped it off, revealing all.

He was magnificent, solid and muscled, his cock tauntingly erect, his stones heavy and pendulant. Every nerve in her body fired with desire, a desire tinged with the possibility of fulfillment for once not by her own hand.

He chuckled. "You look as if you have never seen a man before."

She ripped her gaze from his body only to meet the persistent twinkle in his eyes. "I've not seen such as you."

"Ah," he rumbled. "But you blush. Is there shame in

another man's nakedness?"

She shook her head. "No shame. For God made man in His own image."

He quirked his head, his smile teasing. "Does your god look like me?"

She swallowed hard. It was so very wrong to think of God in the way she was thinking about the man before her. But this Rakki was some sort of god; he had to be. No man she had ever encountered had his height, his coloring, his brawn, his…

She tore her gaze from his crotch. "God looks like no one man, yet resembles all men."

He grunted. "And what does your god's wife look like?"

Nothing like a young woman in monk's clothing entertaining adulterous thoughts. "God does not have a wife," she explained softly.

"Then it is a shame your god cannot enjoy the body he has created for himself." His cock twitched and bobbled.

She had to stop looking at God's magnificent creation. With a shake of her head, Aelfrun gestured to the entrance of the tepidarium. "We will proceed to the bath." She grabbed a towel and a washing cloth from the shelves by the doorway.

Rakki chuckled and followed.

The warm moist air of the heated room prickled Aelfrun's already flushed skin. Rakki's presence was disarming. Never before had male flesh been so exciting and arousing, the soft hair covering the chest inviting touch, tempting her to trail her fingers down sculpted abdominals to tangle in the wiry strands of the groin…

And clutch the impressive attribute hungering for satisfaction.

She had never enjoyed a man's embrace. Instead, she had endured her husband's disgusting girth as he wheezed over her in bed. Once safely ensconced in the monastery, new desires had flared, and she had tried diligently to repress her base urges as she worked alongside novices in the bloom of youth. Now she wanted nothing more than to wrap her legs around Rakki's taut butt, press her mouth to his, sink her nails into the flexing muscles of his back as he plowed into her yearning cunt.

The walk to the caldarium only inflamed her further, the sticky wetness between her legs rubbing with each step. She would not watch him. She would leave him to his bath to fetch a clean tunic.

"Your bathing houses never cease to amaze."

She turned to see Rakki studying the tessellated vault, the colored glass glistening with droplets from the pool's rising steam. His arousal had slackened in his awe, but remained an astonishing attraction. He would feel wonderful inside her. Her breath hitched at the thought.

She had to distract herself. "Do you require oil for bathing?"

He offered a quizzical expression. "Oil?"

"For cleansing the skin."

"There is no soap?"

"Soap?"

"For cleansing the skin." He winked.

"You will make do with water." She indicated the hot bath.

He jumped in, splashing her, drenching her tunica. The linen clung to the curves of her now-obvious female body. She plucked the damp fabric away from her skin, hoping he did not see.

But he had seen. He sat on the marble banquette in the pool with a grin then closed his eyes and leaned his head against the edge.

Her breath raced at the glorious sight of serene masculinity. She should really just leave to fetch his clean tunic.

Rakki opened one eye. "But you will not."

Aelfrun chilled. He had read her mind.

"Because I wish you to join me." He extended his hand in invitation, his silver rings catching the sunlight pouring through clerestory windows.

"No." Instead, she gave him the washing cloth, her fingers grazing his as he took it, the touch thrilling her sex. She recoiled as if he were fire.

He rubbed the cloth along a beefy arm. "You fear me."

She only feared the desire welling within. "I fear the men you sent away. I feared they were the army of Satan, that it was the Apocalypse."

He raised a brow in query.

"The end of the world."

"Ah." He nodded as he swirled the wet cloth over his chiseled chest. "No. I am not a harbinger of Ragnarok."

Now it was her turn to offer a questioning look.

"That is what my people call the end of the world." He patted the edge of the pool.

She removed her sandals then sat out of arm's reach, dangling her legs in the hot water. "We have similar beliefs."

"Yes. We both want power over another."

"Not I." She stirred her feet through the soothing pool.

"No, perhaps not. But your emperor has left to attack a tribe of the east. We found the palace almost empty when we arrived."

"Almost empty?" Her heart thudded. Her husband was not a soldier. He must have stayed.

"We met a courtier—Vaanes," he said with a derisive twist of his lips.

Her gut clenched. So he *had* stayed.

Rakki snorted. "He offered to sell us the palace. Foolish man. We do not buy such things. We take them by force."

Her sycophantic husband would serve any master to save his skin. "What became of Lord Vaanes?" she whispered.

Rakki wiped the blood streaking his face. "I killed him."

Aelfrun tried to choke back her shock but to no avail.

Rakki swam to her, grasping her calves under the water. He narrowed his eyes. "What troubles you? Did you know the man?"

"He was my husband."

He searched her face, concern coloring his expression. "And are you sad for the loss?"

"No," she breathed. "No, I am not. I am relieved. You have freed me from my torment."

"Your husband did not respect you as his wife?"

"Respect?" Tears smarted in her eyes. "No."

"That is why you are in a holy place?"

"Yes. Father Damianos mercifully took me in to protect me."

Rakki gazed deeply in her eyes as his hands skimmed up her legs to her thighs. "Your husband was a fool in many ways."

She should shake him off. Propriety demanded it. But his strength was imbued with a possessive sensuality she wanted, nay, she *needed* to feel. She did not move as he caressed along her thighs, her hips, to her waist, grasping her, lifting her up and into the water. He bent his towering form over her, touched his finger to her lips, wetting them as he licked his own.

"So beautiful, little one."

His mouth covered hers, his soft but insistent tongue exploring, tangling with hers as he wrapped her in a comforting embrace. She clung to his shoulders as his body undulated, gentle waves lapping around them.

He laid kisses down her neck. "How shall I call you?"

"Aelfrun," she panted. "My name is Aelfrun."

Her tunica floated around her waist. In one movement, he stripped off the garment.

Aelfrun gasped and cupped her palms over her breasts.

Rakki urged away her hands, grasping and securing them behind her back. He bent over and pulled a nipple into his mouth.

A thrill shot straight to her cunt, intensified by his thigh rubbing the pearl between her legs. He held her firmly as he moved to the other breast, the luscious torment like nothing she had ever experienced. She breathed his name with a sigh.

He chuckled against her skin. "So responsive. So willing." His left hand gripped her wrists as his right coursed over her curves, his caress somehow familiar, as if he had touched her many times before.

"You are too young, too beautiful for the likes of Vaanes. How did this happen?" He slowly drew his tongue along a deliciously sensitive cord of her neck.

"I am Saxon," she managed. "From a noble family in Wessex. Four years ago, my father gave me to Lord Vaanes to solidify political ties."

"Then you are a foreigner like myself." He cupped her butt and pulled her against him, his cock pressing against her belly.

She wrapped her arms around his neck. "I am. Father Damianos taught me Greek while I lived in the palace." She rolled her hips.

He grinned. "The celibacy of the monastery has made you as wanton as Freya."

She pouted. "Your wife?"

He laughed and picked her up. "A goddess. We have many." He set her on the edge of the pool, licking his lips as he eyed her breasts. "I wish to worship you."

He gently sucked one nipple as he spread her legs wide. He pecked tender kisses over her waist, across her belly, to the hair of her mound. He drew in a breath, then exhaled a muttered oath and pressed his mouth to her sex.

Aelfrun's yelp of surprise melted to a sigh. It was a kiss like no other, teasingly delightful in a new way. He licked and sucked, a ravenous man, tasting all of her, until he fixated on the locus of pure pleasure, flicking his tongue as she writhed against him.

Warmth whorled in her belly, rushing to her feet, curling her toes. She murmured his name in a litany of gratitude. Desire smoldered where his relentless tongue worked, the familiar coiling a welcome sign of what was to come. She grabbed his braids, pulling him closer. She needed this, needed him, needed release—

"Oh, God!"

He jumped out of the pool to slide under her, splaying her knees on either side of his head, his moustache tickling her nubbin, his eyes sparkling with delight as he gazed up at her. His devilish tongue thrust deep inside, plunging in and out forcefully, unsteadying her. She fell forward, catching herself with a slap of her hands on the wet tessellated floor, seeking purchase to ride him. His tongue filled her, the tip reaching a new pleasure spot deep within. She moaned his name with each splendid slide to orgiastic oblivion.

He grabbed her thighs and lifted her slightly. "I want you to see me."

She turned around to face his crotch, his cock jutting proudly toward the vaulted ceiling, the purplish head glistening with his excitement. As his tongue found its aim in her depths, he gripped his shaft and slid his hand up and down slowly, his groan of relief reverberating against her quim. His strokes matched the rhythm of his tongue, languid and leisurely, increasing to a frenzied pace, his stones tightening, his breath hot. She wanted his cock, his glorious cock filling her, slamming into her, releasing his emission inside her, claiming her as his own.

She swallowed her wail of ecstasy as her climax flooded his mouth. With a jerk and a growl he came, the initial spurt surprising, thrilling her to another orgasm. She remained poised, staring at the milky fluid cascading over his fist, over his rings, wanting to taste him as he had tasted her.

She bent over and drew him into her mouth.

He bucked up with a guttural word, thrusting his cock further along her tongue. He was salty and sour, and she relished every flavor, swallowing his enticing liquor, reveling in its burn down her throat.

He handily picked her off him, easing them both into the warm pool to clean away the evidence of their union. He sat on the underwater banquette and pulled her onto his lap, wrapping her securely in his strong arms. "We shall return to the palace where I will make you my wife. You will never know fear again." He nuzzled her neck.

She lifted his chin and pecked his lips, deepening the

kiss when he opened his mouth with a low rumble of approval. His beard chafed her tender skin, his lips and tongue were still fragrant with her musk.

"I would like that, Rakki." His was an embrace she would never flee.

AELFRUN SAT RIGIDLY in the women's balcony of the Church of the Holy Wisdom, struggling to maintain a stoic veneer, grateful that her dark widow's veil obscured the pinched lips and furrowed brow of despair.

Three months had passed since Rakki made love to her. Three months alone without her barbarian Rus. Three months craving his caress.

She had left the bathhouse to fetch a clean tunic, meeting Father Damianos as he approached. Rakki's chieftain had returned. The conquest had failed. The imperial army was quickly returning to the palace from campaigns against the Muslims, and the Rus were retreating. Aelfrun begged Rakki to take her with him. She had nothing now; she was but a widowed foreigner.

He refused, regret in his eyes. "To take you captive would be an act of war. We are not prepared for such battle. Your soldiers are too numerous."

As she sat behind Empress Eudokia, Aelfrun blinked back her sorrow. The smoke and heady fragrance of smoldering incense wafted up to the gallery, burning her eyes, searing her lungs.

Her heart ached at the scene on the dais below. Emperor Michael was investing a new unit of personal guards, a squadron of Rus who had requested baptism to prove their fealty.

A dozen or so men knelt before the bishop and the emperor, their blond heads bowed, each one powerfully built, their strong arms and thick thighs straining chain mail and silk, reminding her of limbs that once secured her.

Tears blurred her vision, falling down her cheeks as the ceremony plodded on. At the emperor's exit, the empress rose. Aelfrun followed her mistress on legs wobbling with emotion. Once in the palace, she hurried to her apartment to wallow in her misery, crying herself to sleep.

Her maidservant gently woke her. The empress was waiting in Aelfrun's reception room and had brought a gift.

Aelfrun composed herself and went to the richly decorated chamber. Attendants lined the marble revetment, their gazes cast to the mosaic floor. The empress reclined on a gilded couch, a soldier of the new imperial unit standing at attention behind her. The empress waved her hand at the man.

The very tall muscular man.

"Aelfrun, here is your new personal guardsman. He is one of the Rus converts."

Aelfrun stared as the guard removed his helmet and offered a slight bow before meeting her gaze.

Rakki.

Every nerve in her body fired with desire and hope. She stilled, not daring to move for fear she would throw herself into his arms.

"His Christian name is John," the empress continued. "He found inspiration from the Book of Revelation."

Rakki's blue eyes flashed with memory.

"He will accompany you when you travel and keep watch when you sleep."

He subtly raised a brow.

"He is yours to command."

Aelfrun had only one command in mind.

The empress stood. "I suggest you communicate your expectations to him." She smiled at Aelfrun, a flicker of understanding in her eyes. "I'll take my leave." The empress withdrew.

Aelfrun quickly dismissed her attendants. She stared at Rakki, disbelieving.

He grinned. "The empress knows it was I who held your monastery. She knows my true name."

Aelfrun blinked. "I told her of the siege of St. John's. That it was you who saved us." Her voice trembled with incredulity. "That I felt safe with you." The empress must have understood the meaning behind her words.

He took one slow step forward, and then another, unbuckling his cuirass, pulling up his hauberk with each excruciating stride. Aelfrun's heart pounded at the smack of leather, the slink of chain mail as both were dropped to the stone floor.

She stepped backwards to keep a view of all of him, until the bed pressed against the backs of her knees. He stopped an arm's length away to strip completely, revealing the sculpted brawn of the warrior she had longed for. He was as she remembered, as she had dreamed every blessed night, her hand between her legs seeking release from despondent frustration.

He was before her in one stride, taking her in a secure embrace, his mouth seeking hers, his tongue exploring her yearning depths, fingers tugging off her veil, unfastening her stola, her tunica, stripping her bare. He smoothed his thick palms over her curves with a heavy sigh, and then lifted her in his arms.

She reached up to cup his cheek, the bristle of his beard like velvet under her palm. His braids were gone, his hair cropped short.

"My hair is longer than yours now," she giggled.

He chuckled. "Just barely." He untied and plucked off her sandals, the familiar smirk playing on his lips, the twinkle still shining in his eyes.

He pulled back the bedcovers and lay her down gently upon the feather mattress. He slithered under the silk sheets to stretch alongside, propping himself on an elbow to gaze down at her.

With the tip of his finger, he traced the outline of her mouth. "Soon, I will make you my wife, little one."

Her chest tightened. "It's impossible now." She was a princess, he a mere guard.

"No, love, it is not." His finger trailed down the heated pulse of her neck, to her breast. "Your emperor has too many enemies. He is not long on the throne." He swirled circles around her puckering areola. "Your future in his court is uncertain." He cupped her left breast, over her heart, his warmth comforting, calming. "I will remain at your side to protect you, but when the time comes, I will steal you away."

Her doubt melted to joy. "And in the meantime?"

He pulled her into his arms, the heat of his skin penetrating every pore, his mouth once again slaking desire too long denied.

His hands smoothed down her back, squeezing her butt before finding her sex. He grinned. "You are wet for me."

She had been from the moment she saw him.

He stroked her pearl, slowly rubbing her to excitement, increasing his rhythm to the puffs of her frantic breaths. Rapture coiled in her belly as she rocked against his hand, murmuring blasphemies. He bore down, wickedly pressing the sensitive nub, willing her climax to burst forth. She bucked up and cried out his name.

He rolled on top of her, crushing her into the mattress, his weight exquisite in its absolute power. She slid her hands along his spine, relishing the ridges of each vertebra, the coarse strands of hair, the solid muscles.

"Aelfrun," he murmured as he drew the backs of his fingers across her cheek. "I have thought of you every minute of every day since we parted."

She kissed the hollow of his palm. "And I, you."

"Let us discuss our expectations as the empress suggested." He grabbed her hands and raised them above her head, holding her wrists tightly against the pillow. "When we are in bed, I command you, little princess." The head of his cock nudged her sex.

Her insides fluttered in anticipation. She opened her legs wider. "Yes, my lord."

He pushed in just an inch.

Sighing at the long-awaited incursion, she clenched around his thickness.

Satisfaction softened his face. "You will do what I desire." Another inch.

Yes, please. She arched with a moan. "Yes, my lord." She tilted her hips, wanting more of him.

"And at this moment, I desire to fuck you."

She sucked in a breath.

"*Hard.*"

He slammed inside, the force lifting her. He pressed her back onto the mattress, holding her steady as he rammed deeper with every thrust.

Her legs hooked around his thighs, hanging on as he took her on a journey to ecstasy. His cock stretched her, filling her perfectly, rubbing the secret spot within. His rasping grunts were music to her ears, his humid breath sparking memories of the bathhouse, his dominance softening her to delirious submission.

His pace quickened and she followed, reckless with pent-up need. He released her wrists to grasp her at the waist, pounding heedlessly, seeking his final pleasure, a pleasure she, too, was racing toward.

She came, gripping him with all her might. He barked a cry and clutched her to him as he let loose his seed, laying his claim, securing her as his own.

With a languorous exhale, Rakki smiled down at her, sweat burnishing his brow, the twinkle in his blue eyes gleaming brightly. He slid to her side, enfolding her in a thick arm.

"My wife." His breath was hot on the crown of her head.

Aelfrun smiled as she burrowed in the shelter of his body. "Yes, Rakki. Until the end of days."

Enslaved

Elle James

The west coast of Ireland, 857 AD

Konrad strode through the small village of Carrigeen in the southwest coast of Ireland, his sword sheathed in his scabbard, surveying the land he and his men had just conquered. For the first time in hours, he breathed deeply, releasing the tension that had kept his body and mind alert to present dangers. The battle was won.

"A fine bit of earth you have now, Konrad." Thorsten strode alongside him, his bravest soldier and friend since they were small children. "Fortunately, the village is intact, save only one cottage that burned to the ground. The men will be content to have women to see to their needs, and you'll have a ready-made roof to cover your head."

"Indeed." He eyed the villagers. The children seemed well-fed, the women strong enough to plow fields, tend gardens, and herd animals. What he did not see were many men. "What do you make of the lack of men?"

Thorsten shrugged. "From the stories the women are

telling, they have seen many battles, and those who conquered them in the past killed their men, but did not stay long. They claim the land is haunted and unhealthy for the Norse. Something about the water making the men sickly. The villagers have built up an immunity to whatever ails newcomers."

Konrad's brow furrowed. This was news he didn't care to hear. The soil was rich, and the sheep and cattle were fat. If the natives and the cattle could survive on the water in Carrigeen, so should he and his men.

After years of battle in his homeland of Norway under the leadership of his older brother Ivarr, Konrad had crossed the seas to fight the Danes. He'd come to this island to stake a claim for land and a home of his own. He was ready to settle, take a wife, and raise children and cattle. Konrad heard Ireland was a paradise of green pastures and strong women, both key ingredients to his plan.

Thus, he had sailed his last journey from Dublin around the isle and let the wind carry him here to the west coast of this lush green land he'd come to love. After a fierce battle led by a paltry lot of old men and boys barely off their mothers' apron strings, Konrad had won. But he wondered that others hadn't claimed this glorious place, haunted soil or not.

Ahead, two women carrying bundles hurried toward a cottage. One was a winsome beauty with light red hair cascading down her back in long luscious waves. The other was tall and raven-haired, her tresses curling in glorious abandon. The latter's hips swayed beneath the dress broader than the redhead's, and with a determination found more often in the men he led in battle.

She handed her burden to the woman standing at the door of the cottage and spoke to her in hushed, urgent tones. The red-haired woman stood by meekly, waiting for the taller one to finish.

Thorsten leaned close to Konrad. "She is a beauty."

"Indeed she is," he said, his gaze never leaving the taller woman.

The raven-haired lovely gave her last command and motioned for the redhead to follow her to the next cottage where she again took charge, handed off the goods the redhead carried, and gave her orders. When she was done, she worked her way from building to building, checking with the inhabitants.

"From what I've learned, the dark-haired woman is the leader of this clan," Thorsten said. "She is the daughter of the previous clan leader. The red-haired beauty is her younger sister."

Konrad had been too busy tending to the wounded and giving his dead a proper send off to Valhalla to learn more about the social structure of the people he'd conquered.

"The old men we captured warned of her iron hand and stubborn streak," Thorsten murmured. "I suggest you establish your claim immediately, and either send her away or make her your slave."

Konrad frowned. "I wish this to be my home. These people will be my people. They need to learn to trust that I will defend them against future attack and provide for their well-being. I don't want them to see themselves as slaves."

"The villagers seem to hold the raven-haired one in high regard. To win them over, you must first win her over or cull her from the herd." Thorsten nodded toward the redhead. "Another suggestion would be to take her sister to wife to secure her fealty."

The raven-haired woman emerged from a home and cast a glance around the village as if to assess the damage. Throughout her visits, she'd avoided looking his direction. At last, she wiped her hands on her apron and glanced his way, her chin tilting high, her blue gaze direct and defiant.

Konrad's groin tightened, his manhood rising to the woman's unspoken challenge.

Thorsten chuckled beside him. "I see you will have trouble with that one. Perhaps if you use her as an example and publicly whip her, she will fall in line."

"A whip would not cow the woman or bend her to my will. What she needs is a firm hand and a reason to accept me."

"Aye, a proper beating is what she'll get. She is strong and young enough she will make a fine slave once you break her will."

Konrad growled a warning. He had no desire to break the woman. Like fine horseflesh, she should be gentled and led to believe she would be better off with him as her rider. He squared his shoulders much like he would walking into battle and marched toward the women.

Brigid O'Ceallachain expected the Norse brute to attempt to bend her to his will, perhaps make her his slave. Despite the fact he was a handsome beast—thick brown hair resting on broad shoulders, a trim waist and powerful thighs—he was still a marauder, a Viking invader come to take what wasn't his.

The previous Norse conqueror had attempted to enslave her, had intended to rape her, forcing her into her own bedchamber with the intention of poking his man staff into her like the greedy, smelly old goat he was.

She had managed to waylay his aggression with food and drink, charging his wine with a wicked herb that made him sleep like the dead. When he woke, he could not eat for days, complaining of the worst belly ailment he'd ever experienced.

Using her skills as a healer to her advantage, she promised to nurse him to health as long as he agreed not to harm her or her sister.

So sick with the ague he could barely climb out of his bed, he'd agreed. While he healed, she had the ladies of the village spread rumors among the men, claiming the river water was poisonous to anyone who had not been raised on it, building a natural resistance to the toxins. They also said the land was cursed by the dead soldiers left unburied.

Soon, the Norsemen succumbed to the same complaint as their leader, each sick and too weak to lift his sword. First one, followed by many, begged their leader to take them back to their homeland where they could die in peace. Still weak of his own complaint, their leader loaded his ships and sailed away, leaving the O'Ceallachain clan tucked in their rocky hills in peace.

Brigid had buried the cache of herbs she'd used to fight her battle beneath the fairy tree and went about the business of clan leader, as usual.

Once again, she ran her gaze over this new Norse conqueror as he stood in the village with his second in command, their gazes taking in what Brigid and her people had built over time with the sweat of their brows.

She had to admit he was ruggedly handsome. He had no boils upon his face and his teeth weren't rotting out of his head. Not that it mattered. Brigid O'Ceallachain would bow to no man. This was her land and her clan. She refused to concede without a fight.

Unfortunately, without an army to back her, once again, she had to seek more unsavory means to vanquish her enemy. One option was to go to Seamus O'Leary, the lecherous brute and High King of County Kerry. He'd had his eye on Caitlinn since she was nothing but a child in bright orange braids. Now that her sister was of age, Seamus wished to negotiate an alliance propagated on his marriage to the fair Caitlinn in exchange for the High King's protection of the O'Ceallachain clan.

Brigid had told Seamus she would give him an answer by the next full moon. To be fair to Caitlinn, she'd presented the proposal. Her softhearted sister begged her to agree in order to save their home and people from the heathen Norse marauders plaguing the lands with incessant battles.

But Brigid had no intention of bartering her beloved

sister for protection of her land and people. She'd offer herself in Caitlinn's place first, not that Seamus would agree. He had a taste for delicate, fair-haired beauties, not for women with hair the color of midnight. Despite their current plight, she still had no intention of allowing her sister's sacrifice.

After admitting defeat that morning in the short, but bloody, battle with the Norsemen, Brigid tied a ribbon to the fairy tree, wishing for an end to hostilities for good, knowing she was out of choices and able-bodied men to defend them from another assault.

Caitlinn laid her hand on Brigid's arm, her fingers digging into her skin. "Brigid, they are heading our direction."

Brigid squared her shoulders and lifted her chin. She had at least one more battle to fight with this hulking Norseman, and she vowed to win.

The big Norseman, dressed in his bloodstained armor, stopped in front of her, his feet planted wide, his arms crossed over his chest. He stared down his arrogant nose at her and announced, "I am Konrad of Kristiansand."

He spoke Gaelic almost as well as an Irishman. As much as she wanted to tell him she wasn't impressed and that he could leave, she held her tongue and nodded graciously. "I am Brigid of Clan O'Ceallachain." His gaze swept her frame down and up, so quickly she wondered if he found her wanting.

"I understand you are the leader of this clan."

Her teeth ground together, but she managed another

nod. "I am." Her nostrils flared as she fought to control her temper. "Or I *was*, depending on your intent."

Again, he looked down on her from his lofty height. "These are now my land and my people," he said, his words measured, his tone firm. "Have everyone assemble to hear my words."

Her first inclination was to spit at his feet and tell him to assemble them himself. She chewed hard on her tongue to restrain herself before turning to her sister. "Caitlinn, please have our people come out."

Caitlinn hurried away to do her bidding. Konrad's second followed her with his gaze, practically salivating like a dog over a juicy bone. Her back stiffened, recognizing the next battle was just beginning.

When all had assembled, the big brute opened his mouth, his voice booming loud enough to be heard. "I am Konrad of Kristiansand, your new leader. I have come to settle on O'Ceallachain lands and make this my home. I will marry one of your people and produce heirs to ensure the protection of these lands for future generations." He lifted his chin higher. "Today, I will choose my bride. All unmarried women of child-bearing age, come to the front of the crowd."

Brigid's fists clenched. She should be happy he was willing to marry the woman he bedded, rather than using her as a concubine to slake his manly lusts. The thought she might be unable to halt this made her belly ache with an anger so great she could barely breathe. When the young women stepped forward, their gazes downcast from fear, Brigid's blood boiled.

Konrad marched down the line of potential brides. He stopped in front of one buxom lass, turned her around, stared at her hips, turned her back around, and made her open her mouth to display her teeth.

Brigid stepped forward, scathing words on the tip of her tongue. Caitlin's hand on her arm kept her from launching herself at the oaf and raking her fingernails down his back.

He moved down the line then back to where she and Caitlinn stood. He turned his attention to Caitlinn. "And you? Are you unwed?"

Rosy color flooded her sister's cheeks, but Caitlinn nodded and bowed her head, her gaze on his boots.

He lifted her chin and studied her face. "Open your mouth."

Rage shivered down Brigid's spine as her sister complied, opening her mouth for his inspection.

"You have all of your teeth," he observed. He lifted her arm. "Strong arms." He turned her around. "Good hips for breeding." He placed a hand on either side of her hips as if measuring. "What do you think, Thorsten? She will make a fine bride and bear many sons."

Thorsten clapped his leader on the back. "That she will. She has child-bearing hips, for sure."

Heat steamed from Brigid's head as the Norse animals laughed.

"I intend to be married before the sun sets this day," Konrad announced and gave Caitlinn a pat on her behind.

Brigid's sister stumbled forward, her eyes wide, her

cheeks flaming.

"Enough!" Brigid stepped in front of Caitlinn, her shoulders thrown back, her feet planted wide in a fighting stance. If she'd had a sword in her hand, she'd have run him through. "These are my people, and I will not have you treat them like cattle."

Konrad's eyes narrowed. "They are no longer *your* people. From the moment your men laid down their arms, they became mine. I will do as I please. And it might please me to make all of them slaves to provide food and entertainment to my men who have fought hard and suffered greatly in many fierce battles."

"Fierce battles." She snorted.

"Brigid, don't…" Caitlinn begged.

Brigid ignored her sister's plea. "Today, you fought old men and young boys, not strong and worthy opponents. Now you stomp in here demanding fealty of women and children like lording beasts. I will not stand by and allow you to harm one woman or child."

The brute crossed his arms over his chest. "And how to you propose to stop me? If I choose to take this pretty red-head as my bride, I will do so. You are not strong enough to defeat me."

Her breath caught as he slowly pulled his sword from his sheath.

"Unless you are carrying a sword beneath that dress…" With the tip of his sword, he lifted her dress, revealing her legs beneath.

Brigid jerked her skirts away from his sword. If she didn't do something quickly, he'd take Caitlinn and ruin her *and* all their chances to bargain with Seamus. "I propose a bargain," she blurted. "My hand in marriage, and with it, the obedience of my people."

Konrad snorted. "You are in no position to bargain." He arched a brow and gave her body another cursory glance. "But for the sake of argument, what will you ask in exchange?"

"You will forbid your men from ruining my women, and they will be allowed to choose their own husbands."

"Again, I see no advantage to me, only you. We could take what we want and disregard your desires."

She nodded. "You could. But as you said yourself, you wish to settle and raise children. Would it not be better to rule women who swear loyalty to husbands, rather than depend on their questionable allegiance as slaves?"

Konrad studied her for a long moment. "I will inspect my prize before I make a decision."

Her chin rose higher, heat again filling her cheeks, this time from mortification. The scoundrel! But she refused to back down. Let him treat her like an animal, as long as he let the other women be.

He circled her, tapping the flat of his sword against her bottom. "Firm and strong."

In front of her again, he sheathed his weapon and stepped closer, staring down at her so long, Brigid grew nervous, and then angry for allowing fear to intrude. "I have all my teeth, and I'm taller and broader of hip than Caitlinn. Surely, I will better bear children."

"I will be the judge." He gripped her hips in both

hands. "Yes, I believe your hips are broader. But what about your breasts? I won't have the mother of my children starving them for lack of milk." He reached out with both hands and plumped her breasts.

Shocked, Brigid slapped his face as hard as she could.

A gasp rose from those gathered as a bright red handprint appeared on his cheek.

Brigid stepped back, her eyes wide, unable to utter an apology and afraid he'd take out his anger on her and her entire clan.

Konrad's lips thinned, and he straightened without shifting his gaze from hers. "I accept your bargain," he said, his voice cold. "The ceremony commences within the hour." Then he turned and marched away without another word.

His second in command followed, a grin stretched across his wretched Viking face.

"Oh, Brigid." Caitlinn grasped her hands in her. "You did not have to take my place as his bride. I would have married him to spare our people."

"I am leader of Clan O'Ceallachain." Her words weren't spoken as firmly as she would have liked, but she could barely catch her breath. "It is my responsibility to protect my people. I must prepare for my wedding."

But first, she had to dig up the herbs from beneath the fairy tree. While she was there, it wouldn't hurt to tie another ribbon around a branch and pray.

LESS THAN AN hour later, he strode through the streets,

washed and stripped clean of his old life and ready to begin his new one. He only hoped his comely bride wouldn't end it before it began by slipping a knife into his throat as he slept. Somehow, he had to convince her their union would be one of mutual benefit and pleasure.

His cock swelled at the promise of the pleasure. Yes, indeed, he would have the most beautiful and strongest woman as his bride, and thus rule this land with the blessing of the people.

From experience, Konrad knew nothing was ever quite that simple. Based on his sore jaw from where Brigid had slapped him, he concluded their union would not be boring. With a grin, he met Brigid in the village commons where a large gathering of people awaited the wedding ceremony.

Dressed in a deep green gown, her raven-black hair hanging long to her waist and a wreath of flowers crowning her head, Brigid stood in the middle of a group of women who brushed her hair and plucked at imaginary flecks of dirt.

The hand fasting ceremony happened so quickly, Konrad barely recalled the words of the priest conducting it. All he knew was that once it was done they would convene in the great hall for the feast, and before the sun set, he and his bride would consummate their marriage.

Would the day never end? His men sat at the head table laughing, drinking, and toasting Konrad and his bride.

Brigid sat beside him, her head held high. She drank not a drop, nor did she eat. She stared straight ahead, her eyes narrowing when one of Konrad's men became too amorous with the serving women.

After many toasts and much food had been consumed, Konrad turned to his new wife. "Brigid, it is time."

She nodded, her face stripped of emotion. Her tight features and pale skin forewarned Konrad that a huge task lay ahead to woo the beautiful Brigid over to his camp. But he was confident that all he needed was to be alone with her for the night to lay siege on her heart. He'd be gentle. He'd give her pleasure. They would talk, because he knew women needed reassurance. By morning, she would understand they both wanted the same things, and that their union made sense. With so few males to protect them, she would come to realize Konrad and his men were needed, not only for their swords, but to share the workload of providing for the clan.

As he helped her to her feet, his confidence grew. By morning, they'd be truly wed. Man and wife. She'd gladly hand over the reins to one stronger than she was. The rewards, she'd see, would far outweigh any loss of pride.

CAITLINN AND THREE other women led Brigid out of the great hall and into the master's chamber where they stripped her of her clothing and helped her into the bed.

She allowed them to do this, but asked that they bring in food and drink for she expected her new husband would be hungry and thirsty during the night.

The women giggled and hurried away to her bidding.

Caitlinn stayed. "If you are unhappy with your husband," she whispered, "I will help you to escape."

Brigid shook her head. "It is my path to secure our future." She had her own way of dealing with a man who would use a woman like a mat and wipe his feet on her. Beneath the mattress lay the bag of herbs she'd unearthed from beneath the fairy tree. Once she and her new husband were left alone, she'd offer him a beverage laced with the sleeping herb. Then she would plot his demise and her liberation.

THORSTEN AND FIVE other men gave the ladies a few minutes head start before they hefted Konrad onto their shoulders and carried him up the stairs to the master chamber.

"Do you need instruction on how to bed the lady?" Thorsten asked. "I would be happy to show you where to jab your sword."

"Perhaps she would prefer one of us to demonstrate the act first." Another man pumped his hips to more laughter.

Much teasing and jostling ensued before Konrad finally reached the master chamber. The men threw open the door and marched him in, dropped him on his feet and ripped the clothes off his body. Then they lifted him yet again, dumping him on the bed already occupied by Brigid.

She lay with the furs fully covering her body, only her creamy white shoulders visible.

When Konrad landed beside her, she scooted over as far as she could, but the bed wasn't that wide, and he still lay against her. If she leaned over any farther, she'd drop off the bed.

Konrad turned to his men. "Enough! Now out with you so that I can claim my bride in peace."

"Not until we bear witness that this wedding has been consummated," Thorsten said with a waggle of his eyebrows.

"Out!" Konrad bellowed.

The man grumbled, backing out.

"If you have any difficulties…" Thorsten grinned from the doorway. "Just call out."

Konrad lifted a candleholder and flung it.

Thorsten closed the door and it clattered to the wooden floor.

Alone at last, he turned on his side and studied Brigid.

She stared at him for a moment, and then rolled from beneath the furs and stood, naked in the light filtering through the shuttered window. Her pale body glowed, the curves soft and flowing, her breasts even fuller than he'd imagined when he'd touched them through her bodice.

While he ogled her fair form, she crossed the room to a small table set against the wall laden with food and a pitcher of mead. "You must be thirsty after the meal." As though she poured drinks while parading naked often, she took her time pouring before facing him and giving him a full view of the prize for which he'd bargained.

From her long raven hair down to the tips of her

narrow feet, she was a vision, goddess-like in appearance, full-figured with milky skin and pink nipples.

His cock grew as hard as his sword's blade.

She approached him with the cup of mead, carefully holding it out to him with meek humility and care.

Konrad had not expected her to become so submissive so quickly. He'd fully expected to have to wrestle her into his bed, and he couldn't deny his disappointment. He liked that she had a temper and a sharp tongue. He'd worried that settling down might dull his battle skills. With a fiery woman, his senses would remain alert.

"Here," she said handing him the cup. "Drink to our union."

"After you." He refused to take the cup, giving preference to her, letting her know that he respected her and would treat her fairly.

She shook her head. "I do not want to dull my senses for what is to come."

He liked that answer, considering the plans he had to ignite her senses. Taking the cup from her hands, he set it on the table beside the bed. "Lie with me, wife."

Her eyes widened, and she reached for the cup again. "I will after you have refreshed yourself with a drink. I fear once we start, you will need the liquid to sustain you through the long night."

"I will drink. Later." Again, he took the cup from her and set it on the table, capturing her hand in the process. "Come, wife. To bed." Then with a sharp tug, he landed her on top of him, her breasts pressed to his chest. "Right now, I wish to show my wife how pleasant marriage can be."

With a fierce frown, she struggled to free her hands. "How can marriage be pleasant if you have to force me to it?"

Relieved there was still some fight in her, he suppressed a grin. "A wife should allow her husband the chance to prove his prowess." He rolled her to his side and released her hands. "You are free to go," he said. When she'd scooted toward the edge of the bed, he added, "But our bargain rests on you being my wife. If our marriage is unconsummated, the contract is broken, and I will choose a more willing woman."

Brigid froze. The damn man wouldn't drink his mead, and now he threatened to break their contract. Her sister's beautiful face and the faces of the other women in her clan flashed before her. She couldn't let them down.

That he was large and well-proportioned, his ruggedly built body attractive in ways she'd never concede to anyone out loud, certainly aided her decision.

Slowly, she lay back against the fur and closed her eyes, shutting out the tempting sight. "Do with my body what you will," she said, keeping her tone even, and hoping he took her words as disinterest. It would never do for him to realize the sight of him caused her breath to hitch. "My body is but a vessel. You will not win my heart or soul."

For a long moment, nothing stirred on the bed. Then Konrad slid next to her.

So tense was she, that the first touch made her flinch. Then the heat from his large body warmed her chilled skin.

"Is that a challenge, wife?" he whispered.

His sweet breath stirred the hair around her ear. She shivered, her body reacting strangely at his nearness—softening, warming. With a jolt, she realized she liked the feel of his solid body against hers. "Not a challenge," she said grumpily. "The truth."

"Challenge accepted." His lips captured the lobe of her ear and pulled softly.

Until that moment, Brigid had never realized how sensitive her ears were. She steeled herself against the pleasure, reminding herself he was only readying for an assault.

But when it came, she was unprepared.

His lips brushed across her eyelids as soft as thistledown.

Her belly tightened and her nipples ached. What was wrong with her? How could this brute arouse her?

Weathered fingertips glided across her cheekbone and down the length of her neck, scraping ever so lightly. When he pressed his lips to hers, he demanded nothing, his tongue leisurely tracing the seam.

Her lips tingled so much she gasped, parting her teeth.

His tongue slipped between and caressed hers.

Curling as if of its own reflex, her tongue dueled with his, thrusting when he thrust and swirling in a desperate battle of wills, taking her mind off where his fingers went until they flicked the tip of a hard nipple. He trapped the nipple between thumb and forefinger, and a moan escaped her lips on a soft puff of air. Deep in her center, blood stirred, flowing thick and hot, spreading fire to every inch of her body.

Where he was tweaking her nipple, she could picture him taking it into his mouth and suckling until she cried out. Instead, his fingers only toyed with the tip until she thought she might scream. "Get on with the bedding," she whispered harshly, frustrated and needy like she'd never been before.

"These things take patience," he murmured.

"Patience be damned." She shoved his hand from her nipple and cupped her breast, squeezing it tight enough to hurt a little, hoping that little bit of pain would bring her back from the insane edge upon which she teetered so precariously.

His hand massaged her breast and moved to the other.

Brigid's breathing grew more rapid, and she twisted against the furs, the soft furry friction causing her to squirm.

Konrad's hand slid lower, skimming across her belly, ever closer to the center of her desire, that warm, wet channel aching to be filled. Rough fingers wove into her mound, parting her to slide across her center strip, flicking it gently.

Brigid dug her feet into the fur and lifted her hips, crying out. When he flicked again, touching her nubbin, her world shattered into a million tiny points of light, each prickling across every inch of her skin. Her hips rocked, and she rode the sensation like waves crashing against the seashore.

At last, she fell back to earth, that place between her legs wet and ready to receive her husband. He slipped a finger inside her and swirled in her juices. It wasn't enough to satisfy her throbbing ache. She wanted more. No, she needed more, or surely she would die.

She grabbed his shoulders and pulled him over her, parting her legs for him to settle between. The sooner they consummated their union, the sooner she could regain her composure and follow through with her plan.

"No," he whispered, capturing her earlobe between his teeth and nibbling. "Not until you are ready."

"Do it!" Her fingertips dug into his hips, urging him to take her.

He resisted, his buttocks tight in her hands. "Only if it is what you truly want it," he said, his voice even.

Why was his not as ragged as hers? Didn't he feel the same keen agony? "It is what I want," she ground out, her mind chaotic with feverish longing.

A kiss brushed her cheek. "Beg me...and I will consider it."

That hint of amusement only spiked her need. Past pride, past the stubborn need to control her world, Brigid cried, "Please. Take me."

"Since you asked so sweetly..." Konrad pressed inward, his cock stretching her entrance. At the bump of his length against the thin barrier of her maidenhead, she winced, well beyond caring and willing to accept the pain to quench her thirst.

Konrad bent to kiss her swollen lips, his tongue pushing past her teeth as his cock breached her barrier and filled her. The sensation was astounding—full, oddly complete—and then she was rushing over the edge again, lights exploding behind her lids.

As he moved in and out of her, she rose to meet him, matching his rhythm until he came to a shuddering stop, his body rigid, his jaw taut as he shot his seed.

Brigid wrapped her legs around his waist and held him there, rejoicing in the newfound sensations so powerful they shook the very foundation of her world.

When at last he collapsed beside her, he pulled her into his arms and held her, his lips pressed to her temple, a hand cupping her breast.

Brigid felt she could die then and there, convinced she would never feel as incredible again. He'd confounded her, choosing a gentle, teasing seduction over force. Perhaps, she'd been hasty in her assessment of his other qualities.

She reminded herself this strong and worthy warrior was her husband, a man who could protect her people. And she could have him in her bed for the rest of her life, doing those things he'd done that night. A warm glow of happiness threatened to make her giddy with delight. One she found impossible to tamp down.

His whiskered face scraped against her cheek. "Making love with a Northman is not so bad after all, is it?"

She lay still in his arms, schooling her expression to boredom. "I could grow to tolerate it."

He chuckled. "Tolerate?" Konrad squeezed her breast and flicked the tip of her nipple.

Her back arched automatically, pressing her flesh deeper into his palm. "I suppose I could learn to like it," she admitted grudgingly. No sense in letting him grow too smug. "Given time."

"Then you are in luck, for I plan to be here for a very long time." He rolled to his side and reached for the cup on the table beside the bed. "You were thoughtful to provide a drink. I find myself quite thirsty after bedding my beautiful wife."

She lay in the heat of his regard, satiated and drowsy.

When Konrad lifted the cup to his lips, memory crawled out from the fog of lust, and Brigid's eyes widened. Without thought, she flung herself across him, knocking the cup from his hand. It flew across the room, spilling its contents across the wooden floor.

"If you were thirsty, all you had to do was tell me. I would have let you drink first." He laughed softly and pulled her into his arms. "Ah well, I can drink of my wife and slake my earthly thirst in the morning."

Lying across the Viking, Brigid found she liked lying on top of this warm mass of muscle and sinew. Perhaps being married to the beast wouldn't be so bad. She could always poison him later if she grew bored or tired of him. But for now, she would partake of what the marriage bed offered and enjoy it. And take her time assessing his many attributes and usefulness before making any hasty decisions.

Brigid slid her hand across her husband's chest and down his belly to his hardening cock. Ah yes. She could think of many uses for such a Viking.

The Oak and the Ale

Beatrix Ellroy

Aarhus, the coast of Jutland, 912 AD

I WATCHED HER get off the ship. She stumbled slightly but moved slowly and steadily once ashore. Slowly enough that Bersi gave her a shove. She turned on him with a snarl, and he raised his hand to hit her. But she raised her own, a nasty little glint in one hand and said something.

As he went very still, I smiled and limped over, cursing the gnarled oak beneath my arm even as it held me up. "Bersi, I thought you'd have known to take knives off your captures."

"No capture, One-Leg," the woman answered. "I'm no thrall. My father gave me over for trade routes. I was guaranteed good treatment."

Bersi snarled back at her. "You stabbed one of my men."

"He made to treat me ill. I thought you'd be used to women defending themselves." She looked over at the shieldmaidens coming off the ship, and a few of them grinned at her. "I'm a valued guest, and I'll thank you for treating me as such."

"She has a point, Bersi," I said over his sputtering. "Come, woman, I'll take you to the Jarl."

She gave a regal nod and walked beside me, leaving Bersi to continue unloading his ship. A grievous breach of courtesy, but no more so than his. Within two strides, she'd outpaced me, and within five, she realized it and slowed.

As it was, the Jarl didn't seem surprised at Bersi's poor treatment, but offered her no apology. Once he heard she had knowledge of weaving and ale-making, he frowned mightily. "We've no huts for you, Aridhe, daughter of Eagher. Would you stay in the great hall?"

"I'd rather not." She made no mention of the other warriors, who'd abused her, but her tone told of her concern.

"She could stay with me." I offered it before I thought better of the statement. "I've no wife, no child."

Neither of them mentioned the bitterness in my tone. She looked me over with her golden-brown eyes then gave a short nod. "I'll stay with One-Leg and come to you if there are issues."

Seeming relieved, the Jarl agreed. "Best call him Teo-thir. Your father has given us leave to trade through his land, and we've given our word to leave his ships alone. That agreement cannot be undone, no matter the fuss you may make, but I will treat you as an honored guest."

With that, we were dismissed, and I led her out into the sunshine. I limped along next to her and showed her the way to my home.

"It is large for one man," she murmured when we ducked inside. "No wife, no child, but it's big enough for them."

I ignored her and shouldered past. I'd made it so, big enough to have an alcove away from the fire in the middle, big enough for a woman and littles, her sisters even. My thigh ached, and I turned away from her questioning gaze.

Too much like the AllFather's, bright and knowing.

Within a few days, we had worked out a routine. She was a strong one, and weaving and ale-making was the least of her work. She began brewing, the most bold and lively meads she said when talked of them, and the children would gather for the sweetened berry cordial she made. The soft rhythm of the loom she'd made Bersi carry from her home filled the longhouse most days. It was a blessed time, for certain.

Which meant Bersi couldn't let it continue. For a few moons, we held steady.

First, it was rumors about Aridhe. Some of the men had been courting her to no real end, and Bersi twisted it as far as he could, setting one man against another, with Aridhe at the centre.

The Jarl pulled me aside on one of my slow, increasingly painful walks into market. "Teothir, what do you plan for Aridhe?"

"You waste no words, do you?" I grunted back, stopping to lean on my walking stick. "I've no plans, other than getting out of the way when she bids me to."

"Then she needs to find a man or leave." He sighed.

"The fighting is turning ill, and she needs to choose one of them. She's been here long enough to find a husband."

Something twisted in my heart, and I grunted again. "I'll give her your message. I don't know that it'll do much good though."

"You, and she, best hope it does." He nodded, looking away from the gnarled bit of oak I leaned on. "Your service, your sacrifice, is a debt that cannot be repaid. I'd not wish to see this come to a bad end."

I watched his straight back and his even stride as he walked away and cursed him.

After I returned to the house, I found her outside, working in the herb garden. When she stood and smiled at me, I felt my heart sink.

My dark thoughts must have shown because she cocked her head to one side as she eyed me. "Teothir, what ails you?"

"Many things, Ari, many things. But the Jarl has a message."

"What is it?"

"You need to marry."

The silence fell, heavy as an axe. My thigh twisted in pain, and I winced and rubbed at it uselessly with one hand. "Men are fighting, with viciousness. He thinks you choosing one will change that."

Her face was still as stone.

I swayed a little on my feet, watching her. Eventually, she returned to the herbs, and I made my way inside. I lay in front of the fire and poured ale into my mug, drank it, and then filled it again. The sun set and the fire burned low, and she came inside with cheeks burnt pink with cold.

"Who exactly would I marry?" she snarled, hanging up her sickle. "Bersi? Hran?"

"I don't know." My voice was soft and cloudy at the edges, far too much ale, but I continued on. "It's not my idea. I'd rather you stayed here with me, and that we stayed as we are."

She turned, hands on her hips. "Would you now?"

"Aye, Ari, nothing would please me more." I paused. "No, a whole and hale body would please me best. If not that, then a body that didn't pain me and a woman to overlook it. If not that, then your company and ale and warm home fires are enough."

"Your leg pains you?"

I snorted. "Pains me. Agonizes me. Twists and burns enough that I'm almost unmanned."

"What do your healers say?"

"I'm lucky to live. That the gods must be smiling on me that I can walk as well as I do."

"They're probably right." She sat next to me, staring into the fire.

I passed her my ale. "It's a good brew."

She swallowed and pursed her lips. "I've made better." Then she stood and busied herself with the fire, with food. After we ate, she poured her own ale and sat beside me again. "Who should I marry, Teothir? None of these men are...I could not imagine the long nights with them."

The night seemed long around us. My stupid, treacherous heart rose up, and I swallowed ale to drown it out. "I don't want you to marry any of them. I would not lose you. This." I gestured with my mug, and then took a deep breath. "You could marry me."

Silence fell again, but it was filled with the snap of wood in the fire, the sparks, and the heat.

"You would want to lay with me," she said, finally.

It was no question, but I turned to look at her through narrowed eyes. "Yes? That is how we have marriages." I swallowed another mouthful of ale, my gut twisting as I considered her words. Why would she lay with a twisted, useless almost-thrall like me? My axe was still beside the door; I hadn't wielded it since I walked out of my sickbed. So I blurted out the first thing to come to mind. "But you don't have to."

She looked at me in surprise. "You'd allow me to say no?"

"I wouldn't force you." The idea was abhorrent, and I swallowed more of the ale to wash the taste of the thought away. The flavor soothed and lingered on my tongue, and transformed, like Loki had laid his mouth on me, I spoke, soft and low. "I would not lay with you until you begged me."

She laughed, short and sudden. "Why would I beg?"

I frowned again. "You don't know?"

"It's not something I would beg for."

I let that comment lay between us as the ale and warmth, and the line of confusion between her eyes made me foolish. "A deal then, *astin min.*"

The line deepened.

"I'll not lay with you until you beg me, but let me have a chance or two at it."

She looked at me, meeting my gaze, the line deep and her mouth flattened into a thin seam. "How? What would that mean?"

I lay back on the rug mat she'd woven, my feet close to the fire, and stared up at the thatch. "Well, kissing is traditional. Some touching." I looked over at her. "Licking, should the chance arise."

She looked utterly bemused. I pushed myself over, shifting close. She stayed still, looking down at me from the corner of her eye.

"You tell me to stop, and I will. Freja strike me down if I don't."

"I'll strike you down if you don't!"

I grinned at her. "That you will."

I could see her back move as she took a deep breath. "So we will marry, but you won't lay with me until I beg?"

"Aye, as long as you let me have the chance to change your mind."

She nodded. "That's as fair and as good as I'm likely to get."

Faint praise, but I took it nonetheless. "So, *erskling*, shall we start?"

"What, right now?"

I shrugged. The ale made me feel soft at the edges, and her mouth looked sweet and lovely in the firelight. "We can. I could kiss you." She looked frantic, and I touched her hand. "We don't have to; we can just sleep."

I stroked along the long bones of her hand, the calluses from the knives, the loom and the needles. Her nails were short, blunt, and ragged in places, and I traced them with my fingertips. She stared down at our hands, and I stroked along the edges of her hand, the crease of her wrist, along the slim bones leading up her arm. The fine hairs rose, and with a prayer to Freja I lifted her hand, and she let me. I placed a kiss in the centre of her palm. I looked up and her eyes were wide and dark, her mouth open just a little.

I smiled. "There you go, Aridhe, one kiss." Her fingers curled closed, and I smiled wider. "Good night, *astin min*, we'll go see the Jarl in the morning, aye?"

She nodded, eyes still wide.

I struggled to my feet and walked to my bedroll. After a moment, I heard her get up and move to hers.

For most of the night, I was hard as iron.

THE JARL SENT me and several of his men to Aridhe's family. They agreed to the handfasting, with nothing like enthusiasm in their eyes as they looked at the oak under my arm, but gave enough of their kin, gold, and their trade to make up for it. How little they valued me was overwhelmed by how much they valued her. When I returned, the Jarl was dark with anger and Aridhe even more so.

"So, Teothir, you return triumphant."

I nodded, eyes narrowed. "Aye, with gold and kin

and promises of trade."

"Good." He paused. "Aridhe had some trouble while you were gone."

A long-absent but achingly familiar coldness took me, and I heard myself speak as if from a distance, looking at him through a haze while I itched to act, my teeth bared. "Did she now?"

The Jarl's smile twisted at one corner of his mouth when he looked at me again. "Oh, she did, and she dealt with it. Well, Fasti did. She stayed with Aridhe while you were gone."

I nodded, slow and careful. Fasti had been on the ship when Ari arrived, had helped her onboard and off. She had also been with me when I'd taken the leg wound, had looked after my longhouse while I lay sick. Still looked after it, praise all the gods.

"Well, Bersi and Varin decided to pay Ari a visit, to try and change her mind, I think. They weren't expecting Fasti, or even Ari, to take all that much offense."

I swallowed down some of the rage, fighting for control. "She's unmarked then?"

"She is now. It happened not long after you left. Bersi will be scarred for life though, and Varin is still limping."

When I smiled at that, his eyes narrowed a bit, pinched and white at the edges. "I thought you'd like that."

The Jarl nodded and left just as Aridhe strode toward me, her gaze raking my frame. "Teothir." Her voice was as strong, as clear as it had ever been.

I let the cold rush of anger out with a growl. "Aridhe."

We stood silently, for far too long, watching each other.

THE WEDDING HAD begun. Animals were roasting, other things baking, and the skald was reciting. Aridhe and I sat together, but not touching. Her cousins, her sister, and one of her brothers were telling tales of her father, her ancestors. And occasionally a story of her as a child—falling out of a boat and being feared lost but finding her way to shore and walking back home in a soaking shift; or getting into the ale and drunkenly telling her grandmother that she'd brewed it wrong. Since birth, she'd been a ferocious thing.

Her ale was working now, brewed beautifully, and making everything smooth.

I held more fear for this night than any battle I'd ever faced. Over the preparations for the wedding, I'd managed to make her breathless, kissing her hands first, then the creases of her wrists and her elbows, her neck and her throat. I'd made it to her mouth, and she'd sweetly breathed into me and made a noise that made me as hard as rock just thinking about it. I'd touched her breasts through her shift. Pressed against her, stiff and wanting, while she met my tongue with her own and made me moan.

I'd not touched her quim, though, or tasted her, and I doubted Bersi and the others would let us be until I'd had her, in the torchlight, while they watched.

If she was worried, it didn't show. Not until the song started and others began gathering us up and holding torches. Then her lips thinned, and her eyes went wide. I reached out and touched her hand, and she clung to it. I drew her close.

"Ari…"

"I know what is coming." Her voice was tight, stretched and dry.

"I will not do it," I growled. "I'll not make you do a thing you do not want."

"If you don't, they'll call off the wedding. They'll say you *can't*. Then they'll leave me here. I'll not stay here for more of Bersi's nonsense. No matter how much I enjoy your company, I won't stay. I'm begging you, Teothir, this has to happen."

I snarled, hiding my face in her hair. It was dark and smelled of flowers.

"I'll miss it," she said, in a small voice.

I'd have missed her words, if not for lingering with my nose so close to her skin. "Miss what?"

She tossed her head and looked away. "The kisses, the…touching. After we're married, when you aren't courting me. When you don't need to do it anymore."

I pulled back. "I wasn't going to stop."

She stumbled and looked at me with wide eyes. "But…"

"Frigga's Hair, Ari. That's not…" I lowered my voice as one of her cousins looked at me. I bent toward her ear. "I'll only stop touching you, and kissing you, when you ask it of me."

She stumbled again and didn't speak until we were in our longhouse, surrounded by our families. "I ought to have let you do this weeks ago." She murmured with her arms around me, "I should have been bold."

I let go of my staff and let it rest against the wall. The rest of the party swarmed inside while I pressed my lips against Ari's softly scented skin. She reached up and pushed my cape from my shoulders, and then I heard her sister speak and heard people begin to leave, content Ari and I would consummate our union. I stumbled over to the bed, my hands on her shoulders for balance then laid her down. With a wince, I lowered myself to lay beside her and pressed my lips to her throat and felt it work against my mouth, felt her breathe.

By the time I'd worked my way to Ari's mouth and gotten her skirts pushed up to her waist, everyone but the Jarl and Bersi had left. I lifted my head and snarled, but Ari grasped my head and pulled me back down to meet her gaze.

"Take me," she whispered harshly into my ear. "Make me yours. In front of them, make it true."

I met her eyes, and she was smiling, though it was crooked and she was breathless. She loosened her grip and stroked down my neck and throat, curling through my beard and drawing me into a kiss. She tasted of flowers and herbs, and I groaned as my thigh spasmed and I fell into her embrace.

"Are you..?" She grunted a little as I landed, but within seconds had twisted her hips, pushing, and rolled me onto my back.

I could hear Bersi clear his throat to speak.

But she snarled at him. "He doesn't need to rut at me like an animal."

I lay on my back, trying to force the pain from my mind. When she straddled me, her sex firm against mine, the twinge fled chased by pleasure fierce like fire. With a swift movement, she stripped off her shift, baring herself completely. A writhe of her hips made me groan. "I can ride him for the same end."

The sudden bravery seemed to leave her, and she folded to press her whole body against me, her face buried in my chest. I stroked my hands down the glorious length of her curves, the soft sway of her back, and the swell of her arse.

For long moments, I let myself have my fill of the sensation; years had passed since I'd been with a woman, years since I'd had even the barest of touches. The past weeks of touching Ari and kissing her had made me hungry for more. My fingers tightened, clutching her, and she shivered against me. I pressed a hand to her face, pulling her into a kiss. She made a noise into my mouth as our tongues met and I thrust up against her.

The noise she made then almost unmanned me. I clutched her hip, and my hand tightened in her hair.

She moaned again.

"Ari." I growled her name, then pulled off my shirt, and wrenched the ties of my breeches apart. At the first touch of her warm quim against my bare cock, every muscle in my body locked.

"Teothir, could you..?"

She pushed her hand between us, and I let go of her arse to join her fingers between her thighs. Her quim was barely damp. She parted her curls and the folds of soft flesh, and I dipped my fingers into the warm wetness. I could feel the back of her hand against my cock, and my own hand sought the glorious slickness hidden within her quim. I pushed up with my hips, and she shuddered against me. I gently pushed my middle finger into her and she thrust back down against me. I praised every god I could think of and pushed a second into her, and she stroked against her jewel while I fucked her with my fingers. I could feel her getting wetter and wetter, and I curved my fingers inside her until she made a choked, wailing noise.

"Remember," I said, my voice low and harsh with need. "Beg me then I'll fuck you."

I looked over at Bersi and the Jarl as she shuddered against me again and whimpered. I held Bersi's ice blue gaze as I pushed my fingers in to the knuckle, my thumb resting on Ari's jewel.

I broke with his gaze when she ground against me with a pleading moan. I pulled my fingers free. "Come up here, Ari," I murmured, my hands on her hips urging her up to kneel astride my face.

Her hand clutched my hair, and I licked from her taint to the top of her slit, and she shrieked. I did it again and again until her thighs shook around me, until I could hear her gasping for breath.

"Are you ever going to fuck her?" Bersi's voice was

an odd mix of scorn and jealousy, and I couldn't help curling my lips into a snarl.

Ari twisted to look at him, too, so I reached up to tweak one nipple while sucking her jewel into my mouth and resting my teeth gently against it. She writhed and shuddered against me, thrusting into my mouth, and the taste of her intensified as she peaked. I could hear Bersi continue but couldn't make out the words over the roaring in my ears. When I pulled down Ari's still twitching hips so I could kiss her mouth, I saw Fasti was still in the room, and that she'd moved to stand between Bersi and the bed, facing away from us with her arms crossed.

Then Ari's mouth was on mine, and I couldn't care anymore. She was shaking, hips twitching, her soaking wet slit pressed against my cock. I held her close lest I take her there and then. With my tongue on hers, biting and suckling, I pushed my fingers into her, and she rocked back down on me.

"Teothir, please," she whimpered, voice gone rough. "Please, I'm begging you."

"Begging for what?" I growled it out, barely holding on. "What do you want, Ari?"

"Fuck me," she wailed, head flung high and hair streaming down her back as she sat upright and ground into me. "Take me, now."

I prayed to every god I could think of then flipped her onto her back and entered her in one swift thrust. Coming home, wetness and warmth surrounding me. I fought for control, that coldness threatening at the edges, and held still inside her. Her quim fluttered around me, her breath hard and harsh in the still, cold air. My fingers gripped her too hard, and I knew she'd wear my fingerprints on her skin in the morning, It was then my control broke and the red haze descended.

With no pain, no thought, I sat back on my heels and wrenched her body upward, one arm around her waist and the other in her hair, pulling her head back. I lifted her, and then hauled her downward, thrusting my cock deep. Over and over I pulled out then thrust into her, slamming her down against me. Her moans, her wails, penetrated the haze and made me beastlike, growling as I hunched over her and fucked her with every bit of strength I could find in my battered body. A small bit of my mind knew I would be in agony when the haze wore off, but I did not care, knowing I should take more care even though Ari was shuddering against me. My balls drew up, heat gathered and flooded, and with a snarl that tore my throat, I came deep in Aridhe.

My wife, true and real.

The haze retreated, and my thigh ached and cramped. With enormous effort, I laid Ari on the bed with as much gentleness as I could muster before pulling out and collapsing beside her. She grunted softly as I pulled out, as my seed pooled on the blanket beneath us. I looked up and Bersi had an unreadable look in his eyes, but he left, the Jarl on his heels.

Fasti turned back to face us and smiled down. "Welcome, Ari, tried and true wife of Teothir."

"Fasti, thank you," Ari said, her voice still uneven and breathless. "For staying, for everything." She reached out and took the other woman's hand and pressed a kiss onto her palm.

Fasti grinned down. "My pleasure. And I'll be off to take mine since you two are joined properly now." She smirked and sauntered off.

I waved as she left, then pulled up a blanket over us.

The silence in the long night was warm and welcoming, and Ari curled into my side, her cool hand stroking along my hip bone. Her fingers touched the fur around my cock, and it twitched.

"Could we do it again?" she asked.

I pulled her up to straddle me, our mingled love pooling and slicking as she rocked against my still-soft cock. The pain retreated again in the soft haze of wanting.

"I don't know if I can fuck you," I said, as I pushed my hand between us. "But I'll make you shake and moan again, as many times as you'd like."

She shuddered and shivered against me, and I praised Frigga and Freya—as well as Sjofn and Astrild and Balder—for what she offered, and then took it.

New Words

Teresa Noelle Roberts

Cordoba, Al Andalus, Eighth Century AD

"YOU ARE TO call me Arnulf," Walladah's new husband said. He spoke slowly, which gave each syllable great weight. The Northman convert whose name was now Faiz ibn Asim spoke Arabic poorly, heavily accented with his angular native tongue, and probably struggled to find every word. But because his voice was deep and rich, he sounded considered, rather than awkward.

It wouldn't do to let him know that his voice affected her. He might be Walladah's husband, but he was a wild Northman, though he had bowed to the yoke of Allah. Faiz was a clever trader as well as a warrior, according to her father, but he must be only a little less ignorant than the dogs and cats that prowled the streets of Cordoba looking for scraps. The rough name Arnulf was part of his old life. He shouldn't cling to it now that he'd embraced civilization.

"Faiz rolls more easily from my tongue than your Northman name, husband," she said, trying to sound mild. She didn't know what Northmen expected of their women, but he was a barbarian after all. He might expect complete subservience, not realizing Walladah was an educated woman, a poet, and raised to be treated as a queen in her own home.

He laughed, a great, booming sound that belonged on the deck of one of his people's narrow ships as it cut over a green-gray, roiling ocean. He looked too big and wild for the room they would share, with the delicate wooden screens that shaded the high, arched windows, the vine-like traceries carved into the walls, the rich hangings. Too big and wild for Cordoba or for her life, like some exotic animal in a menagerie. "I'm sure it does, but in the bedchamber, a man likes to hear familiar words and here, I am still Arnulf." He touched his heart, and then his loins.

Oh, he was a bold one! They were married now, though they'd met only that morning, so there was no reason for him not to be.

Or, for that matter, for her not to let her gaze follow his big hand and speculate about the body hidden beneath the silk and linen robes he wore as if they were his rough native wools and furs. She stifled a nervous giggle as heat rose within her. She'd been trying so hard not to look at anything other than his very blue eyes and pale beard, so fair it was nearly white, which reminded her that he was a foreigner, though he had converted to her faith. Trying so hard to remember why she had been displeased with this marriage. As the youngest of five daughters, a scholar and poet known to be a bit eccentric, she was lucky to get an offer from a young, virile man, not some pudgy old fellow with a first wife possessing a shrewish tongue. But she had hoped for a man who did not butcher her beloved language. She had come to the marriage prepared to feel contempt.

But while her new husband didn't speak Arabic well, he sounded like an intelligent man learning a new tongue, not a lackwit who couldn't learn.

And now that she was letting herself take a good look at him, she had to admit Faiz, or Arnulf, was a handsome man. Tall and broad-shouldered, he moved with grace. He had ruddy skin that had seen much weather, and hawk-like features, severe but well sculpted, softened by a mobile mouth that seemed adept at smiles and laughter. Rather a surprise, that lovely smile, but why should it be? A warrior needed the release of humor or risk running mad, and while Faiz was a merchant, he and all his kin were warriors at the core.

Even his brilliant blue eyes and fair beard were not displeasing. She found herself wondering if he had shaved his head as many men did, or if his turban hid a wild blond mane like those she had seen on other traders from the far north. She almost hoped for the mane. For all his civilized silk and linen attire and his new name, there was something wild about Faiz/Arnulf that the long hair would accent.

He looked like a man who would know his way around a woman's body, she thought, and felt herself flushing. He must have seen her blush, because he smiled at her, a warm, teasing smile, and his blue eyes darkened.

With desire, some instinct told Walladah. She had read much poetry (some of the sort her father would not have approved her reading), talked with the singing girls who performed at the house, and asked pointed questions of her married sisters, and of the old women of the household. She knew about the ways of men and women.

Old women felt free to be gratifyingly direct about the male member and what, when properly wielded, it could do for a woman. And last night, since she was about to get married, the old aunties and married women of the family and several hired singing girls had explained the ways of man and maid, singing erotic songs, dancing provocatively for each other, and telling tales of their own sexual experiences. Moreover, they'd had mimicked sex in great, bawdy detail, at one point employing a cucumber to demonstrate what she might expect.

She hoped her husband was not as large as the cucumber they had used for their pantomime, let alone the stallion they'd all teasingly mentioned. But he was such a big man it was possible.

She imagined that beautiful, mobile mouth on hers, those tall body lying over her, doing the things that her sisters and the old women had explained happened in the dark. Her body caught fire. Walladah's religion taught that men and women should treat another with propriety, but she knew from poetry, tales, and simple gossip how often people fell short of the ideal. But she hadn't understood why until that moment.

For the first time, Walladah understood the sweet madness of lust, understood the poets who wrote they would die for a glimpse of their forbidden beloved, understood the lovers who would risk everything to be together. And her husband had not even touched her yet.

She had to think about something else. There was no sin in desiring one's husband, but she was a reasonable, educated woman of Cordoba, not a wild creature who might throw herself upon her mate without shame. Not a woman of her husband's people; she'd heard they were brazen, openly approaching men they desired.

She'd like to be shameless right now. But she wouldn't know how to go about it. Wouldn't even know how to flirt when she could not charm him with poetry.

Shouldn't they converse as best they could, get to know each other a bit before consummating the marriage? She had to say something. Anything. Even if it was wrong. "Faiz is a strong name. It means *victorious*." She said the word *victorious* in Frankish, a language she knew he spoke with some fluency, better than his halting Arabic.

"You speak Frankish?" His voice was full of wonder.

She shrugged. "Not as well as Hebrew or the Christians' Spanish," she said, continuing in Frankish since he seemed more comfortable with that tongue. "I know a bit of Latin, as well. Most people in Cordoba speak several languages, since we are a city of many peoples. I read only Arabic, though."

He sighed, and the dark light of desire faded in his

gaze. "I can't read any language well. Your letters are lovely, but not easy to learn. They twist so on the page. In my tongue, I know numbers and how to make my mark, but I had no time for scribes' work, and others could do it for me more easily than I could learn."

He couldn't read? "But how can you know the holy Koran if you cannot read?" She knew she sounded shrill, but she was truly shocked. Even those who could never afford a book of their own could read a bit, so if they ever had the opportunity, they might read the Koran.

"Like this. In my heart." Then he began to recite.

His Arabic had been halting before, but now it flowed like a river. He spoke well, inflecting the sentences as if he understood them, and moreover, as if he believed. She realized to her embarrassment that while she knew the passages he recited, she could not join in because she had never memorized them word for word the way she had favorite poems.

She kept waiting for the river of words to dry up, assuming he had learned a passage or two during his time of instruction. But it flowed for an amazingly long time. When he finally halted, he shrugged. Watching his shoulders move, she thought, was like watching mountains dance. "That's all I know so far. I need to hear it several times to remember it, since I'm still learning the language, and I cannot always find someone to read to me."

Walladah blinked a few times, stunned by his memory, and by his obvious respect for words. "I will read to you." Words meant something to him, and out of respect for that, she would call him by the name he preferred in private, once she could shape her tongue to it properly. For now, she'd just avoid addressing him by any name at all. "Better, I will read *with* you, so you can learn the letters, as well as the sound of the words."

How could such a severe face light up so much when the man smiled? "Thank you. The words of the Koran are words of great power, and I wish to know them by heart. Words of such importance you should carry in your heart, like poems. Still, it would be good to read them, since one's memory might need refreshing when a book is so long."

Before she could reply, before she could even react, he crossed the room and embraced her.

The space between them had seemed as wide as the sea, yet it took him only four steps to cross it.

Her husband pressed her harder against his big body. His masculine, clean smell surrounded her. Many foreigners didn't bathe enough; you could identify them on the street by their stench as much as by their exotic garments and curious speech. But he smelled good. Not scented, just good. Either he had adopted local customs along with Islam, or his people knew the value of cleanliness, at least for special occasions like a wedding.

She should say something to him, shouldn't she? She opened her mouth to speak.

Faiz's lips covered hers.

She expected her mouth to be ravaged—Northmen were notorious for raping and pillaging, though she was already learning that much of what she thought she knew of Northmen was wrong. Instead, his lips were gentle on hers, but firm. Inescapable.

Not that she wanted to escape. He tasted rich and spicy. His neat blond beard wasn't bristly on her skin like she'd expected, but pleasant. Soft, but with a little tantalizing scratch. Her body felt languid, liquid, and she found herself leaning more into him.

His tongue darted against her lips and instinctively, she opened them.

One hand cradled the back of her head. The other slipped down her back to rest at the curve of her buttocks. She wore two gowns, a silk qamis or undertunic and narrow-legged sarawil as undergarments, but she swore she felt the heat of that massive hand on her bare skin.

Which made her eager to actually feel him touch her that way, and to explore his body in turn. Even through layers of fabric, she could tell he was strong, muscular.

Aroused.

It wasn't as large as an overgrown cucumber, let alone massive as a stallion, but it seemed immense enough to an excited virgin's imagination.

Her body felt odd, tingly. Her skin was so sensitive she thought she might actually burst into flames, but at the same time, she seemed to be turning into liquid. Only her husband's strength held her up.

When he drew back from the kiss, she was trembling. "I think I will like this marriage, Walladah." Then he said something in his Northern tongue.

"What was that?"

"That your lips are the sweetest I have known. They are like…I cannot remember the words. You know…" He gestured, his big hands flapping like wings, and made a buzzing noise. "What the little creatures with stripes make."

She laughed and clapped her hands. "Nicely done! The word is honey. And it's made by bees." She pronounced the new words slowly.

Then she let herself truly understand what he'd wanted to say, not just the clever way he'd overcome the limits of his Arabic, and her blood sang. "I have known no man's lips but yours, but they are as sweet as wine, and as intoxicating. And happily for me, not forbidden by the Prophet like wine is." She felt herself flushing. When had she become a wanton? A singing girl or dancer might say something like that to a patron, but teasingly. Walladah meant it.

And the blue fire in Arnulf's eyes told her that he knew she meant it. "Then get drunk on me," he whispered, slipping off his open outer robe as he did. It rustled to the floor with a sigh of heavy silk.

He plucked off the light veil, fine enough to pass through one of Walladah's rings, that covered her hair. "Like night," he sighed, running his hands through the heavy locks.

Walladah closed her eyes and leaned into the touch, wishing she could purr like a cat to show her pleasure.

After that, he said little, other than to repeat, "Beautiful" over and over again as he helped her remove her crimson outer gown and the deep green one she wore layered beneath it.

Finally, she stood before him in nothing but sarawil and a long qamis, both made of sheer silk the pale pink of the inner petals of a rose.

Arnulf cupped her breasts through the silk. Her nipples crinkled, dark and obvious through the light fabric, and he laughed that big shipboard laugh. "I lack the words to praise you. My mouth must find other uses." Kneeling before her, he took one nipple into his mouth.

The light fabric didn't block the sensation of his tongue, lips, and teeth all working together to suckle. If anything, the damp silk added its own subtle caress. She could even feel his beard prickling her, which didn't seem like it should feel nearly as delicious as it did.

Heat flared like a lightning bolt from her nipple to the secret place between her legs. She moaned and put one hand on his shoulder.

He still wore his turban. She wasn't sure how to unwrap it without its length getting in their way, so she simply lifted it off his head and tossed it aside. As she'd hoped, he had a lion's mane of white-gold hair, or at least a great deal of it, chin length, but cut in a way that would be tidy if he had been bareheaded all day.

He paused what he was doing just long enough to give his head a good shake, to loosen where it was matted by the turban.

She reached out to touch it with something akin to wonder. It was merely hair, not so different from her own dark locks, and slightly sweaty hair at that. And yet wasn't. There were plenty of fair-haired people in Cordoba, but not like him. His hair was pale as moonlight pouring over the olive skin of her inquisitive fingers.

When he turned his attention to her other nipple, her grip tightened of its own accord and she found herself pressing his head against her breast. He hardly seemed to object. His tongue swirled on one nipple, and he teased the other with calloused but gentle fingers, and he clasped the curve of her ass with his free hand.

She pressed her hips forward, seeking contact. Her sarawil were soaked through between the legs. "I need," she started to say then stopped, unsure what, exactly, she needed. More of Faiz. But she couldn't say that, especially since he'd want to hear her use his foreign name, and she had enough trouble pronouncing Arnulf when she could think clearly.

Luckily, he understood the words she couldn't say. He reached up, grasped the keyhole neckline of her qamis and ripped it open down the front. With surprisingly gentle hands, he pushed the tattered garment off her shoulders. He tried to untie the embroidered drawstring of her sarawil, but seaman though he was, the knot confounded his big fingers. He reached for the knife on his belt. Deftly, he cut the drawstring and pushed the pants down to her ankles.

Walladah held her breath, kept every muscle of her body frozen. A shudder of outrage turned almost instantly to a shudder of stark lust. That was how she'd imagined her Northman husband behaving, destroying things in the wake of his careless passion.

But the destruction wasn't careless at all. It was careful, considered, deliberate. And she hadn't imagined how sensuous and exciting it could be to have her fine garments destroyed like so many rags. She stepped out of the sarawil.

Arnulf kicked them aside. "Beautiful," he repeated as if it was the only word of Arabic he could recall. "Beautiful Walladah." He ran a hand down her naked belly and curved it over her neatly bared mound. "So smooth." He said words then in his own tongue. She couldn't understand them, but his deep voice dropped into a whisper that promised wicked delights, and his gaze went dark and heated. She knew whatever he said must be bold and erotic, and that knowledge, combined with the look and the voice and the teasing caress, aroused her more than she knew was possible.

He slipped two fingers between her legs, not penetrating, but stroking at the slick, sensitive flesh, the place she toyed with sometimes in the night, and she realized she'd been mistaken a few seconds before. It was possible to be far more aroused than she had been earlier, to reach a state where desire for something she couldn't explain might just drive her mad.

She clenched, rocked forward to meet the touch. Blood roared in her ears, and when he withdrew his hand, she found herself grinding at the air.

He smiled, and it was definitely the grin of a warrior who saw victory in his grasp. "Soon," he soothed, stroking her bare back and uncovered hair soothingly.

Then they set to work together removing his garments. Each layer they took off revealed more of the strong lines of his body, more hints of the wild North-man under the civilized clothing of a Muslim resident of Cordoba. By the time they were done, she wished she had the nerve to resort to a knife herself, to hurry the process.

He was very pale where the sun and wind hadn't weathered his skin, as fair as the Circassian singing girl who'd performed at her wedding festivities. But it was the fairness of carved ivory, solid and firm, not that young woman's plump, milky pallor. His broad chest and long legs displayed muscles she didn't know existed. Oh, she could tell his body followed the same human pattern as her own, except for the obvious differences between man and woman. But his size and strength altered that familiar design, so he looked more like a strange creature out of legend—not a monster, but something fierce and beautiful, a djinni, perhaps.

She splayed her hennaed hands on his broad chest. She didn't think of herself as a small woman—she was the tallest of her sisters—but her hands looked tiny against him.

She couldn't help herself. She ran her hands down his body, circled his cock with one hand while cupping his balls with the other. His balls twitched when she touched them, like they had a life of their own. His cock was heavy, hot, thicker than she'd realized, purplish in contrast with his fair skin and the nest of pale hair from which it rose. Intriguingly, it was topped with a pearl of fluid. She caught it with one finger, tasted its musky saltiness. Then she returned her hand and began to stroke. The motion was awkward—she really had no idea what she was doing—but the temptation was irresistible. She managed only a few strokes before he caught her wrists. "Was I doing it wrong?"

"Too right." He breathed her name like a prayer and pulled her closer. "I need patience."

"Please… I want to know what I'm craving." It was all she could think to say as the sheer impact of her husband's body interfered with her ability to think.

He moved his hands, scooped her up, carried her the few steps to the elaborately carved bed, draped with fine white netting and layered in rich red fabrics in celebration of the marriage, except for stark white sheets that would display her virgin blood.

Walladah's heart raced, and she could not tell if she was more excited or frightened. He seemed so huge lying over her, so blond, so alien, and his cock, nudging at her opening, seemed far too large to accommodate. Yet, she *wanted* to accommodate it, wanted to feel it filling her, moving inside her as the older women had described so eloquently. Impatient now despite her nerves, she opened her legs and canted her hips forward to meet him. The broad head of his cock pressed against her, not against her slick opening, but at the hypersensitive pearl of flesh above it. Sensation filled her. She squirmed against him, half-drunk on desire, wanting, wanting…

"You are a maiden," Faiz said—no, she reminded herself, Arnulf. The wild name suited him, even if she could not bring herself to speak it. "And yet you flow like a river for me."

"That's poetic."

He smiled, a fierce, proud smile. "That is the best I can do in a tongue I speak poorly. But this is proper poetry." He began to recite something in his own language.

Walladah caught the rhythm of the ocean in the words, the violent give and take of battle, a few lines that hinted at some wild Northern magic. His blue eyes went distant as he recited, as if he looked, in his mind, at the scene the poem described. It didn't rhyme, but the rhythm was strong music. She could imagine rowing a ship to that beat.

And then the tone changed. She still couldn't understand the individual words, but now he was clearly speaking of something tender and intimate. A long-sought homecoming, a woman's beauty, the wonder of love.

The meter, she thought, was the same as the earlier poem, but it seemed different now, a heartbeat, or two bodies making love. His hips kept rocking as he recited, rocking to the rhythm of the words.

Between steady teasing movement and the deep, rich voice reciting passionate words, she was more than ready when he entered her at last.

There was an instant of pain, a sense of something tearing deep inside her. My old life, she thought. There was no going back now to the maiden she had been, but she didn't want to. She wanted to go forward, to experience the pleasure that the women had described last night.

She wasn't sure what to do next—her pre-marital instruction hadn't been that detailed about how to please a man. So she wrapped both legs and arms around her husband, moved against him, letting her hips take over when her brain failed.

It was overwhelming and frightening and wonderful, all at once. She wanted to say something, wanted to give him a poem in Arabic in exchange for the one he had given her. But that was too much for her brain to handle right now. She opened her mouth to speak, but all she could manage was a moaned, "Faiz."

"Arnulf," he said, a hint of teasing reproach in his voice. Then his mouth was over hers and he was moving faster. Arnulf was big and it hurt a little, she wouldn't lie to herself, but the hurt was edged with gold and she wanted to push to the pleasure she felt hovering just on the other side of the discomfort. Then he eased his hand between their bodies and began to stroke her pearl.

Pain stopped. Thought stopped. Walladah's heart almost stopped as she reached that place of pleasure she'd known was waiting, then went beyond it to a degree of bliss she hadn't known existed. Oh, she'd heard hints in the naughtier sort of poems and songs, had heard the old ladies joking about it last night, but it had seemed like an exaggeration. Those hints were pale shadows of the truth, and the truth was a fire that lifted off the top of her head to let in stars and poems as her body convulsed around her Northman's cock. "Arnulf," she managed to say, unable to worry if she pronounced it properly. "Arnulf."

His body stiffened. His face screwed up as if he were in pain. Then he let out a great roar and his cock leaped inside her, setting off another wave of convulsions, another pleasure so strong it drove away words.

Words stayed distant as Faiz…no, Arnulf… slipped from her side long enough to wet a linen cloth at the wash basin and tenderly clean her. She jumped a bit at the cool cloth, and she was tender and would no doubt be sore in the morning. Still, his touch on her sex and lips set off another release, a milder one than before, but enough to make her groan and make him look down upon her and smile. Words remained far away and difficult as she took the cloth from him and cleaned him, smiling to herself as his cock, though limp from its exertions, jumped at her touch, as if it very much wanted to stiffen for her.

But as she lay curled against his big body, words came back in force. They weren't forming a *good* poem, not yet—and certainly it would be a poem she could share with no one but Arnulf, even when it was complete, for it would be racy enough to make a singing girl blush. She would share it, though, if she thought he could deal with a wife who wrote poems. Meanwhile, another poem came to mind, one of those that she wasn't supposed to know but did anyway, about the night and stars and a beloved brighter than all the stars in the sky. She began to recite.

And to her astonishment, her husband joined in, repeating the poem in his deep voice. When it was finished, she rolled up onto her knees so she could look at his face. "How did you know that?"

"I heard someone recite it after a dinner gathering. It stuck in my head, though I couldn't understand most of the words then. It's a lover addressing his beloved, isn't it?"

"Like the one you recited for me, the second one. The first was something warlike, I think, but the second one talked of love."

"I am very proud of that first poem; it tells of a great battle out of legend. Perhaps you can help me translate it into Arabic. I know you have poems that speak of war and heroes. The second one is rough, but I composed it on the spot, and I was more than a bit distracted."

Once again, the top of Walladah's head opened, and stars and poems flowed in. "You write poetry? Faiz…Arnulf…that's wonderful."

He laughed. "I've never *written* a poem in my life, though perhaps you can help me with that. I've composed many, though." He lowered his voice. "Between the two of us, wife, poetry was what first made me think to open a trading house in Cordoba. Everyone in this city goes about spouting poems, even the woman selling vegetables in the market and the man driving sheep in from the hills, and this fact makes me feel at home even though this place could not be more different from the north. The words of the holy Koran captured me, though I could not understand them at first, because it sounds like a long, wonderful poem. And then I learned what they meant and here I am." He laughed, an abrupt, gruff laugh. "I know. You thought you'd been married off to a wild Northman warrior, and here I lie prattling of poetry."

"I like such prattling. I feared we would not be able to speak of such things, but it seems we have enough words in common for what matters. Even though I didn't understand your poems, I felt them here." She took his hand and placed it over her heart. "Poetry comes from untamed places, though we shape it so it sounds civilized. I think this marriage will suit us both well, Arnulf."

For the first time, his name rolled easily off her tongue. Let him be Faiz to the rest of the world; it was, as she said, a strong and honorable name. But now she could hear the music in his name, wild and fierce and sweet like his verse and his lovemaking.

She said his names again, both of them, for the sheer joy of shaping them with her lips.

Until Arnulf, also known as Faiz, gave her something better to do with her mouth.

The Needle and the Strap

Bibi Rizer

The East coast of Newfoundland, 1015 AD

J ARI SPOTTED THE boat at dawn. He had taken the first watch in his brother's place after losing a game of dice he was almost sure was rigged. The older men had only laughed when he protested. As the youngest in their remote settlement, with no woman to give him prestige, Jari had to bear their fun at his expense like a Norseman. Stoically. He filed away his anger to make use of one day in battle or on a raid. Perhaps he would picture his brother's face as he cleaved open one of the Skræling warriors.

In truth, he had no wish to face the Skræling again. Their shrieks and painted faces gave him nightmares. A Norseman—having nightmares about battle! Jari thought the Skræling gods had cursed him with cowardice because he accidently desecrated a grave site. How was he to know these wild people didn't burn their dead like proper warriors? It was hardly fair to be cursed for ignorance, but other people's gods were like that, Jari knew. Unfair.

He gazed out at the boat, silhouetted by the rising sun over the silver ocean. He hoped they had women with them. And ale. First ale, then women. Jari found women almost as terrifying as Skrælings without a little fortification. Two or three ales in him, though, he could perform respectably well. When he'd had the opportunity, that is. Which had been a while ago. And with whores.

"Eighteen summers old," Jari muttered. "Stuck in this desolate *drit*-bucket, watching ships like an addled thrall-child."

He sighed heavily and began the climb up to the longhouse to inform his brother of the approaching ship.

His brother, Iver, roused eventually, untangling himself from the limbs of his pregnant wife, who protested with suggestions that made Jari's cheeks burn and cock twitch.

Iver slapped his back as they made their way down to the shore. "I should slit your throat for looking at my woman's teats," he said with a grin.

"I wouldn't have looked if she hadn't been shaking them in my face," Jari replied. "I was in grave danger of being concussed. I had to look to dodge a lethal blow to the head."

His brother roared with laughter all the way to the beach.

The long ship had not moved any closer. Its mast was down, but even at this distance, Jari could see the small craft had oars. The ocean was relatively calm.

"Why don't they row in?" Jari asked.

"Pull up the faering. We'll go out to meet them."

"Should we not…wait? What if they're not friendly?"

Iver slapped him again. "That's a Norse boat, boy. What Norseman would lurk off the headland like an eel if they had intentions to attack?"

They climbed into the faering, a small narrow dinghy with two sets of oars, and set to row out to the forlorn longboat.

When they reached the bobbing ship and pulled up to her port side, Iver called out, "Hey! Brothers? Show yourselves!"

No answer came. Iver threw a loop of rope to an oar lock and pulled up close alongside, hoisting himself upward. Jari clambered up beside him. No sooner had he poked his head over the gunwale and witnessed the horror therein than Iver had lunged at him, tearing him away and hurling them both into the frigid water below.

"Pestilence!" Iver shouted as they surfaced.

Jari blinked the salt water from his eyes and considered the after image of what he had seen. A pile of bloated bodies, grey in death, their faces contorted in their last agony.

"Did you touch one?" Iver asked.

Jari shook his head, treading water, feeling his feet grow numb, his stones shrinking in his sodden breeches. "No, I didn't even have time to take a breath."

"Good. Let's away. We'll come back with flames and arrows and send these poor souls to Valhalla, if they've earned it."

They returned with more of the men from the settlement, and bows and arrows dipped in pitch. Jari carried a flame with which to light them. Their holy man spoke some inscrutable words, beseeching the gods to look kindly on these most ignoble deaths.

Jari thought it was pointless, but he said a silent prayer to Freya that these Norsemen's wives might find peace somehow. It galled Jari to think of women waiting for men who were never coming back. He would dream of them tonight, he thought. Dream of easing their grief with his under-used manhood.

"Jari! The flame!" his brother snapped. The other men had their arrows at the ready.

Jari lifted the lantern so each could light their missiles. They let fly and soon the small ship was smoldering then burning, dark smoke rising with the souls of the dead men.

Jari blew out the lamp as they turned the faering and began to row back to shore.

Halfway to the beach, the air was torn with a wild screech. They all turned to look at the burning ship just as a spectral figure, black clothed and flaming emerged onto the gunwale, hung there for a moment, writhing, before tumbling into the churning water.

"Gods preserve us," said one of men. "A sea draug!"

But when the creature surfaced, screaming and thrashing, Jari could see it was no monster. It was a woman. And she was about to drown.

Without thinking, Jari dove into the waves, pushing

through the current. The woman disappeared from view as he swam, sinking with a weak yelp. He dove down, opening his eyes under the murky brine and just spotted a falling shadow. His hand shot out and grabbed a tendril of the poor creature's hair. He kicked his legs hard and dragged them both to the surface.

"Are you mad!?" he heard his brother cry. "She'll have the fever!"

The woman wasn't breathing. Jari kicked and swam for the faering, but as he arrived, the other men set on him with oars. One even drew an arrow.

"You'll not be getting back into this boat with that," the holy man said, not sounding very holy at all.

"Please," Jari spluttered, as a wave overtook him. "She's not breathing."

"Give her back to the sea that took her then," another man said.

"Iver!" Jari pleaded "Pull us up!"

Iver frowned darkly. "Throw down a rope," he said. "We'll tow them to shore."

Jari grabbed the rough rope and wound it around one wrist as the men set to rowing. By the time they got to shore, he was numb from his toes to the tips of his hair. The men pulled the faering up onto the sand while Jari dragged the woman out of the water.

"Don't come near me with that pestilent creature," someone said.

"It's just a girl!" Jari said, pushing hair from his eyes. The girl was grey and cold. Jari had seen fishermen pull unlucky friends from the sea several times. Sometimes they died, but sometimes…

He pressed his hand hard on her ribs, once, twice, three times. Then he lowered his lips and blew into her mouth.

"Gods, Jari," someone said with a cruel laugh. "Are you that hard up for female company that you must kiss a drowned girl? And a poxy one at that?"

"Go fuck a sheep!" Jari shouted. The girl still wasn't breathing, and he couldn't hear her heartbeat over the crashing of the incoming tide. He pressed her breast again, hard, and this time a torrent of brackish water streamed out. Jari turned her on her side and squeezed her.

After vomiting more water, she began to cough.

Jari looked up to see that all the men had left but Iver, who glowered down on him.

"If she has the fever, you are a dead man," he said. "I don't think the gods will…"

"Shut up about the gods!" Jari said. The girl was stirring, her coughing subsided, she whimpered. Jari helped her sit up.

"Take her to the fishing shed on the headland. Provisions are there. If neither of you are infected, you can come back to the long house, Wodensday, after the new moon. If you are infected… well, we'll burn down the shed with you both inside."

Iver turned and left, striding up the beach without looking back.

"I love you, too, brother," Jari yelled after him as he disappeared in the scrub.

Jari looked down to the girl, whose color was returning, though she was shivering, and trying to cover her pale shapely legs with her sodden dress. He gave her a sip from his wineskin, which added some rose to her cheeks.

Now she was alive and with her eyes open. Jari could see that she was a young woman, maybe a bit older than him, with a soft feminine shape, golden hair and bright grey eyes. Miraculously, she didn't seem to be burned, not even her hair. Perhaps the gods looked on him with favor today, after all. The Skræling gods or his gods, he cared not if they delivered a pretty woman into his care.

Unless she had the fever, of course. Then he was fucked. But it was too late to change that now.

"Come," Jari said, "We should get you warm." He helped her stand, but when she stumbled, he picked her up and carried her along the beach toward the headland. Jari found having a pretty girl wrapped in his arms made him feel like a Norseman carrying off the virgin daughter of a pillaged hamlet. His cock stirred for the second time that day, despite being half frozen.

Jari couldn't actually picture himself ever carrying off an unwilling virgin daughter. The screams of women made his heart ache. Iver said he was too soft, but a priestess of Freya once told him he was wise to revere women. That one day Freya would bless him for it. Maybe this was that day.

"Do you speak my tongue?" he asked the girl, who had cuddled into his chest.

"Yes," she said. "I'm a Norsewoman."

"And your name?"

"Gull. Gull Grímsdóttir."

"I'm Jari Sturlason. Do you know where you are?"

Gull looked doubtfully at the bleak landscape of rocks, scrub, and grey ocean. "The end of the world?"

"Near to it," Jari said, with a laugh. "We call it Vinland. But for no good reason. There are neither grapes nor wine of any sort. Only rocks and ice and wild men throwing axes at your head."

"Sounds like my father's house," the girl said.

Jari laughed so hard he nearly dropped her.

They were both warmer when they arrived at the small fishing hut, and Jari soon had a lantern lit and a fire underway.

"You're not burned?" he said. "You seemed on fire when you leapt from the boat."

"It was just my cloak. Moth-eaten thing. Good riddance." She pulled off a boot and emptied water onto the floor. "Can I tell you a secret?" she said, as she unlaced her jerkin.

Jari tried to look away from the shapeliness of her bosom in her clinging wet tunic, but failed.

Gull smiled up at him. "Like what you see?"

"No! Uh, I mean yes. That's a very nice tunic. Finely made." Jari made much of tending the fire. "What is this secret?"

Gull slipped off her wet skirt and threw it over the back of a chair. "There is no fever," she said. "No pestilence. Those men died from bad drink."

Jari stopped poking the fire and stared. "Truly? What

kind of bad drink?"

"Something they bought from honorless monks in Wessex. To do trade with men and sell them poison! I hope their god makes their cocks fall off."

"You took none of this drink?"

"A lone shieldmaiden on a boat of men?" She snorted. "Hardly. I needed to keep my wits about me. And so I kept my life, and they did not."

Jari thought the girl didn't seem very upset about losing her fellow sailors. As she sat cross legged on a straw mat in nothing but a soggy tunic, he thought he could just see the outline of her pubic hair, which seemed to be as rich and golden as the thick tumble of damp curls on her head.

"We should go back to the longhouse, I suppose," Jari said, his nerves lighting up. "If there's no danger, there's no need to stay here."

Gull nudged his knee with her pale slender foot. "Isn't there?" she asked. She moved her foot up his thigh and pressed gently on the hard bulge in his breeches. "We should get you out of these wet clothes." Gull stood and wrapped her arms around Jari's waist. She squeezed him, laying her head on his chest with a sigh. "Thank you for saving my life."

Jari caught his breath. He couldn't remember the last time anyone had expressed gratitude for anything he'd done. Maybe the act had never happened. His brother and the other men of their settlement mostly treated him like a burden, though he worked as hard as any of them. The three women in the settlement – his brother's wife, the chieftain's wife, and her elderly thrall mostly ignored him, unless something heavy needed to be moved. And then they never thanked him, certainly not with a warm cuddle.

Jari felt he would be content to stand there with her head resting on his chest until Wodensday after the full moon came, and they were allowed back in the long house.

But Gull began to unlace his knife belt, and it soon clattered to the floor.

Jari watched her as she tugged his tunic out of his pants, and he lifted his arms obediently as she slid it off him.

"Oh my," Gull said, brushing her hands over Jari's hard stomach.

He was mostly hairless, another thing the men teased him for, but Gull didn't seem to mind.

She leaned down and bit one of his nipples rather hard.

"Ow," Jari squeaked. "You vixen, that hurt."

Gull just shook her head and slipped off her own tunic.

Jari thought his cock might spend right there and then. Gull stood in front of him, naked but for a rune stone and a small pouch on a thin leather strap around her neck. Her breasts were everything he imagined—full and fair with dark red nipples like berries ripe for picking. He slid his rough hands up to cup one in each, feeling the weight and warmth of them, the intoxicating *woman* of them. He felt light-headed, longing to spread her legs and plunge between them with his cock, mouth, fingers, everything he had. His brush with death had ignited him like a Solstice bonfire, and he needed to be doused. To blazes with being content with a cuddle.

He picked her up and sat back on the chair with her in his lap. She wriggled and pressed down on his manhood, sending jolts of pleasure coursing through him. Nothing was between his cock and her cunt but the fabric of his breeches as Jari laced his hands into her tangled hair and pulled her forward for a kiss.

She tasted of salt and wine, and oh sweet gods, he had never been kissed like this. Gull kissed with her whole self: her lips, her teeth and, Freya's cats, her tongue. It darted in and out and wrapped around Jari's until he could no longer think.

"Let me fuck you," he said, tearing at his breeches, trying to pull them off. "I beg you."

Gull leaned back, a little smile on her face. "Begging is not necessary," she said. "But you will have to do it my way."

"Gods, anything," Jari said.

Gull slipped the leather rope from her neck, removed the rune and the pouch, and set them on a bench. Then she slid her hands down Jari's arms and lifted them above and behind his head.

"What are…"

She pressed her lips on his, quieting him. "Don't speak unless I tell you to. Nod if you understand."

Jari nodded. He was breathing so quickly his lungs burned.

Gull wound the strap of leather around Jari's wrists and tied them tightly to the back of the chair.

When she stood, the beauty of her naked body made Jari's cock throb; when she knelt before him, he thought he might expire from the sudden rush of blood from his skull to his manhood.

Gull slid her fingers around the top of Jari's breeches and gave a little tug. Jari lifted his behind to help her until his garment was around his ankles. His cock sprang free and bounced on his stomach eagerly.

Gull bent over and removed Jari's boots before slipping his breeches completely off. Then he was as naked as she, the little fire warming away the last vestiges of the cold of their unscheduled swim. With his boot laces, Gull tied his ankles to the chair.

"Mouth or cunny?" she asked, standing.

Jari tried to say something but nothing came out.

"I asked you a question, boy," Gull said, a stern expression on her face. "Mouth or cunny?"

"Mouth," Jari bit out. He desperately wanted to shove his cock so deep in this girl that it bent with the force, but he'd never had a mouth on him before, not even from a whore, and he wanted to know how it felt. If it was anything like kissing her, he'd be shooting his seed down her throat in seconds.

Gull dipped her head, taking a deep inhale of breath, running the tip of her nose, and then, gods, her tongue along the line of hair beneath Jari's navel. She kept going, her tongue traveling through his pubic hair to the base of his cock and along its length to the swollen tip. Gull glanced up at him, a wicked look in her eye as she wrapped her lips around the head and swallowed him, inch by blissful inch until he was half inside her mouth, and more. He could feel the back of her throat just rubbing against the tip of his cock.

"Sweet Freya," Jari said.

Gull let his cock slip out and pinched him so hard on his nipple that he yelped.

"*No* talking!" she said, before wrapping him in her warm lips again.

Jari pressed his own lips tightly closed as Gull moved up and down, sometimes scraping her teeth along his length, which was a paradise of sensation, and sometimes twirling her tongue towards the base. As she moved, her breasts stroked across his knees, the hard pert nipples tickling through his fine blond body hair. Jari felt he might lose his mind. He was desperate to touch her, desperate to say something, above all desperate to come. He could feel it building, every muscle in his body tensing with anticipation.

It was as though she knew. Cupping his aching stones in her cool hand, Gull slid back and focused her magical lips on the engorged head of Jari's cock, sucking and swirling her tongue, until he couldn't hold back a whimper.

"I…I…" he bit out. But it was too late. His seed surged into her mouth in hot bursts, while his entire body rocked with wave after wave of tingling ecstasy. When the stars faded from his vision, and he was finally fully spent, Gull was sitting back, wiping her mouth with the back of her hand.

"You may speak," she said.

"I'm sorry," Jari said.

"For what?"

"For coming in your mouth. I…couldn't help it."

Gull stood, bent down and kissed him on the lips, letting her tongue find his and swirl with it together.

She tasted different now, less wine and more salt, but it was no less intoxicating. Jari felt his cock harden completely again, though he had only emptied it seconds before.

"Do you taste bad?" Gull asked.

Jari shook his head. If that was his taste, the rich saltiness, it *wasn't* bad, not at all. He would come in her mouth and kiss her clean every night for the rest of his life if she'd let him.

Gull looked at him with a little smile.

Jari had the awful sensation that she'd read his thoughts and knew what soft and sentimental things he was thinking. He should probably bend her over the bench and take her from behind just to reestablish his position as a man and a Norseman, but as he was currently tied to a chair and completely at her whim, it was impossible. Jari was grateful Iver wasn't around to witness this. The very idea made him laugh.

"Is something funny?" Gull asked, stepping forward, straddling his legs and dropping down to sit on him, her wet sex pressed against his throbbing erection.

"No…"

"No, *Mistress,*" Gull said.

Jari thought he had misheard. Thralls called his mother "mistress". He was no thrall, and this girl was not his mother. Thank the gods for that.

She reached down, sliding the head of his cock into her warm opening, lingering there, not moving.

Jari tried to rise up to fully penetrate her but she moved with him, always just keeping the tip of his cock inside, but nothing else. He wanted to impale her, slam into her and fuck her until she screamed the name of every god she knew, and some new ones. "Please…" he said.

"Please, *Mistress.*"

"Please, Mistress. Fuck me, Mistress, please." Jari felt natural saying it, and the sensation of her pushing downwards until he was enveloped, balls-deep in her warm wet cunt, only helped. If she was to be his mistress, so be it. A thrall could do worse.

She moved languidly, trailing her fingers all over his scorching flesh, over his chest, down his hard abdomen, back up to tickle the hair under his arms. And just when he thought he'd have to beg again, she wrapped her arms around his head, gripping his hair in her fingers and kissed him, her hot tongue darting in and out.

Jari pulled at his bindings; he wanted to hold her, to touch her, pull her hair, grab a handful of her magnificent ass, and slide his thumb over that glistening pink slit that opened and closed teasingly with every thrust. He knew of the button of nerves there that if stroked with a deft finger or thumb would send a woman into paroxysms of ecstasy. He wanted to give her that. The chair rattled beneath them as Jari tugged at the leather strap.

Gull scowled at him. "Are you trying to escape?"

"No."

She moved up and down, her cunny squeezing his cock.

Jari felt his eyes rolling back in his head.

"No, what?"

"No, mistress."

"That was a lie, boy," Gull said, "What happens to boys who lie?"

She reached over, pulling something from the small pouch she had removed from her neck. A sewing needle. "Why aren't you adorned, boy?" she asked, fingering his earlobe. As he was still being fucked, frustratingly slowly, the slightest touch made him shiver. So she was going to pierce his ear. That seemed a small price to pay for the privilege of filling her with his come. And he wasn't about to tell her that his lack of adornment was because of his youth. He turned his head willingly.

Gull reached over and held the needle in the flame of the lamp for a few seconds. Then she tugged down his earlobe and jammed the needle through it.

"Odin's arsehole!" Jari said at the sudden pain.

Gull continued to move her hips as she pulled a tiny gold ring from the pouch and held it over the flame before looping it through the stinging hole.

"Did you just curse one of the gods?" she asked. "That's very naughty." Her hand slid down over Jari's right nipple, circling it with her fingertips. She rose up and down on his cock.

Jari's reason was leaving him. As the tingle subsided from his ear, he found himself craving it, craving more. The pain combined with the pleasure of her hot sex was tearing him apart. He snapped his hips upwards, trying to get deeper into her, trying to regain some control, but she just rose, almost to the point of him slipping out, and lingered there.

"Hold still," she said, and pressed the burning needle through his nipple.

"Mother of … Christ," Jari said, in Latin, a curse he'd once heard a Northumbrian monk say.

Gull calmly looped another gold ring through the hole in his nipple, wiping away the drip of blood with her finger, which she popped in her mouth and licked clean. "Have you abandoned our gods?" she asked, as she stood and let him slip out painfully.

His dripping cock bounced back and slapped his glistening sweaty belly, sending a jolt through him as the tiny wound in his nipple seared. Pleasure. Pain. One or the other. He could no longer tell the difference.

Her finger swirled around his other nipple. "Are you a Christian now?"

"Gods, no…Gull, mistress…" He said the first thing that came to him. "Let me taste you. Let me lick you and suck you until you scream for mercy."

"Your sweet temptations won't save you. I like you, Jari Sturlason, but you're still not adorned enough for me."

She slid her hand down his chest, over his navel and down the path of hair to his straining swollen manhood.

She grabbed him tightly and pulled upwards, clenching until she had a finger full of his foreskin pinched up above the tip. The needle re-appeared.

"Gods, no!" Jari cried.

Gull paused, needle raised, a wicked grin on her face.

"No, mistress," Jari tried to free himself, pulling at his bindings.

Gull ignored him, reaching over to hold the needle in the flame once more. She pulled his foreskin, stretching it painfully.

"No, demon whore, not there!" He writhed in the chair, but the rough wooden wall of the shed prevented retreat.

"Did you just call me a whore?"

"Bitch, I'll …I'll…" Jari was afraid he would start crying. What had he gotten himself into pulling this lunatic from the waves? She was likely to sew shut his manhood so that he could no longer come or piss and would die a horrible death from both. He did the only thing possible, trussed up as he was, the tip of his cock firmly clamped in her fingers. He planted his feet on the ground and stood, lunging for her.

She took a shocked step backwards, and they both tumbled to the floor, the chair crashing down on top of them. Her hand was mashed between them but in the fall she had let go. He wriggled off her, releasing one of his feet in the process.

That was enough for him to rise and slam himself against the wall, splintering the chair. Free from his bindings, he dove for her, pinning her down with his knees and clasping her wrist.

"Ahhh, you brute! You'll break my bones!"

"Drop the needle! Drop it!"

As the needle dropped to the floor, Jari swept it up and cast it into the fire. Then he flipped her over and tied her wrists behind her, using the same leather strap she had bound him with. Jari fell back, resting against the wall, panting and still infuriatingly as hard as ice. He wondered if his cock had a desire for pain that he didn't share.

Gull lay silent, face down on the dirt floor. Then she started to laugh. "Now that you've got me like this, what will you do to me?"

"For the love of nine mothers, woman, are you mad?"

She turned her head, smiling sweetly. The smudge on her face from the dirt floor made something in the region of his heart flicker.

"Gods. You were only playing? You weren't really going to pierce my cock?"

"Not if you didn't want me to. You Norsemen are not so brave. In the south, men have the tip cut right off when they're just babes."

Jari clamped his hand over his cock at the thought.

Gull struggled to her knees and edged closer. She sat back on her heels, her head turned, fixing him in a stare so deep and inviting he thought he would drown in it. "Come and kiss me, boy."

Jari leaned over and kissed her, and wiped the smudge of dirt from her brow. They rested there, forehead to forehead, breathing deeply, the smell of sweat and sex and salt water swirling around them. Jari pressed his lips on hers until he felt them twitch upwards into a smile.

She turned away and bent forward, raising her glorious round ass into the air, exposing her glistening nest.

"Sweet Freya's bosom…"

Jari grabbed her hips, and guiding his cock into place, he impaled her so eagerly that he felt his tip bounce against something inside her. She yelped, whether from pleasure or pain he neither knew nor cared. But soon Gull's cries melted into delicious moaning. And begging. For more, harder, deeper.

Jari reached around and ran his hand down her smooth tummy and into the bed of soft curls below. He parted her lips and slid his fingers into the wet valley between them, like an explorer with no map, but Gull's soft whimpers and words guided him.

"A bit higher. Make circles ov…oooooohhhhh yes, like that…"

Jari wrapped his free hand around her shoulder, holding her body so he could penetrate her with more force as his fingers moved over her swollen bud. The sensation of having her bound hands between them, pressing on his stomach was thrilling and maddening; she kept curling her fingers into claws and scratching at him. Each time she did, he pounded his cock into her with more force, as though that might make her submit, and stop inflicting the pain which he both dreaded and craved.

Somehow, she got two fingers around his newly pierced nipple and pinched with fierce pressure. He gasped back a yelp and pressed down on her wet slit, sliding his fingers through her juices. She released his nipple at last, her body lurching forward as she writhed under him.

"Oh, gods, I'm so close…" she whimpered. "So close. Jari, fuck me!"

Jari was close, too; he bit down on his own tongue to forestall it as her muscles pulsated around his cock in rhythmic waves. He slid one knee between her legs and lifted her right off the floor until he was holding her there, impaled on his hammering cock, writhing and screaming for release. "Gods!" Jari shouted.

When it came, it was like a violent tempest they rode together. Jari moved his hand from her slit to her waiting mouth where she muffled her ecstasy by sucking her own juices from his fingers. His manhood surged inside her, pumping her full of his seed. He could feel the cream of it dripping down over his balls, onto her lush thighs, and the floor beneath them.

They stayed like that as their spasms subsided. When he could think again, Jari reached over and pulled a caribou skin off a shelf, throwing it down on the floor. He eased out of her and gently lay her face down on the soft fur. With shaking hands, he undid the ties on her wrists then bent to kiss them, the red welts further inflaming the inferno in his heart, and elsewhere.

"I'm sorry," he said. "I didn't mean to hurt you."

Gull rolled over and gazed at him curiously. "What

Norseman apologizes for fucking a woman until she screams his name?"

"I'm a terrible Norseman," Jari admitted. He could see this now. He was soft and emotional and would let this woman lead him off the edge of the earth if she wanted to.

"But a very good *man*," Gull said, curling her fingers around his waning cock. "I think I will keep you. If I'm to stay here, I'm in need of a man since my foolish husband drank poison mead."

Jari sat up so quickly he saw stars. "You're not… truly? He was one of them on the boat?"

Gull nodded, biting her lip. "Pay it no mind. I hated him. He was a brute. And his men were no better. They made sport of raping virgins and wasted all their plunder on gambling and whores."

"I hate gambling," Jari said, truthfully. "I always lose."

Gull smiled at him, so beautifully that he thought he might dissolve into a puddle.

"And whores?"

"What whore could compare with you? With them, it's like fucking an ice-wraith, and with you, it's like fucking a goddess."

That pleased her. She sighed happily. "And what will you do with your plunder?"

"Give it to you," Jari said without hesitation.

"And what if I want to put another hole in you? Pierce you again. What will you do?"

Jari ran his hand over the welts on her wrists. "Tie you up and fuck you."

Gull laughed and kissed him, soft and sweet on his bruised, salty lips. "Tie you up and fuck you, *Mistress.*"

About The Authors

Lizzie Ashworth has everything she has asked of herself—a lifetime of living—and the fruit of her effort appears in her writing. At her deep woods refuge in the western Arkansas Boston Mountains, she toys with words, battles with paragraphs, and muses on the wind in the trees.

lizzieashworth.com | facebook.com/AuthorLizzieAshworth | pinterest.com/ashworthlizzie

Evey Brett lives in southern Arizona with two cats, a snake, and her Lipizzan mare. She's written erotica and romance for numerous publishers including Loose Id, Ellora's Cave, Carina Press, Lethe Press and Cleis Press.

www.eveybrett.wordpress.com

Beatrix Ellroy is a lover of words, and has written several short pieces collected in a variety of Cleis anthologies.

beatrixellroy.wordpress.com | twitter.com/BeatrixEllroy

Melissa Fuchs is a graduated translator and interpreter and has translated several erotic novels. Born and raised in Tyrol, Austria, in the center of the Alps, she has been spinning tales since she can remember, and now indulges in her fascination with history and those personalities who helped to shape it.

Elle James spent twenty years livin' and lovin' in South Texas, ranching horses, cattle, goats, ostriches and emus. A former IT professional, Elle happily writes full-time, penning adventures that keep her readers begging for more. When she's not writing, she's traveling, snow-skiing, boating, or riding her ATV, concocting new stories.

www.ellejames.com | facebook.com/ellejamesauthor | ellejames.com/ElleContact.htm

Emma Jay has been writing longer than she'd care to admit, using her celebrity crushes as inspiration for her heroes. Emma, married 27 years, believes writing romance is like falling in love, over and over again. Creating characters and love stories is an addiction she has no intention of breaking.

emmajayromance.com | facebook.com/pages/Emma-Jay/154235604624868 | twitter.com/EmmaJayromance

Regina Kammer is a librarian, an art historian and an award-nominated, Amazon best-selling, multi-published writer of erotica and historical erotic romance. She began writing historical fiction with romantic elements during National Novel Writing Month 2006, switching to erotica when all her characters suddenly demanded to have sex.

kammerotica.com | kammerotica.com/blog | facebook.com/Kammerotica

Megan Mitcham is a *USA Today* bestselling author who pens sizzling suspense novels that whisk you across the globe, wedge your heart in your throat, make your hands sweat and your naughty bits tingle. Check out her special forces heroes in the Base Branch Series.
www.meganmitcham.com | meganmitcham.wordpress.com | facebook.com/meganmitchamauthor

Mina Murray is an Antipodean and whisky aficionado. Her work appears in Cleis and Mischief anthologies, including *Dressed to Impress, Lords and Ladies, Brief Encounters, Sudden Sex, The Mammoth Book of Quick & Dirty Erotica, The Big Book of Orgasm* and *Three of Hearts*.
minamurray.wordpress.com | twitter.com/murrmina | pinterest.com/murrmina

Nym Nix hails from Canberra, Australia. She lives with her family at the foot of a mountain, where kangaroos occasionally visit her front garden. Her imagination, on the other hand, lives anywhere but in reality.
nymnix.wordpress.com | twitter.com/NymNix

Teresa Noelle Roberts writes stories for lusty romantics of all persuasions. Her short fiction has appeared in anthologies including *Best Bondage Erotica 2011, 2012, 2013* and *2014*, and *The Mammoth Book of Erotic Romance and Domination*, and she has written numerous erotic romance novels. Her persona in the Society for Creative Anachronism is an Andalusian Arab.
www.teresanoelleroberts.com | www.facebook.com/AuthorTeresaNoelleRoberts | twitter.com/TeresNoeRoberts

Bibi Rizer is a writer and blogger who lives in Vancouver, Canada. When she's not writing about sexy Vikings, she designs book covers featuring sexy vampires, trolls, millionaires and lifeguards. If you enjoyed her story you can read more about Gull Grímsdóttir in *The Shield Maiden's Revenge.*

bibirizer.com | bibirizer.com/news | facebook.com/pages/Bibi-Rizer/845707895448516

About The Editor

Delilah Devlin is a *New York Times* and *USA Today* bestselling author of erotica and erotic romance. She has published over a hundred forty erotic stories in multiple genres and lengths, and is published by Atria/Strebor, Avon, Berkley, Black Lace, Cleis Press, Ellora's Cave, Grand Central, Harlequin Spice, HarperCollins: Mischief, Kensington, Montlake, Running Press, and Samhain Publishing.

Her short stories have appeared in multiple Cleis Press collections, including *Lesbian Cowboys*, *Girl Crush*, *Fairy Tale Lust*, *Lesbian Lust*, *Passion*, *Lesbian Cops*, *Dream Lover*, *Carnal Machines*, *Best Erotic Romance (2012)*, *Suite Encounters*, *Girl Fever*, *Girls Who Score*, *Duty and Desire* and *Best Lesbian Romance of 2013*. For Cleis Press, she edited 2011's *Girls Who Bite*, and 2012's *She Shifters* and *Cowboy Lust*, 2013's *Smokin' Hot Firemen* and *High Octane Heroes*. In 2014, she added *Cowboy Heat* and *Hot Highlanders and Wild Warriors*.

www.delilahdevlin.com | facebook.com/DelilahDevlinFanPage | twitter.com/DelilahDevlin